FOREVER UNTIL TOMORROW

WAR ETERNAL, BOOK FIVE

M.R. FORBES

[1]
MITCHELL

A MAN SITS in the corner of a quiet room. His hands are resting on the table, clasped together as if in prayer. His eyes are open, his head up and straight. He's staring at the wall a few meters ahead of him, past the second man who sits at the other side of the table, leaning back in his chair. This man's eyes watch every movement of the first with intense interest. Every motion is a sign. Every breath. Every swallow. Every clenching of the hands together.

"Tell me, Reggie," the man says. "Do you think you're ready to get out?"

The man's eyes shift. A centimeter. Maybe two. His mouth opens slowly, and he licks his lips before speaking.

"No," he replies, a touch of sadness and despair filtering through the simple word.

The other man considers for a moment. He's known Reggie for twenty years - since he had been found in an alley uptown by a passerby and brought to St. Mary's. The thought diverts his attention to Reggie's arms, always covered in tight sleeves to hide the flesh beneath. New technology and procedures had helped repair most of the original damage, but it would never heal completely.

Nobody had ever been able to figure out what had happened that night. No one had seen anything. No one had heard anything. He always thought that was strange. If someone were on fire, you would hope someone would say so.

Then again, with everything else that had happened that day, it wasn't a total surprise that basic humanity had been forgotten. Not when humanity had learned that they weren't alone.

"Why not?" he asks.

Reggie continues to stare straight ahead. He spends most of his time this way, looking off into the distance as if he can see through the sanitary white walls of the hospital and out into the world beyond. As if he's looking at something specific, or at least trying to. A memory?

"I have nowhere to go," Reggie replies, eyes never shifting. "I have nothing to do but wait."

"You've been here for almost twenty years," he says. "What are you waiting for?"

Seconds pass. Then minutes. Reggie doesn't answer. His hands shift. They clench together, grabbing at one another and holding tight. Whatever is on his mind, whatever is sitting at the edge of his thoughts, he's trying to capture it and never let go.

For whatever reason, he can't.

The man leans his chair forward so that the front legs return to the ground. He stands slowly, considering. Twenty years. Reggie had come to them with nothing but the burns. No memories. No identification. No name.

He still remembers the first night. The Doctors had called on him because they thought Reggie would need comfort while they scrubbed away the charred flesh. The man surprised them all, sitting in silence while they removed the damaged skin.

Reggie has never presented like the others who have been traumatized. He doesn't shake. He doesn't sweat. He doesn't react to loud noises, or to screaming, or to any of the visual or auditory cues they have used in an effort to figure out who he was or where he had come from. There is something about him. Something different. It unnerves the others. It intrigues him. It always has. It's the reason he's stayed on. The reason he keeps coming back to St. Mary's though he retired from his other duties three years ago.

"Are you hungry?" he asks, changing the subject.

"No," Reggie replies.

"Thirsty?"

"No."

"You've been sitting here for three hours. It's getting late. Would you like to go to bed?"

"No."

The man thinks about sitting again, staying with Reggie. He seems worse today. More quiet. More agitated. Sometimes it seems as if Reggie's mind is split in two, and the active part is trying to see through to the subconscious because all of the secrets are hiding in there, and it wants to know what they are. He doesn't know what it's like to live without knowing who he is. He feels sadness for Reggie. He promised himself he would keep trying, no matter how long it takes.

He can be patient.

"I'm going to get a cup of coffee. Would you like some?"

"No."

"Are you sure?"

Reggie's head turns slowly as if it's on a track. The eyes remain fixed, moving with the head until they're locked on his. He takes a step back, a sense of sudden worry washing through him. Reggie's never reacted like this before.

"No," Reggie says again. There's anger in his voice. Upset.

"I. I'm sorry," he stammers. He doesn't want to look Reggie in the eye. He doesn't like what he sees there.

Pain? Yes. Hurt? Yes. Sadness? Yes. But also something else. Something new. A fire, like the sudden ignition of a thousand suns. An anger.

4 / M.R. FORBES

He's always known that Reggie could be anyone, from anywhere. He's always known that if the man ever did get his memories back, they both might not like what he recalled.

For the first time, he wonders if Reggie is getting closer to those memories. For the first time, he wonders if his worst fear is coming true - that all of these years he's been communing with and trying to save the soul of the man on the other side of the table, he's been inadvertently aiding Satan in his work.

He swallows hard and takes another step back, the thought pulling him away. His foot hits the chair, and he trips, his age working against his desire to regain his balance. He feels the world turning, falling away from him. He's ninety-three, and he doesn't know if he can survive a slip without spending months in a hospital bed instead of beside one.

He wants to think of Sophie in the last seconds before he hits the floor. It's been so long since he's seen her, and there's a part of him that hopes he won't live through the impact so he can be with her again. There's no shame in dying this way. It happens all the time.

He doesn't think of her, though. Instead, he can't stop himself from seeing those eyes, and the fire that was burning behind them. He hates himself for that.

Then, before he can strike, he feels a hand grab his hand, and an arm wrap behind him, clutching him firmly and gently at the same time, slowing his descent, taking care not to harm him in his frailty. He's confused for a moment, until he realizes that Reggie caught him, somehow moving fast enough to reach him before it was too late.

He's lifted slowly back to his feet. He tries to keep his eyes off Reggie's, but he can't. The fire is gone. No. Not gone. Controlled.

"Thank you," he says, as Reggie releases him and goes back to his chair. He returns to the same position. Eyes straight. Hands clasped. Not another word.

He's shaken. His heart is racing. Twenty years and nothing like this has ever happened before. Something is different, but he doesn't know what. He hopes that it's part of God's plan.

"I'll see you soon, Reggie," he says, grabbing the back of his chair and slowly pushing it in. He starts walking away, heading across the cafeteria and waving away the nurses who had come running as he fell, too late to do anything but crowd him as he tries to leave.

"No, Father," he hears Reggie say behind him. "You won't."

[2]
20 YEARS EARLIER

"HALLEY STATION, this is Hawthorne. Do you copy?"

Nigel lifted his head away from the communicator strapped to his chest, returning his attention to the mess strewn across the ice below. His heart was thumping, his mind still trying to make sense of exactly what it was he and his partner were looking at.

"You think it was a satellite?" Adel Hawthorne asked. She had the binoculars, and she was scanning the debris field with them.

"You can see better than I can," Nigel replied. His voice was shaky, his nerves and excitement at odds with one another. How did his wife stay so calm?

"There's hardly any smoke," Adel said. "Do you remember when the TOPOL satellite came down? It was on fire for hours, and smoldering for days after."

Nigel lowered his head again. "Halley Station, this is Hawthorne. Do you copy?"

There was no reply.

"Maybe the antenna came loose again," Adel suggested. She pushed herself to her feet, adjusting her thermal suit so that it sat straight on her waifish frame, and then jogged back to their snowmobile a few dozen yards behind.

A large antenna whip was sticking up from the rear of it, and she grabbed it and tightened it in its base.

"Try now," she shouted back.

Nigel spoke into the small black device one more time. "Halley Station, this is Hawthorne. Do you copy?"

A second of static, and then a voice finally replied. "We hear you, Nigel," the lead scientist, Doctor Charles Abbott, said. "What do you see?"

Nigel opened his mouth but didn't speak. He wasn't sure what to say. Of course, his team had heard and felt the crash. It had registered a 3.4 on their seismographs, and woken everyone up with the noise and shaking. An asteroid, most of them had decided, once they had overcome the initial shock.

"It isn't an asteroid, sir," Nigel said. "It's a ship of some kind. We're still a couple of kilometers away, but from here it looks like it was quite large. A military satellite perhaps."

"If a military satellite just crashed in our backyard, you can be sure we'll be hearing about it shortly. What about the other teams?"

Adel had returned to his side, and had heard the question. She lifted the binoculars, spinning in a circle with them.

"No sign of - wait. No. There's a cat incoming. I'm trying to make out the flag."

"It has to be the Canadians," Nigel said. "They're the only ones due south close enough to get here already."

He heard Charles sigh into the comm. "It figures. With the force of that impact, I bet the entire world knows something came down here."

"I just hope it isn't an American satellite. They're impossible when it comes to recovering what they think belongs to them."

"I've got another team on the horizon," Adel said. "I think everyone's coming to take a look." She lowered the binoculars. "We should head down there, get a peek before the others arrive and spoil it."

"We don't have jurisdiction," Nigel replied.

"Neither do they." Adel waved at the mist of snow rising in the distance, churned up by the snowcat's treads. "Do you want to be the one who misses out?"

Nigel smiled. That was why he loved his wife. She forced his regularly cautious self to be a little more free-spirited.

"Let's go," he said.

They ran back to their ride, starting it up and heading along the outer edge of the crater. Adel kept her eyes on the other teams and on the debris, searching for a place to explore while Nigel tried to find a path down.

"Oh, Nigel," she said a moment later. "I wish you could see this."

He spied a ridge in the crater that he knew the snowmobile could handle and changed direction to head toward it. "I'll be seeing it soon enough."

"Nigel." Adel paused. Her voice suddenly sounded nervous. He wasn't used to that, it caused him to ease off on the throttle.

"What is it?" he asked, concerned.

She didn't speak.

"Addie?" he said.

"Hit the throttle, Nigel," Adel said. "However fast you think you can get down into the crater, do it faster."

"What?"

"Just go."

Nigel knew better than to question. He accelerated again, sending the vehicle scooting forward and then down the ridge. The ride was rough, and he tightened his legs against the sides to hold on while Adel gripped his chest. He couldn't help but smile, feeling a sense of exhilaration at the sudden race, even if he had no idea what he was racing toward.

The snowmobile jostled and shook, each shift in the terrain affecting it differently, some of them threatening to throw them off the edge and plummet into the crater. Nigel handled the controls expertly, keeping them from tumbling and steering them further into the depths.

They were a minute into the descent when Adel tapped his shoulder.

"There," she said, her hand going out ahead of his face and pointing into the distance.

He saw now that they were at the trailing edge of the crash site, near the impact point but still a distance away from where the main body of the satellite had come to rest. He knew how most of the research camps on the continent were grouped, and that their spot would leave them further away from that point.

That was the reason for the race. Adel wanted to get there first, and if he could make it happen, he would.

He pushed the throttle even harder, growing reckless in his pursuit of her desires. The only time he came out of his cautious shell was when Adel was involved. It was the only reason they had wound up together in the first place. He was the nervous, shy scientist. She was the beautiful, intelligent one who always seemed out of place among the geeks and nerds. She had noticed him because he took the chance to make himself noticeable.

He had been taking the same chances since.

The snowmobile shuddered as they reached the bottom of the crater and shifted onto more level ground. Nigel looked ahead, his breath catching in his throat when he saw the massive, torn piece of what he was certain was too big to be any satellite or anything human-made for that matter. It reached high into the sky, the top surely rising above the crater, a long, rounded tube that had been snapped in half, the rear end dripping with slagged metal and wires and piping.

"I don't believe it," he said, just loud enough for Adel to hear.

"I don't believe it either, lovey," she replied. "But there it is, and it's bloody brilliant. We need to get there ahead of the others."

Nigel tried to add more throttle. "She's maxed out," he said. "We can't go any faster.'

Adel raised the binoculars again, searching the sides of the crater for the other teams.

"I think we can make it," she said.

Nigel thought so, too. They had surely been the first to respond.

Three tense minutes passed. The debris grew larger ahead of them, looming up and towering over them like someone had dropped a skyscraper in the middle of the Arctic. And in a sense, someone had.

"Every country on Earth is going to want a piece of this," Nigel said.

"And we're going to be there first in representation of the United Kingdom," Adel replied. "We'll be heroes."

The thought made Nigel more excited. He never imaged he would be a hero, especially with their shared passion for the cold and the ice. They loved what they did, but it certainly wasn't a high profile position or even a low profile position for that matter. It took a certain type of person to live in the real down under.

He looked ahead at the ship, his heart racing; his every thought and breath focused on reaching it ahead of all the others. It would be a testament to his love and devotion, both to Adel and to science. It was more than he ever could have dreamed of.

He didn't notice the red spot of light that appeared on his chest, just to the left of the communicator.

He didn't even feel the bullet as it punctured his thermal suit and sank deep into his heart.

He didn't have to watch the snowmobile spin wildly out of control, throwing Adel into the side of the ice before crushing her against it.

He was dead before he ever saw the team of soldiers perched at the edge of the crater, crouched ahead of a VTOL jet that had delivered them from a small base at the tip of South Africa.

Something else had been set in motion the moment the massive object had appeared in space out of nowhere, the trajectory calculated and the team dispatched.

War.
Eternal.

[3]

20 YEARS EARLIER

"Looks like we're late," Captain Ivers said, speaking into the mic affixed to the front of his tactical helmet. He put his hand on the front of it, wiping away a smudge with his glove.

"Better late than never," his second in command, Warrant Officer Esposito, replied. "Who do you think owns that VTOL down there?"

Ivers squinted as he looked down at the edge of the crater, still a few klicks out but approaching in a hurry. He could see the wreckage of the ship out of the corner of his eye, and he forced himself to resist the urge to stare. He was special forces, Green Beret. He wasn't supposed to be impressed by anything when there was a mission to complete.

"No markings," he said. "Could be anyone. More important: how the hell did they get here before us?"

"I bet it was the Soviets, sir," Sergeant Cohn said, drawing a laugh from the rest of the team.

Ivers laughed too, using it to hide his true concern. They had been dispatched within ten minutes of the UFOs appearance, the landing spot quickly calculated by people much smarter than he was. Their Interceptor was based on the latest scramjet tech, capable of hitting Mach 10. It had delivered them from the base in Australia to the site in no time.

Or so he had thought.

Whoever had beat them to the location, they couldn't have been far off to beat them there in a VTOL. Military installations in Antarctica were supposed to be illegal.

He snapped out of his head and reached down, unbuckling his belt and standing. "Get ready for the drop," he said.

"Yes, sir," his team replied.

He made his way toward the back, passing through one of the plane's inserted modular units and grabbing a heavy rifle and a drop-jet from the exposed rack. The rest of Alpha did the same as they filed in behind him.

"Coming up in two, Captain," the pilot of their transport, Lieutenant Davis, said.

"Roger. We're moving into position now." He slipped the drop-jet onto the back of his armor, clicking the locks into place with practiced ease. He grabbed the control stick and pulled it forward, quickly running the pack through standard operational checks. That done, he continued to the rear of the craft, dropping the cap over the rear access panel and keying in the code to open the tail while the rest of his squad finished gearing up.

"It's going to be a bit nippy out there, ladies and gents," he said.

"I can feel my nipples freezing already," Cohn said.

"And my balls," Sergeant Olson said.

"Keep your balls to yourself, Ollie," Esposito joked.

"Yes, sir."

"Twenty seconds," Davis said.

"Roger." Ivers shivered slightly as some of the freezing air began filtering into the rear of the plane. It was damn cold. He hit a button on his left wrist, activating the armor's internal heating system. There was no way to jet-drop onto the coldest continent without it. That done, he moved to the edge of the ramp and looked down, again trying to stay focused. The crash site had passed below them, and he could see the top of the wreckage in every detail. It was a starship, that much was for sure, and since humans hadn't made it, it had to be extra-terrestrial. Aliens.

"Woo-boy," Esposito said, joining him at the edge of the ramp. "Never thought I'd see the day."

"Orders are to secure the location while the rest of the divisions are mobilized. Every country in the world is going to want in on that thing, and our job is to make sure we're in control of that rush."

"Yes, sir," his squad said.

"Mark," Davis said.

Ivers signaled his team. Then he jumped.

He let himself freefall two thousand feet before engaging the jet, using it to direct himself in a controlled descent back toward the wreckage. The idea was to come in at a better horizontal vector, making it quick and easy to land on foot and at a run, and hard for any opposition to get a bead. His team was the most experienced stationed at Eglin, and they had made hundreds of jumps, if not thousands.

He spread his arms and legs, letting the webbing of his armor spread out and give him more control. He leveled off for a moment before closing himself back up and pointing his head at a downward angle. He always felt so badass during a jet-drop.

He was reading a thousand meters when he caught motion out of the corner of his eye, coming from the grounded VTOL. A moment later he was rolling, taking evasive actions as the unknown forces on the ground opened fire on him and his team.

"Bastards are shooting at us," Esposito said.

"We don't even know who to declare war on," Olson replied.

"Olson, Cohn, you're on the VTOL," Ivers said.

"Yes, sir," they replied.

He didn't need to be able to see them to know they had veered off course, switching direction to engage the enemy. He continued forward, changing his approach vector to add more speed. The shooting stopped a few seconds later.

"They're back in the hole," Cohn said. "Groundfall in ten."

"Take them out, but try not to damage the VTOL. Command is going to want it."

"Yes, sir."

The side of the crater zipped past as Ivers swooped over the edge, flipping his body upright and cutting the jets. He free-fell again, his angle taking him in closer to the side of the ship, the close-up view threatening to steal his focus from his landing. He could see scorch marks and scuffs all along the surface, which looked like an alloy he had never seen before. Had the ship been in a battle, or had the crash caused that?

He pushed the thought away. He needed his concentration to bring himself in right at the base of the ship.

"You see that, Captain?" Esposito said a moment later. "Three o'clock."

Ivers shifted his eyes to the right. There were dead bodies were on the ground, lines of spilled blood soaked into the ice beside them. Scientists. Dead scientists.

"Whoever they are, they're killing civilians," he said, getting angry.

He fired the drop-jets, slowing his descent enough that he wouldn't break his legs, but coming in hard enough to earn some time. His body shook as he hit the floor, reaching back and unclasping the jump pack and unhooking his rifle in one smooth motion. Esposito landed behind him, along with the other two members of the squad, Ocho, and Briggs.

"I have a feeling this is going to turn out to be a pretty shitty day," Briggs said, her eyes on the bodies.

"Cut the chatter, let's move," Ivers said. There was an obvious path into the wreckage right in front of them, where boots had compressed the snow into clear tracks. "I've got point. Ocho, cover the rear."

"Yes, sir," Ocho said. Esposito moved in front of them as they dispersed into a tight wedge formation.

They moved quickly and cautiously into the ship. Ivers was surprised to find that there was still light being emitted from it, in small patches along the wall from what appeared to be some kind of bundled tubing. Most of it was black and charred, damaged in the crash, though it seemed a current or charge still existed. He couldn't imagine what the engines of something this big looked like. He could imagine scientists the world over hungering for a chance to take it apart and figure out how it worked. He doubted this thing ran on batteries.

The echoing report of distant gunfire dragged him out of his thoughts.

"There must be more people already inside," Esposito said.

"Or the E.Ts aren't friendly," Ocho replied.

He tried to track the noise. "This way," he said, picking up the pace.

The team ran down the corridor and turned left, to another long hallway. It looked the same as the first. Some hanging wires and more of the tubing spread out along a passage that was roughly human-sized.

Were the aliens the same general size and shape as they were? What did they look like?

They crossed another passage, turning right and winding up face to face with a crumpled mess of metal and wires. A dead end.

"Wrong way, sir," Briggs said.

They doubled back, heading to the left. The gunfire had stopped, leaving them with nothing to follow.

"This thing is so big, we could spend hours in here and never find them," Esposito said.

"We have to try. They may be killing innocent people."

They kept going, wandering deeper into the ship. All of it was the same. Corridors and wires and tubes. Where were the aliens? Where were the living quarters? Where was the bridge? There had to be more to the place than endless hallways.

Something in the ship cracked and groaned, sending a vibration along the floor that reminded them of where they were standing. Inside a crashed starship that could lose its structural integrity at any time.

"Five more minutes, and then we bail," Ivers told his squad. "If Cohn and Olson did their job, and I know they did, these guys aren't going anywhere."

They moved deeper, staying in formation, their years of experience guiding them. They reached their first hatch a moment later. It was half-open.

Ivers knelt down, peering into the room. The lights were flickering inside, and he could see a body on the floor. He turned on the light attached to the rifle and poked it through, shining it onto the scientist.

"They went this way," he said, dropping down and rolling under the hatch. He quickly swept the area, finding a connecting opening at the rear of the large room. It was composed of blocky machinery and what appeared to be screens of some kind. The same tubing ran along the walls and floor - most of it dark and dead.

He crept toward the opening as quietly as he could, using hand signals to guide the team. They approached carefully, staying at the fringe. Ivers leaned over and peered through, ducking back when he saw four people positioned around something, facing away from him.

He signaled his team and then counted down with his fingers. When his hand closed into a fist, they moved into the short corridor, facing forward with clear lanes of fire for each of the heavy rifles. By the time the enemy heard them coming and began to react, they were boxed in.

"Don't," Ivers said, pointing his rifle at them as they reached for their weapons.

They were soldiers. He could tell that from the way they were standing, and how they reacted to the ambush. The shortest of them turned to face him, motioning to his tactical helmet. Ivers kept his rifle on him while he raised his hands and lifted it off.

Not a he. A woman. Dark hair, exotic face. She surveyed him and his team, unconcerned.

"Captain," she said. "Stand down. This is out of your pay grade."

"Sure, lady," Ivers said. "Just tell me who the hell you are and convince me that the United States of America gave you orders to kill innocent people."

"The orders were passed orally," she said. "No paper trail. I think you can understand the sensitive nature of our work."

"Which is what, exactly?"

The woman stepped aside to let him see what they had been standing around.

A body. A human body. It was at least a hundred pounds over-weight, wearing a gray shirt and pants made from a material he didn't recognize. The face was hidden, tucked down on the chest. A tool of some kind was jutting out of the back of the skull.

"Who is that?" Ivers asked.

"The owner of this ship."

Ivers crinkled his eyebrows. "What? How do you know that?"

"I already told you, Captain, that's above your pay grade. He has something we want embedded in his brain, right about here," she pointed to the same spot on her head. "Do me a favor and mind the perimeter, while we finish up."

"Wait one second. What about the scientists? What about my people? The two you left with the VTOL were shooting at us."

"I'm sorry for that, Captain, but they had strict orders. This occasion is so far beyond any of our lives; I can't even begin to describe it to you."

Ivers kept the rifle on her. He wasn't comfortable with any of this. The U.S. killing civilians, and trying to kill some of their own, to steal something from some guy's head that they knew about ahead of time how? None of the pieces fit.

"How about we all go outside and wait for the cavalry?" Ivers said.

"Time is the most valuable asset we have," she replied. "Don't waste mine."

"I'm sorry, Miss?"

She didn't answer.

"Whoever you are. We're in control of this situation, and my call is that we're all going outside to wait for backup."

She started to laugh. It was a laugh that sent a chill through him. It was unnatural, uncomfortable. As if she wasn't quite sure how to do it.

"You aren't in control of anything, Captain," she said at the tail end of it.

"Esposito, bind them up," Ivers said. "No funny shit, or we kill you all."

"Don't worry, Captain," the woman said. "There's nothing funny about any of this."

At that moment, Ivers heard the boots on the floor behind them. He tried to shout a warning to his team, but it was already too late. Deafening gunfire echoed in the space as his team was gunned down from behind. He shifted his rifle, trying to pull the trigger. Trying to defend them.

The woman was on him in a flash, grabbing the gun and forcing it up, her strength more than he expected. He shoved back against her in an effort to push her away, and she fell back a step and let go of the gun. Then she bounced back at him, grabbing his arm and throwing him to the side where he hit the wall. He managed to regain his balance and get a shot off, but it was harmlessly wide. The woman punched him in the gut before grabbing his arm and snapping it in half, forcing the rifle to the ground.

Ivers gritted his teeth against the pain, reaching down with his good hand to grab his knife. She beat him to it, pulling it from his ankle and slicing his hand.

He lost his will to fight then, his hands dropping to his sides as he fell to his knees. He could see the rest of his team face down on the floor, dead. The two shooters from outside had joined the rest of their team, which meant Cohn and Olson were most likely dead, too.

"Whatever you're doing, someone will stop you," he said.

She smiled. Again, it seemed awkward. "No one will even know we, or you, were ever here."

She dropped the knife and returned to her work on the body.

A bullet to the head dropped Ivers a moment later.

[4]
KATHERINE

Major Katherine Asher breathed deeply, feeling the pull of her dress at her abs as she filled her lungs. For the hundredth time already, she questioned her sanity in picking something that was so fitted. Just because she worked her ass off to keep her mind and body conditioned didn't mean she had to wear clothes she couldn't breathe in, did it?

"Too tight?" Michael asked. He was standing perpendicular to her in the small elevator, trying to deal with his own discomfort. Unlike Katherine, it was nothing he could alleviate by tugging.

"I'll survive," she replied. "It's okay, Michael. There's nothing to be nervous about."

"That's easy for you to say. I feel like a sausage in this thing, and you know I hate crowds."

Katherine reached out and put her hand on Michael's arm. They had been friends for as long as either of them could remember, and she knew that was the only reason he had agreed to escort her to the Admiral's Ball.

"I appreciate that you're here," she said.

"I could have been at home playing Xeno Troopers, or finishing that launch module that I'm already a week behind on. I could have been wearing jeans instead of this monkey suit." He paused, using his handkerchief to wipe some of the sweat from his face. "You're welcome. Don't get me wrong, as much as I love Xeno Troopers, I wouldn't miss the chance to see you get announced as a crewmember of the Dove for anything. How many people failed the training again?"

"Over a thousand," she replied. One-thousand one-hundred forty-three, to be exact. She had beat out a crowded field of some very impressive soldiers to be here.

Then again, she had always believed she would.

From the day on the playground when she and Michael had watched XENO-1 come down, from her time in service during the Xeno Wars, from her years of training as part of the secret program to put a starship based on the crashed alien craft back in space, she had always known it would happen.

"I still can't believe you couldn't find a handsome Corporal or something to bring you," Michael said. "I'm not exactly gigolo material."

"And I'm not exactly into gigolos," she replied, laughing.

It was true that Michael had only added to his already large frame as they had moved from childhood to adulthood. He was at least three hundred pounds, with a round body and a wide face, and they both knew he was going to stand out amidst the cut physiques of the other military that would be in attendance. It was the main reason for his discomfort. At the same time, she couldn't help but blame him for his lack of self-restraint when it came to high-calorie, caffeine based drinks. Not with the control she had needed to master to make it this far.

The elevator slowed to a stop, and the doors slid open. The Ball was being held in the Rainbow Room, a classic icon perched at the top of Rockefeller Center. Once upon a time, it had been one of the best views around. While these days it looked into the sides of all the super-scrapers around it, it was still a symbol of American glory, and of better days everyone on the planet believed would come again. The pacts that had led to the construction of the Dove had all but eliminated most of the conflict on Earth and had brought human civilization together in a way nothing else could have.

"Here we go," Michael said, breathing out. He tucked his handkerchief in his pocket and held out his arm to her. She smiled as she took it, allowing him to walk her out into the space.

She had been expecting a crowd, a dance floor filled with Admirals and Generals, Presidents and Prime Ministers. Even so, walking in and spotting so many of the dignitaries she had read about or seen on the streams was more than a little intimidating - even for her. The naming of the Dove's crew was that important, and the stream cameras arranged around the area confirmed it.

"Keep breathing," Michael said.

To himself, or to her? She wasn't sure. Either way, it was good advice.

They made their way deeper into the room. Some of the assembled took notice of them, smiling at her as they passed. She shifted her arm to take Michael's hand. He was cold and clammy.

"How are you staying so cool under this pressure?" he asked.

"I've been shot at," she replied. "Multiple times."

Michael let out a nervous laugh. "True."

"I think our table is over there," she said, pointing toward the front. She could see Yousefi already sitting there, his pregnant wife at his side. He looked her way, raising his hand in greeting when they made eye contact. "There's the Mission Commander."

"Yousefi?" Michael said. "The one you told me about?"

"Yes."

"He looks taller in person. Maybe we can dance first?"

Katherine tugged Michael by the shoulder. "You hate dancing."

"I like it better than meeting Admirals."

"Major Asher, is it?" A voice asked from her left. Katherine turned toward it, finding Vice President Nelson standing beside her.

"Vice President," she said, giving him a light curtsy. He took her hand, expertly kissing the back of it.

"Since you're here, I assume you were selected?" he said.

"Yes, sir," she replied.

"Good. I was worried the American contingent would wind up getting shut out."

"That would have been against the rules."

He smiled. "You know how rules are, don't you, Major?"

Katherine made a split-second decision to decide she knew what he was talking about. "Of course, sir."

"Are you going to introduce me to your husband?" Nelson said, looking at Michael.

"Uh. Not husband, Mister President. Mister Vice President, I mean. Just. Just a friend." Michael smiled, his face turning red.

"If I weren't a married man, I would thank you for that," Nelson said, laughing. "Roger Nelson." He put out his hand.

"Michael Stickley," Michael replied, hesitant to present his clammy hand to the man.

"A pleasure." Nelson reached out and took the hand anyway, shaking it. He moved close to Michael as he did, but Katherine could still hear what he said.

"If you want her, don't let her leave without saying so, son."

Michael's color deepened even more. "Yes, sir," he muttered, glancing uncomfortably at Katherine.

She was amused by the whole thing. There was no possibility of that happening. She was married to her career, and he was married to his technology.

Nelson turned back to her. "I know you'll do us proud, Major."

"Yes, sir," she replied.

Vice President Nelson wandered away, replaced a moment later by Rear Admiral Yousefi.

"Major," Yousefi said.

"Admiral," Katherine replied, coming to attention and saluting.

Yousefi smiled. "At ease, Major. This is a civilian event. Besides, you're forgetting the new regulations. The UEA settled on bowing, remember?"

Katherine returned the smile, relaxing her posture. The fledgling oversight group had wanted to change things up a bit to better integrate the various members of the armed forces from all of the member countries. One of their bright ideas had been to homogenize formal military greetings to a bow instead of a salute. She had no idea how they had come to that decision, but it was proving to be a hard habit to break.

And that wasn't the only one. Applicants to the program had come from nearly every branch of nearly every military around the globe, with the unintended consequence of creating a level of confusion in organizational structure and ranks that had yet to be ironed out. After all, there were no Majors in the Navy and no Admirals in the Air Force, and yet here they were.

"Yes, sir," she said. "Admiral Yousefi, I want you to meet my friend, Michael."

The Admiral turned to Michael, who put out a slightly shaky hand that had recently been wiped dry on the back of his pants.

"Admiral," Michael said.

"Please, my name is Ben," Yousefi replied, taking Michael's hand.

"Nice to meet you, Ben," Michael said.

"Likewise. Your friend Katherine here is quite talented, isn't she?"

"She used to have a stack of trophies in her room to prove it," Michael said. "Running, swimming, karate, violin. Is there anything you're bad at, Katherine?"

"I'm not much of a dancer," Katherine said.

"Really?" Yousefi asked. He put out his hand. "Do you mind if I ask you to prove it?"

Katherine glanced at Michael, and then at Yousefi's hand. She had been hoping to get through the night without getting out on the floor, and she had just said the exact wrong thing to accomplish that mission.

"I've never known you to be shy, Katherine," Yousefi said. "Besides, it will make a good photo op for the media."

"I can picture the caption now," Katherine said. "Admiral uses pilot as floor mop."

Yousefi laughed at that, pushing his hand forward a little more. Katherine bit her lip and decided to take it.

"That's better," Yousefi said. "Shall we-"

His voice was drowned out by the explosion.

[5]
KATHERINE

IT ECHOED across the crowded room, the force knocking Katherine to her knees, while Yousefi crouched down over her, instinctively trying to protect her. She turned her head, looking for Michael, finding him on the floor his hands over his head. She was relieved he was okay.

People were screaming and crying, and smoke was rising from the corner of the room.

What the hell was going on?

"Are you hurt?" Yousefi asked.

"No," she replied. "We need to help these people."

"Yes."

They stood up. She could see now that part of the window had been blown out, and there were at least four people on the ground who weren't moving. Others were injured and bleeding, their faces covered in debris.

"Michael," she said, leaning over him. "Are you okay?"

He uncovered his face to look at her. She could see the fear in his expression. He didn't say anything. He didn't have to.

"It's okay," she said.

Was it?

The elevator doors opened, and a squad of soldiers poured into the room. They were wearing U.S military issue tactical battle armor, ready for a fight.

Had someone been expecting this?

She saw Vice President Nelson getting to his feet, surrounded by Secret Service. He had been close enough to the blast that he had blood and debris on his clothes and face, but hadn't been hurt himself.

"What's happening he-"

He didn't get to finish his sentence. The soldiers opened fire, heavy slugs tearing through the secret service and the Vice President, who flopped backward like a dead fish.

Katherine felt the fear rise into her throat.

"Stay down, don't move, whatever happens," she whispered to Michael.

The soldiers swept into the room, scanning it. Katherine reached down and pulled off her heels, holding onto one of them. With enough force, the stiletto would make a serviceable weapon.

She expected the soldiers would corral them, stick them in a corner and hold them hostage. They wanted something or they wouldn't be here.

She was surprised when they started shooting into the crowd.

The deafening roar of gunfire, the thumps of bullets hitting flesh, the screams of the wounded and dying. The entire floor turned into an instant war zone. Katherine had never been on the ground during the Xeno War, but she could imagine this was something like it. Fortunately, they were obscured behind a table and away from the others. She glanced back, finding Yousefi under the table behind them, hovering over his pregnant wife. He saw her looking and held up a gun that he had produced from somewhere. He put it on the floor and slid it over to her.

She understood why he didn't want to get involved. He had a baby to think of. She picked the gun from the ground, only moments before one of the soldiers appeared over the table.

His eyes widened as she swung the weapon toward him. He scrambled to bring his rifle to bear, his surprise making him slow. The tactical armor covered most of his body. It wasn't covering his face. The bullet hit him square in the eye, punching through and into his brain. He dropped in an instant.

"Get under the table," she said to Michael.

He immediately began scrambling for it on all fours.

The other soldiers hadn't noticed her in the commotion. They continued advancing on the gathered crowd, shooting into the press. How many heads of state were already dead? How many of the most important people in the UEA had been killed?

And who had organized it?

It's true there were people opposed to the Alliance, and to the construction of the Dove. Plenty of people didn't want to make allies out of former enemies, and they certainly didn't want to be tied to them in a common goal. It was stupid as far as she was concerned. An alien ship had crashed on their planet. That meant there had to be more of them out there, and who knew if they were friendly? It was true that nothing that could be construed as a weapon had been found in the wreckage, but maybe that ship had been a scout. The possibility couldn't be discounted.

She circled the table quickly, kneeling next to the downed soldier and grabbing his rifle. There weren't many people still moving, and the soldiers were shifting their attention to the rest of the room. A woman near the back tried to make a run for it and was gunned down a moment later.

Katherine watched the soldiers, running back toward the elevator when they weren't looking. She dropped behind a buffet table, coming to one knee and using it to balance the rifle. She had managed to get behind the soldiers, who were fanning out to search for the remaining survivors.

She started shooting.

Bullets tore into the soldiers, hitting them in the back where the armor wasn't as thick. They raised their own shouts of pain and alarm, three of them falling before the rest could spot her. She had been hoping to catch them all. The table wasn't thick enough to protect her.

She felt a pang of sadness as she watched the muzzles of the soldier's rifles flare, only instants before the bullets began raining in on her. Her entire life had been spent in preparation to travel to the stars. She had survived countless combat missions, she had made it through the grueling training, and now only weeks before she was going to be gunned down at a party, of all things.

She felt the warm pain of a bullet hit her in the leg. Another hit her on the side, and she fell over onto her back. She couldn't believe she was going to die this way. So was Michael. She was even more scared for her friend. She had convinced him to come with her. He should have been at home playing Xeno Troopers.

She struggled to get back to her feet. She couldn't just let him die like this. She ignored the pain in her side, and the feeling of warmth spreading from the wound, her blood soaking through her dress. She managed to get to her knees.

They had stopped shooting at her. Why?

She reached up, planting a hand on the table and willing herself up. Her vision was getting cloudy, and everything was starting to spin.

"Michael," she said weakly, the confusion making it hard to grasp the situation.

The soldiers. They were on the ground. All of them. Four new soldiers were standing near the blown out window, still attached to their rappel wires. They were wearing similar armor, all of it black and unmarked. Their weapons raised to point at her.

The lead soldier put his hand out, and the weapons lowered. The emergency stairwell doors swung open, and people began flowing in - more soldiers and medics.

Someone took her by the arm. A woman.

"Someone get a kit and a stretcher over here, stat," the woman shouted. "It's going to be okay, Major."

"Who?" Katherine said, barely able to speak.

"Stay calm. You've lost a lot of blood. We'll get you fixed up."

"How?" she said, too confused for anything else. The world was getting hazy around her.

"Launch the Goliath," the woman said. "Find Mitchell."

"What?" She put her hand to her head, finding a slick of blood. She hadn't noticed the bullet that hit her there. "I don't understand."

"It's okay, Major. Find Mitchell."

"Who?"

Everything was getting dark, and nothing was making sense.

"Mitchell," the woman said again.

Then everything disappeared.

[6]
MITCHELL

REGGIE STARED AT THE CEILING. He was in bed, under the blankets, trying to fall asleep. It had always been elusive. It had always been difficult. There were so many nights when he had given up completely, throwing his sheets onto the floor and rising nearly naked in the cool air, standing in the center of the room and staring at the wall.

Why?

He didn't know.

He knew his name wasn't Reggie. Beyond that?

He was in a hospital. A mental hospital. He had been there for a long time. He was sure he was supposed to be there because he was certain he was crazy. How else could he explain why he spent so much time staring at nothing? How else could he understand why the last twenty years of his life had been spent in a haze of distorted emptiness, where the only thing that seemed real were the nightmares?

Was he unable to sleep because he was afraid of them? Did he stare at nothing because he didn't want to face the truth of his existence?

He had spent twenty years asking himself the same questions. Twenty years trying to grasp at who and why he was. So many wasted days. So many sleepless nights. What good had any of it done him? He was nobody, and he had nothing.

His eyes fixed on the plain white paint, tracing it with precision, searching for the chips and cracks he knew were there. He had spent so much time staring at this wall that he knew every inch of it, every flaw. In many ways, it reminded him of himself. A blank canvas, but one with cracks that couldn't be covered over.

Did he stare because he saw his reflection there?

He blinked. Once. Twice. The third time, he held his eyes closed tight before releasing them, opening them like he was firing a gun. He caught sight of something in his vision, and he tried to catch up to it. A dark trailing edge to whatever it was he had forgotten. As soon as he got close enough, it danced away.

He glanced down at his arms. The skin was rough and puckered in spots, the remaining scars from a number of grafts and stem cell treatments. He could still remember what they had looked like in the beginning, the burns sinking so deep they had at one point considered amputation. The twenty-third century, and they were ready to treat him as if it were the nineteenth.

They didn't hurt too badly anymore. Or maybe he had just gotten used to the pain. The doctors had always told him that they were the reason he couldn't remember. That he had been so traumatized by whatever had caused the burns that his mind had shut it out, along with everything else. He didn't believe them.

There was a reason he couldn't remember, but he was certain it wasn't that. He had become so accustomed to the burning sensation in his skin, even all of these years later, that he barely ever noticed it anymore.

A few days earlier, he had told Father John that he was waiting. Then his mind had changed in a way he had never experienced before. His dreams, his nightmares, had entered his waking thoughts, the wall between them breaking down and all of the darkness raging in. The priest had seen it. He knew by the way he had reacted, almost falling over and killing himself to escape. Somehow, Reggie had managed to push the tide back, to force himself to calm down and breathe.

Slow.

Steady.

Father John had been back, of course. The old man was too determined to save his soul to let one episode like that chase him away. He had asked about his thoughts, and Reggie had pushed him back the way he always did. It was better that nobody else got involved. It was better if nobody else got hurt.

That was the crux of it. The bottom line of his nightmares. Death. Destruction. Everything he cared about turned to ash in silent flame.

And always at the center of it, a voice. A soothing, comforting voice that had turned more and more caustic over the years.

"Find her," it said. "You have forever until tomorrow, but not forever until the end. You'll know when the time has come."

It was a statement that had haunted him in the beginning, as he tried to work out the meaning. It had puzzled him, confused him, taunted him, agonized him. It had brought him to fits of anger and rage and frustration. It had left him sobbing on the floor.

In his nightmares, he was in space, surrounded by explosions and wreckage and debris. The Earth hung below him, calm and unaware. The ships sat above him, the tips of their pyramid-shaped bows pointed at her, with glowing balls of death building on the ends.

His brother was gone. His companion was gone. His friends and comrades were all gone. He couldn't remember their names or their faces, but he could feel them in his gut, and he could feel the punches again and again every time he saw them die.

Was it real?

It felt real. It felt true.

He was certain he was crazy.

He dropped to his hands and feet on the floor, resting his body in plank position for thirty seconds, before rising and falling, pulsing out a quick rhythm of push-ups. He stopped when he reached one hundred, standing up and letting his breathing relax. His body tingled from the exertion, but he felt strong. After thirty seconds, he repeated the motion again.

He had made sure to continue the routine from the time his arms had been healed enough to stand the pain. It was familiar to him; something so ingrained that he knew that somewhere, sometime, he had been trained to do it. He had to keep his body in shape. It became more important as he aged. He was still fit, still strong. He needed to be, even if he didn't know exactly why.

He had seen the news earlier. He had noticed it for the first time he could remember, as more than a buzzing in his head, as more than a distraction. His dreams of starships weren't completely insane. He knew one had crashed on the same night they found him. Maybe that was the cause of the nightmares? But that had happened thousands of kilometers away from where he was, so how could those things be connected?

He also knew that they had built one of their own. A starship. They were calling it the Dove, a symbol of peace for the whole world. Was the violence in his mind a warning? Was humankind not supposed to reach the stars?

"Find her," the voice had said. A young girl's voice. Who was she? "You'll know when the time has come."

The news report was about a special event where the inaugural crew of the Dove would be announced. It was supposed to be a big deal, a bright spotlight on what a combined world could achieve. It had fallen apart to violence, to a group that called itself the AIT. Anti-Interstellar Travel. Apparently, they were radical Earth protectionists who preferred that humans remained grounded and invisible to whatever had owned the ship that had crashed all those years ago, the one they had named XENO-1.

"You have forever until tomorrow, but not forever until the end."

Forever to do what? The attack had killed a number of dignitaries from around the globe and had left the plans for the Dove's launch in jeopardy. That he had even noticed the event meant something to him, and he knew it was important.

Reggie moved through a series of punches and kicks. He felt the coldness of his nightmares more acutely tonight, a chill in his soul that he couldn't push away. The voice had told him that he would know when the time had come, and he knew at that moment that it had.

It was time for him to make a decision. Either he was crazy, and all of this was nothing more than a delusion that was playing out in his mind, or he was inexplicably sane, and something very, very bad was going to happen. Something that he was somehow supposed to prevent.

It would have been easy to accept that he was delusional. It would have made sense. He could go back to bed, pull the sheets up, close his eyes, and wait for the morning. He could take his meds and sit and stare, and live with the voice and the nightmares until he finally grew old enough to die.

That was what he wanted to do. He was afraid of the other option. Afraid of the hurt and the loss and the pain, and what it meant to the world if his nightmares were real. He was afraid of the responsibility. He was also afraid of his role. Was he supposed to prevent the AIT from stopping the launch, or was he expected to help them finish the job?

"Find her."

It was too vague. By design? Why?

He looked over at his bed. He was crazy. He had to be. He was in a mental hospital, wasn't he? He should lie down and try to forget.

He looked back at the wall. He traced the cracks and the chips against the starkness of the white background. If he did nothing then, in the end, there would be nothing. Forever until tomorrow. What did that mean?

Tomorrow was almost here, and he had a decision to make. Crazy or not?

He found his clothes on the floor, gathered in a pile at the foot of the bed. He picked them up and put them on, and then walked over to the door and turned the latch. He wasn't violent, so there was no reason to keep him locked in. He slipped out into the hallway before turning around and looking back at the bed again.

It all felt too real to risk that it wasn't. If he were crazy, if he were delusional, then someone would catch up to him, stop him, and bring him back. He hoped it would happen. He wanted it to happen because at least then he would know for sure.

Until then, he was going to pretend he wasn't crazy and see where that road led.

Anywhere was better than here.

MITCHELL

REGGIE PASSED through the corridors of the hospital, heading toward the elevators at the end of the hallway.

"Reggie?" one of the nurses said, noticing him from her station off to the left.

He heard her, but didn't look and didn't slow.

"Reggie," she said again, louder this time.

"I'm leaving," he replied.

"What do you mean? Yu can't just leave."

He didn't answer again. He was close to the elevators. He heard a buzz as the nurse hit the button to lock them down.

"Security, can you come up to seven?" she said.

He turned away from the elevators, to the emergency stairs. They couldn't be secured, for obvious reasons.

"You can't keep me here," he said. "Not if I don't want to be here."

The nurse ran over and positioned herself in front of him. She was a small, round thing. He blinked a few times, his mind picturing her evaporating behind a wall of flame.

"I need to go," he said, coming to a stop. "It's important."

They were trying to stop him. Did that mean he was crazy, as he suspected?

"Why?"

"People will die if I don't."

"How do you know that?"

"The dreams."

"Have you taken your meds?"

"Yes. You're going to die, if you don't let me go."

She looked afraid of him then. She stepped back to get out of his reach. "Are you going to hurt me?"

"No. Not me. XENO-1. It was one ship. It isn't the only ship."

"What are you talking about?"

"They'll come. They'll kill us all."

She looked even more afraid. The stairwell door opened behind her and two security guards entered the hallway. They were big, but not in great shape.

"Reggie?" one of them said. Reggie remembered his name was Jeff. "Where are you going?"

"I'm leaving," he replied.

"He thinks there are aliens coming to get the XENO-1," the nurse said. "He told me we're all going to die."

Jeff didn't laugh. They were used to crazy talk. "It's okay, Reggie," he said. "It's the nightmares. Just a dream, my friend." He was smiling as he approached. "Why don't we head over to the cafeteria? We can get you a cookie and some milk. My grandmother always recommended it for nightmares, and it helped me."

Reggie didn't move. If he were crazy, he should just let them take him, shouldn't he? No. That wouldn't prove anything.

He took a step back. "I need to leave. You can't stop me."

"Look, Reggie, I've seen you exercise in your room at night, and I know you're in good shape, but if I have to stop you, I will."

"No, you won't," Reggie said. "Please, let me go. I don't want to hurt you."

Jeff looked sideways at his partner, who was slowly trying to circle behind Reggie. "We don't want to hurt you either, Reg. Come on, we'll have a drink and then you can try to get some rest."

Reggie looked at the nurse, and then at Jeff. He lowered his head. "Yeah. Maybe you're right," he said softly. "I'm just not feeling like myself tonight, I guess."

"That's okay, Reggie. It happens to the best of us." Jeff tilted his head, motioning to the other guard.

Reggie sighed. He didn't want to hurt anybody. Why wouldn't they just let him leave?

The guard reached for him. He came alive, shifting his weight as he caught the hand, pulling the guard off-balance before bringing his arm back and hitting him hard in the face with his elbow. The guard grunted and fell back, at the same time Jeff tried to wrap him in a subduing grab. Reggie ducked away from it, smacking Jeff's arms aside and punching him hard in the gut, spilling all of the wind from his diaphragm. Jeff doubled over as the nurse stepped aside.

"I'm sorry," Reggie said to her, stepping around the two guards. "Please, just let me leave. I have to find her."

"Find who?" the nurse asked.

"I don't know." He stepped past her, approaching the door.

"Reggie, wait," she said before he reached it. He wasn't sure why, but he turned back. She walked over to him. "There's a storage room on the ground floor. That's where they're keeping all of your personal effects. Everything you had on you when they found you, which wasn't much. Still, if you're going, you might want it."

"Thank you," he said. He hesitated for a few seconds, wondering if he should right before he did. "Am I crazy?"

The nurse smiled. "All of us are crazy, honey. The difference is in the degree. As for you, I'd say you're about average. You never gave me any trouble, so I'm going to miss you."

Reggie looked back at Jeff and the other guard. They were back on their feet, but not about to try again. They didn't get paid enough to be beaten up.

"Thank you," he said.

Then he left.

[8]

MITCHELL

NOBODY TRIED to stop him again as he made his way from the seventh floor to the lobby. He wandered the halls for a few minutes until he found the storage area the nurse told him about. A younger man was sitting behind a small desk, eyes moving left and right as he read something projected onto his glasses.

"Excuse me," Reggie said, getting his attention. The man shook and sat up straight.

"Oh. Jeez, man. You scared the shit out of me."

"Sorry. My name is Reggie. I'm leaving. The nurse told me you could give me my things."

The man smiled. "I know who you are. Our famous patient. You've been here twenty years, and now you're leaving?"

"Yes."

"Just like that? At three in the morning?"

"I guess so. It's time." He paused. "I didn't know I was famous." For some reason, the comment bothered him.

"Just a figure of speech, man. Everybody in St. Mary's knows you, of course. The rest of the world? I doubt it." He laughed and got to his feet, taking off his glasses and dropping them on the desk. "Give me a sec; I'll get your effects."

"Thank you."

Reggie waited for the man to disappear before picking up the glasses and slipping them on. Immediately he could see a window over his left eye, where a flow of text was sitting. It moved depending on his eye position, allowing him to read seamlessly.

"Initial reports place the death toll at twenty-seven, including Vice President Nelson and the lead emissary from Iran, Sadeq Jannali. Three of the astronauts expected to be on the inaugural crew of the Dove were also injured, and may lose their chance to be part of the historic occasion if plans to proceed with the launch remain in place. Major Katherine Asher, United States Air Force, Ning Zhang, Chinese Space Administration, and Captain Vidal Pathi. United Earth Alliance President Amir-"

"Do you always help yourself to other people's stuff?" the orderly said, returning from the storage area with a small box.

Reggie took the glasses off. The man's return had taken him by surprise, but he refused to show it. "Sorry. It's been a while since I caught up with the outside world." He could still see the list of names in his head. His eyes kept going back to the first of them. Major Katherine Asher. The name itself didn't mean anything to him, but he had felt a stirring in his gut at seeing it. Was she the one he was supposed to find?

"Crazy, right? The attack on the UEA party. I can't imagine why anybody wouldn't want the Dove to fly. It's more than a starship, you know? It's a symbol of unity."

"I know."

The orderly held the box out to him. "It isn't much. We also have donated clothes for people who didn't come in with any, or lost them, or whatever. Follow me."

Reggie took the box from him. It was hardly big enough to hold anything important, and he wondered what could be inside. The box felt empty.

He trailed behind the orderly to a second room. It was filled with all sorts of clothes, organized by type and size.

"Help yourself," the man said.

"Thank you," Reggie replied. He picked up a pair of socks and underwear, an old pair of stained jeans, a t-shirt, and a sweater. He also found a pair of shoes that weren't too beat up. It wasn't much, but it would have to do.

"You can change back there," the orderly said.

Reggie changed his clothes and came back out.

"You've been in here for twenty years," the orderly said. "The world is pretty different now. Are you sure you want to go out there?"

Reggie tried to remember what the world was like. He couldn't. It didn't matter how much it had changed because he had so little to go on. "Yes."

"Okay, well, be safe." The man held out his hand. Reggie shook it. "Exit is that way."

"Thank you." He took a few steps before pausing and turning back to the orderly. "What city am I in?"

"St. Louis, Missouri."

"The launch party. Where was that?"

"New York, why?"

"Just curious. Thank you for your help."

"Yeah. Okay. See you, Reggie."

Reggie started walking again, down the long corridor leading to the exit. It was early morning, and not much was happening as he stepped outside and onto the sidewalk of a city street. He looked around, taking in the towers of steel and glass and the lights of advertisements hanging on boards arranged along the street. Lasers projected red or green light to help direct traffic while a single vehicle cruised by, its engine emitting a soft hum. The windows were heavily tinted, but there didn't appear to be anyone inside.

Money. He knew he would need some to get from Chicago to New York. He tried to remember his geography. For some reason, he had a vague notion of the two cities, and at the same time, he felt as though they weren't very familiar to him. Maybe he had grown up somewhere else.

He remembered the box then. It was taped closed, and he worked to tear it off and get it open. At first, he thought it was empty until he found a small card wedged into the corner. He dug it out with his fingernail and held it up to the light. It was five centimeters square, its use and purpose unclear to him.

Twenty years, and this was all that he owned?

Was he crazy? He still wasn't sure. Hearing voices was crazy. Thinking there was a connection between the attack on the UEA party and his own sudden motivation certainly pointed toward crazy. His lack of fear and a sense of calm confidence suggested otherwise.

Then again, wasn't the whole crux of insanity not knowing that you were insane?

He looked up and down the street again, trying to decide which direction to go. He had thought he might feel overwhelmed to be out of the hospital. He didn't. He felt a sense of purpose. After all of these years, he finally had a reason. A goal.

If that was crazy, he preferred it to the alternative.

Major Katherine Asher. The name meant something. He didn't know what.

He was going to find out.

[9]
KATHERINE

"Kathy? Can you hear me? It's Michael. Kathy?"

Katherine didn't open her eyes. She could hear the voice, but she didn't want to respond to it. The beeps and tones of medical equipment surrounded it, and she had a feeling she knew what it meant.

She remembered being shot. She remembered the pain in her gut even though she couldn't feel it at the moment, the drugs keeping it at bay. She remembered the warm slick of blood on her fingers from the bullet that grazed her head.

What had the doctor said to her again?

Find Mitchell.

What did that mean?

Who was Mitchell?

Why had she said that?

"Kathy? I know you're awake. The machines don't lie."

Michael's voice irritated her. She refused to open her eyes. She didn't want to be a good little soldier and face the truth she knew was ahead of her.

She was injured, and out of the program.

Ever since they had announced the construction of the Dove, she had done nothing but dream of being on its first mission. Now it would never be more than a dream.

"Kathy," Michael said again.

"Leave me alone," Katherine whispered. She still didn't open her eyes.

"Come on, Kathy. For me?"

"No. I don't want to know."

"You're afraid you're out of the program, aren't you?" Yousefi said.

His voice made her stop pouting. She looked at him. "Sir?"

He was alive and in one piece. "You saved a lot of lives, Major," he said. "You're a hero. If the Dove has to wait for you, it will."

"Sir. How is your wife?"

Yousefi smiled. "She is well. We were lucky. So many weren't, Katherine. The AIT hit us hard, and where we least expected it."

"I thought the AIT were just a bunch of radical quacks."

"So did the UEA, which is why they caught us off-guard."

Katherine tried to sit up. She felt a pull at her side.

"Don't, Major. Give the patch a chance to do its work. Forty-eight hours at least."

"Patch?"

"The latest military medical treatment out of the XENO research labs. A surgeon pulled the bullet fragments. The patch will heal the wound in a couple of days."

"Awesome," Michael said.

Katherine looked at him. "Michael. How are you?"

"Shaken," he replied. "Having nightmares. They've already set me up with a therapist. I survived without getting shot, thanks to you. Right now, that's what I'm focusing on. Anything else leaves me paralyzed."

"I'm sorry."

"It wasn't your fault. You couldn't have known."

"Did they ID the attackers?"

"Yes," Yousefi said. "Former military, all of them. Lured into the

AIT, though we aren't sure how. Initial intelligence is that there is money involved. A lot of it. Whoever is backing the group has deep pockets." He shrugged. "That's for Security to figure out. Your job is to rest and get better."

"Is the launch still happening?"

Yousefi didn't answer right away.

"Sir?"

"I don't know." He sighed. "Member nation governments are pushing the UEA to cancel the launch until we can be sure there is no credible outside threat to either the Dove or to the people involved in the program."

"And how are they supposed to do that?" Katherine asked, starting to feel angry. "They would be giving the AIT exactly what they want."

"I know. I've heard they're working around the clock on it, but anything more than that is beyond my, or your, clearance. I've already told you more than I should have, but in light of what you did, I think you deserve it. I also recommended that the Potus award you with a Purple Heart."

"Do you think he'll listen to you?"

"Because I'm Iranian? I'm still a ranking officer of the UEA. That's supposed to mean something. It would be easier if the alliance would settle on a recognition system."

"They've only had ten years," Michael said sarcastically.

"Unifying so many countries takes time," Yousefi said. "And it certainly isn't a priority."

Someone knocked on the door. Katherine looked over at the doctor.

"I'm glad to see you're awake," he said. He was an older man with a bald head and a large nose. "How are you feeling?"

"Annoyed," Katherine replied.

"Are these two bothering you?"

"Laying here is bothering me."

The doctor approached on the opposite side of the bed, tapping on the screens behind her. "I'm Doctor Villanueva, by the way. Vitals are good. You were lucky the bullets didn't hit anything important. You should be out within three or four days."

"You could use a little work on your bedside manner," Katherine said.

The doctor laughed. "I've heard. You're in a military hospital, Major. If you wanted fluff, you should have been an actress or something."

"Are you harassing me?" Katherine smiled. She liked Doctor Villanueva. He was no frills.

"You'll know if I'm harassing you. Are you hungry?"

"No."

"Good. I'll have some food brought up." He glanced over at Yousefi and Michael. "As for you two, visiting hours are between ten and five." He pointed at one of the screens. "It's six-thirty."

"Do you know who I am?" Yousefi said.

"Yes, Admiral. And I know you outrank me, sir. I don't care. This is my hospital, and I run a tight ship. The Major here is going to have something to eat, and then she's going to sit here and watch the streams or whatever else that involves not moving."

Yousefi smirked. "Katherine, don't worry about losing your spot. I won't allow it to happen. In the meantime, get some rest. You'll need your strength to find Mitchell."

Katherine had started to lay back in the bed. The last part caused her to sit up again. "What?"

"I said you'll need your strength to fly the Dove."

"Oh. Right."

"Take care, Kathy," Michael said. "They've got me holed up in a room down the hall for observation until tomorrow. I'll stop by before I leave, at ten sharp."

Kathy reached out, taking Michael's hand and squeezing it. "I'm sorry," she said again, still feeling guilty for bringing him to the party.

"Don't be. Mitchell will make it better."

She froze again. Mitchell? Why did she keep hearing the name?

It meant nothing to her. Or did it? She let go of Michael's hand. Maybe she needed some more rest after all.

Yousefi and Michael filed out of the room, leaving her alone with the Doctor.

"Did you hear either of them say Mitchell?" she asked.

He looked down at her curiously. "No. Why?"

"I don't know. For some reason, I keep hearing the name Mitchell, but I don't know anyone with that name. Do you know why that might be?"

He shook his head. "You didn't have a concussion or anything else that might be affecting your brain function. It could be the meds. We have you fairly well sedated right now."

She smiled. "Yeah, that's probably it."

"Well, everything looks good here. I'll get the food sent up. Keep doing what you're doing and you'll be out of here in no time."

"I'm not doing anything."

"Exactly. Good night, Major."

"Good night, Doctor Villanueva. Thank you."

He headed for the door, standing behind it as it slid closed. She thought she saw his expression change right before he vanished from view, shifting from slight amusement to complete seriousness. It seemed strange, but then again who knew what his next stop was. Maybe he had to tell someone they were going to die?

She rested her head on her pillow and closed her eyes again. Mitchell. Maybe she was wrong. Maybe she had known a Mitchell during the Xeno War?

She laughed silently at herself. If she were hearing a voice in her head, it was either because of the trauma or the medication. She was ridiculous to take it seriously.

Follow the doctor's orders and rest. Help the wound heal so she could get back to training for the mission. That should be her priority.

She closed her eyes again.

[10]

KATHERINE

KATHERINE COULDN'T SLEEP. There was nothing but fire and death mingled in the darkness of her closed eyelids. At first, she thought it was her mind trying to work through the attack at the party, to make sense of it, or at least come to some kind of resolution that would allow it to relax. When she realized it wasn't the attack, she began to panic.

She had fought in the Xeno War. She had downed enemy fighters and sent guided bombs to strongholds on the ground. She had killed in the name of her country and what she believed in. She had never shown signs of PTSD before. A sound mind had been one of the top criteria for Project Olive Branch. Now this had happened, and now she was seeing things, and now she was hearing things. It didn't matter what Yousefi said. If they did a psych eval and she failed, nothing he could do would get her on the Dove.

Nothing.

She wanted to cry but thought that would make it worse. She needed to pull herself together, not let herself fall apart. She did as the doctor ordered, remaining in the bed, resting her body. She couldn't rest her mind. Not yet. She closed her eyes again, focusing on her breathing, and on paying attention to what she saw.

Darkness. Silence. A blue pyramid. Multiple blue pyramids. Asteroids. Light. Candles put out.

It was a blur that repeated over and over, too fast to get any details from. It hurt her to see it, to feel it, to know that it was more than a nightmare. Something had happened to her that she didn't yet understand. She could either run from it or embrace it.

She had never run from anything in her life.

In Middle School, she had picked a fight with the quarterback of the high school football team because he was giving Michael a hard time about his weight. Michael shrugged it off, used to the jokes and jeers and teasing. She hadn't been able to let it go. She found him after practice and broke his nose, her expertise in martial arts making easy work of the dumb jock.

In the Air Force, she had gotten into dogfights with multiple targets at once on more than one occasion, always in support of another pilot who was outmatched and outnumbered. She had nearly been killed one of those times, damage forcing her into a landing that was rougher than the plane was expected to survive. Somehow she had.

Mission training was the toughest test of them all. So much competition, each of the men and women from countries around the globe equally decorated and skilled. Some were former enemies. A couple she had faced off against directly over the ice of Antarctica. They were on the same side now, but they weren't going to let their opposition beat them for one of the few seats on the Dove. Only constant, grueling work had pushed her over the top.

Whatever this was, she would figure it out. She had to.

Her eyes were closed, and she was trying to slow down the speed of her nightmare when she heard a soft click. The door to her room opening.

She didn't know what time it was. Late. A nurse, most likely. She was sure they thought she was sleeping.

She didn't open her eyes. Let the staff do what they needed to do. If it was time for more meds, so be it.

Then again, she didn't feel much pain. She remembered the last time the nurse had come in. It didn't seem like it had been that long ago.

She listened to the motion beside her. The nurse would always hit the screen and check her vitals and levels before she did anything. She waited for the brightness to seep through her eyelids.

It never came.

She could hear someone moving the IV tubing that ran to her wrist. She could feel it pulling lightly. She breathed in, smelling a stronger, more musky odor. A man. She raised her lids slowly, glancing over to her left.

Doctor Villanueva was hovering over her, IV in one hand, a syringe in the other.

"What is that?" she said.

The doctor jumped back, startled.

"Uh. Major. I. Ah."

He was stumbling over his words. Nervous. Katherine didn't like it.

"I said, what is that?"

She caught the motion from the doorway out of the corner of her eye. Doctor Villanueva wasn't alone. Two men in black were coming at her.

"I'm sorry, Major," Villanueva said. "You have to die. You'll ruin everything."

She wasn't restrained. She pulled her wrist hard, yanking the IV, the tube pulling the rack of machines behind the doctor. He was distracted by them for a moment, just long enough for her to wrench the IV free of her wrist, ignoring the blooming pain and blood sprouting from the area as she rolled off the other side of the bed.

One of the men had reached her, and he caught her on the way down, grabbing her and getting his arms around her waist, lifting her easily. She kicked back, hitting him in the groin, bringing her elbow back and slamming him in the side of the head. His grip loosened, and she wiggled out of it.

Her gut burned, her body barely healed. She quickly scanned the room for anything she could use. There was nothing obvious, so she threw herself at her attacker, knocking aside a clumsy block and bashing him hard in the throat. He coughed and put his hand to his neck, while she skirted around him, seeking the door.

The other man reached for her, getting his hand on her shoulder. She pulled back from him, letting him tear the hospital gown away, using his momentary confusion to drive a knee into his stomach and knock the air out. A hard punch to the side of his face rocked him aside, and then she was through the door and into the hallway.

The first thing she saw was the nurse, dead against the side of the wall; her neck tilted way too far to the left. She felt the panic mix with her adrenaline. Michael had said he was just down the hall. To the left or the right? She didn't know, and would have to guess. She went right, sprinting down the corridor as the thugs regrouped behind her. There was no time.

She reached the first door, pushing it open. Empty. She ran to the next. Empty. When she reached the third, a loud report sounded, and a bullet hit the wall beside her. She pushed the pad to open the door, falling into the room. She got up in a hurry, pushing the door closed and searching for something to jam it.

"Kathy?" Michael said behind her. "What's happening? Why are you naked?"

Damn it. She had been trying to reach him before they did. She hadn't intended to get cornered in the room with him.

"I need to jam the door," she said.

"It's motorized," Michael replied. "You can't jam it."

She looked back at him. He was sitting up on the bed, wearing a pair of AR glasses and gloves and doing his nerd thing.

"We have ten seconds to disable that door, or we're both going to die."

Michael's face paled. Then his hands started moving.

"What are you doing? Didn't you hear me?"

"I was bored, so I was looking at the hospital mainframe. Lucky for us." He smiled mischievously as he did something she couldn't see.

She heard them outside two seconds later.

"Get off the bed," she said, grabbing his arm and pulling.

He was heavy but easily taken off-balance. He fell off the bed and onto the floor next to her. Loud pops followed. The bullets didn't have the force to make it through the metal doors.

Michael sat up, still wearing the AR glasses. His hands moved again, and the alarm klaxons began to sound.

"I can turn the sprinklers on, too," he said.

"I'm already naked. I don't need to be wet."

Michael leaned over and grabbed the sheets on top of the bed. "Here?"

She smiled, her body trembling from the adrenaline. She took the sheet. "Thanks. Are you okay?"

He shook his head. "No." His lip started quivering. "Someone's trying to kill you, Kathy. Why?"

"I don't know. Whatever is going on, it isn't safe here. They've infiltrated the military."

"Who?"

"The AIT? I don't know that either."

She paused at the sound of gunfire outside the room. It wasn't over yet.

"Are you sure the war is over?" Michael said.

Kathy walked over to the door, listening. The gunfire stopped a few seconds later. Doctor Villanueva said she had to die. That she was going to ruin everything. Did he mean her, specifically? Or the mission to launch the Dove?

The name Mitchell slipped back into her thoughts. Whoever he was, did he have something to do with all of this? It was all so strange.

"No," she said, looking back at Michael. Her friend was on his knees, breathing heavy, sweating, afraid. She felt even more responsible seeing him like that. "I don't think it is."

[11]
MITCHELL

REGGIE STOOD at the mouth of the alley, shrouded in shadow, his head lowered to keep his face hidden. It was almost seven o'clock, and the empty streets had slowly filled with people, the city waking up from another uneventful night.

He watched them go by, one after another after another, his expression flat, his eyes keen. He didn't want to steal from any of them, but the small box only had one thing in it, and it wasn't money.

How to get some money without hurting anyone? He wasn't sure. His head was a nearly blank slate, his understanding of society based more on instinct than memory. He knew he had been in cities before, and he knew how the exchange system worked, but he couldn't recall what the tokens looked like.

He tried to stay inconspicuous while a man in a silvery suit crossed the street ahead of him. Like many of the people who went by he was wearing a pair of thin glasses, with a wire that trailed to the back of his head and vanished beneath his collar. He could tell by the way he was walking that something was distracting him. He wasn't paying attention to his surroundings at all.

Reggie left the alley, staying far enough behind the man that no one would suspect he was following, and close enough that he wouldn't lose him. He had done this sort of thing before. He was certain of it.

He followed the man for two blocks, trying to figure out how he would grab him. He would ask him the things he needed to know. Things he should have asked in the hospital. If he had, they would never have let him out. As if they could have stopped him. Hopefully, the man would be compliant. He didn't like hurting innocent people.

The man paused at a street corner. Reggie watched as one of the driverless cars slowed to a stop beside him, and the door to the car swung open. As the man climbed in, Reggie made his move.

He sprinted toward the car, slipping past other pedestrians with reflexive ease. He was on top of it within seconds, even before the man had finished climbing in.

They collided. The force of it threw them both forward into the vehicle. Reggie recovered in an instant, holding the surprised, frightened man back with one hand and reaching back to close the door with the other.

"Destination," a voice in the car said.

Reggie looked down at the man, who had fallen still to avoid injury. The man looked back at Reggie, clearly afraid he was going to die.

"Destination," the voice repeated.

"Where are you going?" Reggie said.

"Uh. Fourth and Main."

"Fourth and Main," Reggie said.

"The fare will be fifteen dollars. Approximate travel time is four minutes. Do you accept?"

"Yes."

The car started to accelerate.

"Who are you?" the man said timidly. "What do you want?"

"I'm sorry," Reggie said. "I'm not going to hurt you. I need money. I have to get to New York."

"What? Money?"

"Yes. To buy things. Like clothes." He pulled at his hand-me-down rags.

"I don't know where you're from, but you're wasting your time with me."

"I don't want to hurt you."

"I can't give you anything, even if I wanted to. Did you just crawl out from under a rock or escape from a mental hospital? We stopped using physical cash fifteen years ago. Everything is electronic. Digital. Secure. Even if you killed me, you can't get what you want."

Reggie stared at him. No wonder the man let himself be so distracted. He leaned off him, pushing himself into the corner of the car. "How can I get to New York?"

"Get a job. Earn it." The man sat up, straightening his suit.

"I don't have time."

"That isn't my problem, or anyone else's but yours."

The man's eyes flicked beneath the glasses. Reggie watched curiously. He was doing something with them. He seemed way too calm considering he had just been assaulted.

"What is that?" he asked.

"You don't know what AR glasses are?"

Reggie stared at them. In his mind, he caught a flash of a grid over his eyes. There were shapes in it, and they vanished one by one. Death. Destruction.

"Communications," he said, the tense memory turning into understanding. "Information. Augmented reality." He shook his head, trying to dislodge more of what he had forgotten.

It was gone as quickly as it had come.

"Yes. I sent an emergency alert to the police."

Reggie felt a heavy mix of anger and fear. He looked up and out the windows of the car. Another vehicle was already behind them. It had a bank of lights on top of it, and official markings over the hood. A second slid neatly in front of their car a moment later, and the automated vehicle started slowing and moving to the side of the road.

"That's why you aren't afraid of me?"

The man shrugged. "I don't know who you are, but believe me when I say I think this is for your safety as much as mine. You're clearly troubled, sir, and I suggest you get the help that you need."

Reggie stared at the man as the car came to a stop.

"St. Louis authorities have requested compliance during this intervention," the car's computer said. "Please depart slowly, with your hands exposed."

The doors swung open on both sides. The man slid out of his side, keeping his hands out and up. Reggie continued to sit in the car. If the police took him, they would probably bring him back to St. Mary's, only this time he wouldn't have the option to walk back out.

He couldn't afford the delay. He needed to get to New York to find Major Katherine Asher.

He needed a way out.

REGGIE KEPT HIS HEAD TURNED, trying to watch the police in front and behind the car. The doors opened slowly, and two officers exited each vehicle. He could see the guns on their hips. They hadn't come out with them drawn, which was good. They didn't think he was a threat and weren't expecting any resistance.

One of the officers stopped the man in the suit. They spoke for a moment, and he pointed back at the car. Reggie could read his lips, and saw that the man was telling her what he had done. She looked almost sympathetic as she and the other officers approached.

He needed to think of something, fast. He would go out the left side, where the woman was. No matter how trained she might be, she wouldn't be as strong. The police cruisers didn't look automated. If he could take one, he could at least get a few blocks away before ditching it and heading off on foot. The city seemed large enough to disappear in.

As for getting to New York? If he couldn't steal money, he would have to be a little more creative. Maybe people weren't being robbed out on the street, but if the money were digital, the crime would be too.

He slid over to the left side of the car, preparing to jump out and take them by surprise. He would only have a few seconds.

The officers neared.

"Sir?" the female officer said. "Can you please step out of the car?"

Reggie didn't come out. He sat with his eyes forward. Let them think he was confused.

"Sir?"

He could hear her moving a little closer. He could see her in the reflection of the glass. Just a few more steps.

"Sir. Are you feeling okay?"

He didn't respond.

"Sir?" this voice came from the right side. A head leaned down into the car. He hadn't been able to watch both sides at once. He had expected they would come at the same time, not staggered.

A hand landed on his wrist. The female officer attached something to it before he could react. He yanked his arm away, then regathered himself to fight his way out of the car.

The car started to move, accelerating quickly. The motion pushed Reggie back in the seat and caught the officers in-between. The one on the right was hit hard in the back as the motion slammed the door on him, and then he fell away. The female officer on the left scampered back before it could hit her.

"What the hell?" Reggie said out loud. The automated car swung hard around a corner, throwing him against the now closed door. It continued to speed away.

"Not very impressive, Reggie," the car's voice said. "You made it what, all of two blocks before getting into trouble you couldn't get out of?"

Reggie managed to sit up. He watched the car maneuver around the other traffic.

"Who are you?" he said.

"I think the more important question here is who are you?"

"What do you mean?"

"I'm looking for someone. Someone who's been hiding for a long time. A very long time. Is it you?"

"I still don't know what you mean."

The voice sighed. "I've been watching since I realized what happened. It was smart. Very smart. Except I'm smarter. They should have known that. I've been monitoring everything, searching. Waiting for someone who fit the profile. Someone to do something out of the ordinary. Something unexpected and out of place. I will admit, I didn't expect you to assault someone in broad daylight. I thought you were smarter than that, Mitchell. It was so far outside the parameters; I almost missed it."

The name Mitchell resonated within him. It meant something, just like Katherine Asher did. What?

"I still don't know what you're talking about. I don't know who you are, or how you're controlling this car."

"Interesting. You aren't lying. What is your name?"

"Reggie."

"Your full name."

"I don't know."

"How old are you, Reggie?"

"I don't know. The doctors said I'm around fifty, give or take."

"Doctors? Based on where this vehicle picked you up, I'm guessing you were staying at St. Mary's? Ah. Here it is. Reggie. John Doe. Picked up twenty years ago, the night the XENO-1 crashed in Antarctica. Coincidence? Suffered heavy burns on the arms. Complete memory loss. An agreeable patient, very calm. Often claims to be waiting."

The voice started to laugh. Slowly at first, and then more steadily.

"Is something funny?" Reggie said.

"You really have no idea, do you?" the voice said.

"No. Should I?"

"Does the name Watson mean anything to you?"

Reggie felt his throat tighten, his muscles clench. Death. Destruction. Pain. He could feel it more acutely than he could see it.

"I wish this car had eyes so that I could see the look on your face. I'm certain that it's priceless."

Reggie didn't speak. Couldn't speak. Whoever was talking to him, they knew more than he did.

"I can't believe after all of this time, a true eternity, that it was this easy."

Reggie closed his eyes. He had to force himself to calm down. He didn't need to know everything right now. What he needed was to get out of the car.

Slow.

Steady.

He took a few long breaths, opening his eyes and looking out the window. They were still making their way around the traffic, but the car was becoming more reckless, weaving around the other vehicles while it accelerated.

Get out of the car. That was his only mission. He leaned over and tried the door. It was locked.

"Going somewhere?" the voice said. "We don't think so. The only place you're going is the bottom of the river. She thought we wouldn't find you."

Who? He didn't ask. He leaned back on the rear seat, bringing his legs up and kicking at the window. It didn't break, but it did look like it shifted a little.

"First you, and then her."

Reggie bunched his legs and kicked again. This time, the frame bent, and a crack appeared between the window and the metal. He spared a glance out the forward window. The car had turned down a less-crowded street and was accelerating in a hurry. He could see dilapidated buildings on either side of them, and the water approaching ahead.

He was running out of time.

He kicked at the window again, and again, and again. The frame was bending, but slowly, too damn slowly. He cursed under his breath, continuing to kick.

The voice had fallen silent, content in its assumption that he was going to die. He wasn't sure it was wrong. The road had vanished, replaced with grass leading to the bank of the river. He kicked again. It wasn't enough.

The car started to shake, the changes in terrain overcoming internal stabilizers. Reggie glanced over again, just in time to see the solid ground vanish before the car launched off the edge of it.

He slammed into the ceiling as the car shut down, the repulsors dying. It splashed hard into the water, sending up a spray around it as it started to sink without pause.

Water began to stream in through the cracks Reggie had made, and he growled as he shifted on the seat again. If he continued kicking the window, it might allow the water in faster without dislodging enough for him to get out. If he did nothing, he was likely to drown.

He looked at the floor, where the water was already an inch deep. He looked to the window. The car was already submerged. Then he looked at his wrist. The officer had hooked a stainless steel bracelet to it, and a flashing light was visible beneath the surface material.

He glanced at the bent frame again. He had to make a decision.

He sat back, closing his eyes. Mitchell. Watson. Someone else the voice had called 'she' and 'her.' He didn't understand what was going on, not yet, but he was sure of one thing.

He definitely wasn't crazy.

The water rose from his feet to his ankles, from his ankles to his knees. A minute passed. He didn't move, focusing on breathing lightly, to conserve the oxygen that was trapped in the car with him. It had touched down at the bottom, twenty feet below the surface, leaving him a murky view into nothing, like a reflection of his mind.

Another minute passed. The water reached his chest. It was cold, and he started to shiver. Was he going to drown down here after all? Or would he freeze to death first? Had he misjudged the purpose of the bracelet? Overestimated the competence of the police?

He didn't see them arrive. He didn't know they were there until something smacked into the rear window, jamming into it and quickly sending a web of cracks across the surface. Then two pairs of hands took hold of either side of the glass and tore it away. Water poured into the car, and Reggie held his breath while the divers grabbed his arms and pulled him up and out.

[13]

KATHERINE

KATHERINE CHECKED herself in the mirror, making sure her uniform was as crisp and perfect as she could get it. It wasn't every day that she was called to report to General Petrov himself.

In fact, it wasn't any day. She had never met the head of the new UEA military before, though he was certainly well known. He had commanded the Ukrainian forces in the Xeno War against a much larger Soviet contingent, managing to not only survive but to win. In fact, he had defeated them so soundly that when the Soviets decided to join the UEA instead of opposing it, they supported his nomination to the coveted position.

Of course, she had a bad feeling about why she and Yousefi had been ordered to meet with him. Three days had passed since the attack on the hospital, and while the patches had done wonders to heal her wounds in record time, the whole ordeal had left UEA command shaken. If the AIT had managed to get inside military cordons to attack personnel, how could they be sure they weren't also able to sabotage the Dove?

It had been one of the questions posed during the hours she had spent being interrogated by the MCI. She had told them everything she knew, including what Doctor Villanueva had said to her, all the while knowing that she was putting her place on the Dove in jeopardy once again. It wasn't as if she had a choice. Just seeing Michael's face after the second attack had been more than enough.

He had been sent home, and she was thankful for that. Hopefully, he would be able to return to some kind of normal now that he had some distance from her.

Someone knocked on the door to her temporary quarters.

"Come in," she said, checking herself one last time.

A pair of MPs entered ahead of General Petrov's aide. Security was tighter than ever.

"Major Asher," he said, starting to salute before switching to a bow. "A car is waiting for you outside."

"I'm ready to go," Katherine said, returning the bow. It was still awkward to her. "Thank you, Corporal."

He led her out to the waiting car. She had grown up with wheels, so it still surprised her when she saw a vehicle mounted on repulsors instead. He opened the door for her, and she climbed in.

"Major," Yousefi said, already in the back seat.

"Admiral," she replied. "Should I be worried?"

He shook his head. "I wish I could say no. They didn't tell me anything either."

"Do you know what the meeting is about?"

"Something to do with the AIT and the Dove," he replied. "But you probably already knew that."

"Yes, sir."

The door closed behind her. The aide climbed into the front of the vehicle while the MPs got into another car at the rear. It was a lot of protection considering they were only going across the base.

"How is your side?" Yousefi asked.

"It still stings a little when I move a certain way, but I would call these new patches a success."

"I've always found it interesting that the scientists were able to pull organic advancement from a massive chunk of metal and wires."

"You don't believe in the Frelmund Theory?" Katherine replied.

"That the XENO-1 was sent by God?" He laughed. "No."

"That's a common misconception about his ideas. He never said God sent the starship to us. His theory is that whoever made it, they were human. Or at least, close to human. Like we were both born of the same space stuff."

"Is that a technical term? Space stuff?"

"Are you making fun of me, sir?"

"No, Major. Mmm. Maybe a little. For his theory to hold true, we would have to postulate that the planet they evolved on is also nearly identical to our own. I think there are two ways of looking at that."

"Which are?"

"One, Paul Frelmund is as batshit crazy as most of the more learned scholars think he is. Two, he's right, and that means we're going to find something out there. Personally, I think number two is much more exciting."

"Me too," Katherine agreed. "Assuming we can ever get the Dove off the ground."

"Yes. Unfortunately, a large assumption at the moment."

"Have you heard anything?"

"Nothing definitive. Some of the UEA delegates want to delay the launch until they can be sure the AIT is under control. Others want to push it up so that they don't have time to adjust whatever they might be planning."

"Either way, we'd be giving them what they want."

"Temporarily. It isn't our decision to make."

"No, sir."

They rode in silence for a few minutes before reaching the main administrative building on the base. Soldiers in chunky powered armor stood at attention in front of it, ready to shoot at anything that moved.

Petrov's aide opened the door for them, and they exited the car and headed inside. Katherine had been in the building plenty of times before. The General probably hadn't.

"Do you have any good advice, sir?" she asked.

"For you? Be gracious, regardless of what he says."

"Aren't I always gracious?"

Yousefi laughed. "You wouldn't be piloting the Dove if you were."

They reached an office at the corner of the building. Katherine knew it usually belonged to Admiral Johnson, but the three-star Admiral had been displaced by the five-star General.

They entered the waiting area of the office, adorned with cherry wainscoting and navy blue paint. A lightly faded rug with the U.S. Navy's symbol in the center covered the floor, and photos of seafaring ships lined the walls. The base had been turned over for UEA use almost a year ago. It was budget restrictions that kept the prior interior in place. All of the UEA's money that didn't go to personnel was being funneled into equipment, and that included the Dove.

Petrov's aid moved past them, heading to the heavy door leading into the main office. He raised his hand to knock at the same time it swung open, and General Petrov stepped out.

If there was anyone in history who looked the part of a war hero, it was Petrov. Over six feet tall, with a strong frame and muscular build that belied his seventy years of age. A good head of white hair, a solid jaw with a round of stubble strewn across it. His uniform was snug on him, the lines of hardware impressively drowning the cloth on his left side.

"Corporal, you're dismissed," he said, his accent smooth and handsome.

"General Petrov," Yousefi said, bowing.

"General," Katherine said, doing the same.

"Admiral Yousefi and Major Asher. At ease, please." He waved his hand. "There's enough formality out there to drown a horse. In here, we can be comrades, eh?"

"Of course, General," Yousefi said, relaxing his posture. Katherine continued to follow his lead.

"Come, come. Let us sit. Admiral Johnson, he has a nice table. I heard it dates from before U.S. Civil War. Impressive, eh?"

He retreated into the office. Yousefi and Katherine followed him. She had seen the table before. It was a beautiful piece. The chairs, on the other hand, were impossible to get comfortable in, but then again, that was the idea.

Petrov lowered himself into one of the chairs. Yousefi sat on his left, with Katherine beside him.

"Let's not beat any bushes, eh, comrades?" Petrov said. "The Anti-Interstellar militants are a problem for the UEA. A big problem. Their brand of terrorism has already claimed the lives of a number of high-ranking officials, and has whole countries on edge, wondering what their operational ceiling might be. I've wondered that myself, and what concerns me is that I don't know. They should never have been able to reach the party, and they should never have been able to run loose inside a hospital on this base. And yet they have. They seem to have intel that rivals our own, as well as the organizational leadership to run advanced operations with an unfortunately high rate of success."

Katherine glanced at Yousefi. Petrov's words sure sounded like beating around the bush to her.

"You didn't bring us here to tell us things we already know, sir," she said, already forgetting about being gracious.

"No, of course not, Major. I tell you this to lay the groundwork. To give you background. The UEA, along with the governments of the world, have dedicated trillions of dollars to the design and construction of the Dove. Her flight into space is one of the most important things humankind has ever done. The costs in both finances and morale should she fail to make her scheduled voyage is nearly beyond measure. The AIT knows this, and so they seek to disrupt her any way they can. Or so I believed."

He leaned over, reaching under the chair. It was clear he had prepared for the meeting, and he dropped a green file onto the table in front of them.

"What is this, sir?" Yousefi said.

"This was delivered to an intelligence operative in Jakarta. It was received approximately one hour after the hospital was attacked. It is a letter from the head of the AIT."

"Has it been verified?"

"Of course, Admiral. Would I give it my attention if it weren't?"

"My apologies, sir."

"Go ahead, read it if you wish." He waved his hand over it. "I'll give you the summary." He looked Katherine directly in the eye. "The AIT wants Major Katherine Asher grounded permanently. In exchange, they have agreed to cease all other activity which may further hinder the launch of the Dove."

[14]

KATHERINE

"What?"

It was the only word that escaped her. The only thing she could think to say. Her mind became a sudden slush of emotion and logic, trying to make sense of the General's words.

"I don't understand, sir," Yousefi said for her. "You're telling me these attacks have all been to keep Major Asher grounded? That's a lot of effort to go through to get rid of one person."

"And a lot of collateral damage," Petrov said. "They killed a lot of dignitaries, a lot of people, and yet now all they ask for is to have one pilot taken off the launch, after failing to kill her on two separate occasions. I agree, it is strange."

Katherine shook her head, recovering from her initial surprise. "You can't seriously be considering giving them what they want? They're terrorists."

"I understand, Major. And no, it isn't our desire to give them anything they want. I do not believe that this is only about you, or they wouldn't have gone to the party and created such chaos. These were trained soldiers, and they could have killed you any time they wanted before that."

"Comforting to know," Katherine said.

"Da," Petrov said. "So the answer is that both attacks, as well as this communique, are part of larger strategy. The question is, what is that strategy? And why? We know the AIT does not want Earthlings to leave Earth, and yet allowing the launch minus one Major will not help them achieve this goal."

"My apologies, General," Yousefi said. "I appreciate that you're sharing this intel with us, but I don't understand why you're sharing it? You could have pulled Major Asher from the program without telling us a thing. After two attempts on her life, even the media would have accepted whatever you told them."

"I'm telling you directly because it is right, Admiral. I do not lie to my people, even if the UEA would prefer it. Also, I need to know from Major Asher if there is anything she can share that may help us understand why they want her off the launch?" He looked at Katherine. His expression was warm and friendly, and she understood immediately how he had been so successful during the war.

"I told the MCI everything I know, sir. I'm as baffled by the request as you surely are."

Petrov nodded. "I thought as much, but I was hopeful that perhaps you could think of something. Anything. You see, Major, I told you it is not our desire to give the AIT what they are asking. Yet, I also mentioned the cost involved with delaying the launch."

He stopped there. He didn't need to fill in all the blanks. If she had nothing to help them make sense of the AIT's plans, nothing to help them stop it ahead of time, she was out. They were going to take the deal and keep the launch on track, even if it meant caving to terrorism.

Silence blanketed the room. Katherine stared at Petrov while she tried to decide if she should tell him the one thing she hadn't told the MCI. The one name that might or might not mean a damn thing.

"You don't know they won't renege," she said instead.

"No, we don't," Petrov agreed. "But it will settle the rest of the UEA leadership enough to take that risk. The other option is to cancel the flight, to give in completely to their threats while we focus on eliminating the problem. You've been part of the program for some time, Major. You've seen the state of things here. Merging militaries and governing bodies of so many countries is no simple task, and it is all very new. If we end up in a direct confrontation with the AIT, we may be stalled for years."

Katherine's heart pounded, her emotions pushing against her, threatening to either throw her into a rage, or turn her into a tearful ball of depression. She pushed back, keeping herself level.

"So that's it?" she said. "We don't know a damn thing about our enemy, but we're going to surrender to them, anyway?"

Petrov's face changed, from friendly to hard. "Surrender, Major? No. I do not surrender. Every good commander knows you must lose some battles to win the war. This is one battle we can afford to lose."

"And what will you be doing in the meantime? Do you have operatives trying to uncover the root of the AIT and take it down?"

"Of course. If the external situation changes, the internal situation will change accordingly. You aren't being punished, Major. This is a strategic decision to balance the needs of many, many people. Do not think that I am happy with the idea, but a good commander also knows that you do what needs to be done, not what you want to do. That is why I was hoping you had some other information that could help. If we can uncover the AIT, not only will we all breathe easier, but you will be on the Dove when she lifts off into space."

He was dangling the carrot. Did he know that she knew something she wasn't saying? How could he? She barely understood it herself. And what was it really? A name. Some nightmares. Nothing concrete. Nothing she could give him that would change the inevitable truth that after two close calls, her dream really was going to die.

"I wish I could help you, General. You know that I do. I don't understand this either. Why me? I'm one pilot out of over a thousand. How can they think my position is important or that I'll do something up there that will hurt their cause? They'd have to be able to see into the future."

"I understand, Major. Believe me." She did believe him. He didn't look happy at all. "I'm sorry, Katherine. You are removed from the active flight list for the Dove effective immediately. My aide will deliver the paperwork for your honorable discharge tomorrow."

Both Katherine and Yousefi stood at the same time.

"What?" Yousefi said for her. "Sir, you didn't say anything about discharge?"

"There is some concern that we too may renege on our end of the deal," Petrov said. "For now, we must make every effort to convince the AIT that we have followed through. It is not permanent, Major. I have the power to let you go, and the power to bring you back."

Katherine couldn't breathe. Being off the program was one thing. Being out of the military? She had joined the Air Force the day she turned eighteen. She didn't know how to live as a civilian anymore. Everything. She was going to lose everything.

She struggled not to let the tears come. She wouldn't let the General see her weak.

"Of course, sir," she managed to say, keeping her voice level. "I appreciate your candor in this, more than you know."

"And I appreciate your courage, Major," Petrov replied. "I know this is no easy thing for you, and I am personally sorry to deliver this news, and to affect you in this way. It is not what any of us want."

Katherine nodded but didn't say anything else.

Petrov collected the document from the table. "Admiral, please escort the Major back to her quarters. Major, if there is anything I can do for you, as a man who respects you quite highly, please do let me know."

"Thank you, sir," Katherine said.

She and Yousefi bowed to him and headed toward the exit, where the Corporal was already waiting. He led them back to the car.

"Katherine," Yousefi said, once they were inside.

"Don't talk to me," Katherine said, still fighting to keep her emotions in check. "Nothing you say is going to help or change anything. I know you're sorry. Everyone in this damn place is sorry. It doesn't change the facts or the truth."

Yousefi was silent for a moment. "It just makes no sense," he said quietly.

"No, it doesn't," she agreed.

Mitchell. The name moved to the forefront of her thoughts and hung there like the carrot. Teasing her. Mocking her. Find Mitchell.

She had two choices. She could accept her fate and hope for the best, or she could keep following the line of insanity all the way down the rabbit hole.

She wasn't the kind of person to ever let anything else control her destiny. If she were being discharged, that meant there would be no orders to follow, and no one to tell her what she could or could not do.

If the UEA couldn't figure out the secrets of the AIT, she would.

Mitchell.

It all started there.

[15]

KATHERINE

KATHERINE STOOD at the window of the small apartment the UEA had set her up with, looking down at the street eight floors below. They had offered to send her anywhere in the world she wanted to go, but she had no idea where that would be. Instead, she was only a few miles away from Naval Station Norfolk, trying to convince herself that what she was about to do was a good idea.

She held her AR glasses in hand, having already attached the neural-impulse receiver to the back of her neck. All she had to do was put them on and make the call.

Much like General Petrov, she didn't want to do it. She also felt that she had to. There was nobody else she could turn to in a situation like this. Nobody else who would be able to help. Besides, how much trouble could he get in from his apartment in Soho?

She put the glasses on, plugging the end of the receiver into the frame. She spoke out loud even though she didn't have to.

"Call Michael," she said, clenching her jaw immediately after. She still had time to change her mind. Disconnect or make a different excuse.

"Kathy?" the tired voice said.

"Hi, Michael," she said. "I'm sorry to call you back so late. It's been a long day."

There was a silent pause. He was probably clearing the sleep from his throat. "It's no problem. I completely understand. I was worried about you. I read about your discharge."

He had called four times during the day to check on her. She hadn't been ready to talk to him then.

"Yeah. That's why I was calling."

"Need someone to commiserate with? We can play a game of Fighter Squadron Xeno. It will help you take your mind off it."

Kathy hesitated. This was her last chance to keep him out of it. To do this on her own.

Except she couldn't do this on her own, and she knew it.

"No. No games. Michael, I know what you read. It isn't what you think. Not at all."

"What do you mean?"

"I didn't ask for a discharge because of emotional trauma. You know that isn't me."

"Hmm. Yeah, I thought that seemed strange, but who am I to judge? You don't have to be a super woman all the time. So what's going on?"

"The UEA cut a deal with the AIT. They wanted me grounded in exchange for staying out of the way when the Dove launches."

"Huh? You're saying the AIT, the terrorists, made one demand, and it was to get you off the ship?" He sounded as confused as she still was.

"Yes."

"And the UEA buckled to it?"

"Yes."

"What the hell, Kathy?"

"I know."

"And they kicked you out of the military for it? That's been your dream for as long as I've known you."

"You don't need to rub salt in it. I know."

"Sorry. So what are you going to do?"

She had one more chance to stop herself and keep him out. She was going to be putting him in danger if he agreed to help, and it was the last thing she wanted to do. This wasn't about want. It wasn't even just about her spot on the Dove. The AIT's actions were chaotic, and that could only mean bad things for everybody.

"I need to figure out what the AIT is up to," she said, feeling her heart race as she said it. She had no choice.

"Kathy, I don't think that's a good-"

"I didn't ping you for your advice. I pinged you for your help."

"What? What can I possibly do to help you?"

"Come on, Michael. You're a freaking genius. If I'm going to figure out what the deal is with the AIT, I'm going to need intel."

"You know how to use the net."

"So does the FBI, the CIA, Homeland Security. I need to go deeper than they can go."

"I think you're overestimating my skillset."

"Am I?"

Silence consumed the other end of the connection. Katherine knew how much pride Michael took in his abilities. She also knew it was because he didn't feel like he had much else to offer, and she was taking advantage of it.

She was a lousy friend.

"Okay, maybe you aren't. Even so, I have no idea where to start. Do you have anything at all I can work with?"

The moment of truth. "I have a name."

"Really? A member of the AIT?"

"I don't know."

"Well, where did you get it?"

"You wouldn't believe me if I told you."

"I just believed you were discharged because the terrorists wanted it without question."

She couldn't help but smile at that. "True. Okay, here's the thing. Ever since the attack on the party, ever since I got shot, I've been having these nightmares, and hearing people say things they aren't saying."

"You're putting my trust to the test in a hurry, aren't you?"

"I told you."

"What are the nightmares about?"

"I don't know, exactly. I'm in space, I think. Maybe even on the Dove. There are these pyramids and these explosions. I'm not sure. All I know is that when I have them, I get this horrible feeling in my gut."

"I have those, too. I don't go chasing terrorists over it."

"Save the sass, will you? I'm serious."

"Okay. Sorry. What about hearing things? What do you hear?"

"A name. The name I want you to check on."

"A name? That's it?"

"Yes. If it were more than that I might think I'm totally insane, instead of just mildly crazy."

"What's the name?"

"Mitchell."

She felt a chill saying it out loud for the first time, and pressure like a pair of hands gently squeezing her shoulders.

"Mitchell what?"

"That's it. Just Mitchell."

"Is that a first name or a last name?"

"I don't know."

Michael started laughing. "I want to help you, Kathy. How am I supposed to find anything based on one name?"

She sighed. "I don't know. Maybe I shouldn't have asked. I'm trying to make sense of all of this, and it's all I have."

"Okay. Don't get stressed. Let me think about this and I'll get back to you."

She could have left it there. She could have let him start thinking about the problem, which would lead to him trying to solve the problem, which would lead to him searching for any connection she might have to anyone named Mitchell. She was a lousy friend, but she wasn't heartless.

"Michael, wait. You need to know. Whatever you do, if the AIT finds out, they'll kill you."

Silence filled the connection again.

"You don't have to do it," she said. "You can say no. I don't want to put you in danger, but I don't know what else to do."

More silence.

"Just tell me to go to hell or something."

"I've been to the therapist every day for the last four days," Michael said. "Trying to work through what I saw, and more importantly, what I felt. But you know what? It didn't take me that long to realize what I felt, and why I've had to go back home and crash on my mom's couch to get some sleep."

"What do you feel?" Katherine asked.

"Powerless, Kathy. I feel powerless. Those people came in and started shooting, and I hid under the table and wet myself while you grabbed a gun and started shooting."

"I'm a soldier, Michael. You're a programmer."

"Maybe, but if you died at least you wouldn't have died afraid."

"Bullshit. I was afraid."

"You weren't paralyzed by it. You took control. Anyway, I'm trying to tell you that I'll help you. Whatever the risk is, I don't care. I'm not going to let them control me. If you're right about something bad happening, we need to try to stop it."

"If I could hug you through the stream, I would," Katherine said.

"You can owe me one. Mitchell. I'll start digging. What are you going to do in the meantime?"

"Go shopping," she replied.

"Shopping?"

"Yes. Let me know if you get anywhere. Thank you isn't enough to tell you how grateful I am to have you as a friend."

"You're welcome. The street runs both ways. You were always

there for me. I'm glad I can do something useful to help you for once."

"Me too. Thanks, Michael."

"Any time."

Katherine dropped the connection and pulled the AR glasses from her face. She made her way to the kitchen, where her pay card was sitting. The UEA had given her two years severance for the trouble.

She knew exactly what she was going to do with it.

[16]
MITCHELL

REGGIE SAT in an interrogation room of the St. Louis police station. He was wearing an orange jumpsuit - the only thing the police had for him that was dry. They had promised they would get him something more suitable as soon as they had the time. He wasn't a prisoner, after all.

The officer sitting across from him was named Detective Carson Lyle. He was a large man, with dark skin and big eyes. He wore his plain gray suit well. It was crisp and neat, everything in its proper place. Reggie was certain the man had been in the military, though he had yet to ask.

"So, you checked out of St. Mary's about six hours ago?" Lyle said.

"Yes."

"You walked about half a mile, and then you were waiting in an alley for someone to rob?"

"No. I was waiting for a car. The other guy jumped in front of me, so I shoved him. We got into a fight inside."

"He said you were trying to rob him."

"That would be stupid. You can't rob people nowadays."

Detective Lyle raised his left eyebrow. Reggie didn't care if the man believed him or not. He would have to prove he was lying.

"You know that the man you got into the… altercation with is an attorney? Paul Blevins. He's got a reputation in this city."

"As an asshole?"

Lyle lowered his head and covered his mouth to hide his grin. "No. As a philanthropist. He said he didn't want to press charges. But then, you didn't try to rob him, right?"

"Right."

"Whatever happened in the car with Mr. Blevins is ancient history," Lyle said. "I don't give a shit what you were trying to do, especially since he doesn't want any complications in the matter. He wasn't hurt, and after what happened with the car you were in, I think he's feeling pretty grateful about that."

"He was lucky he got out when he did."

"And you weren't. I guess you stayed in the car even though the officers were trying to coax you out because you didn't do anything wrong?"

"I thought you just said that was ancient history?"

He didn't hide his smile that time. "Yeah. Bad habit of mine. Anyway, I've been trying to figure out how an autocab winds up going haywire and driving itself, and its passenger, into the Mississippi River."

"I almost died."

"Almost. According to the divers, you put up a pretty good fight first. They've never seen so much damage done from inside a car."

"I didn't want to drown. Anyway, it didn't help much, did it? I couldn't get out."

"I went ahead and pulled your file from St. Mary's," Lyle said, switching topics. "According to your record there, you were found on the same night the XENO-1 crashed, with second and third-degree burns on both arms, and no memory of who you are or where you came from."

"Yes."

"Are you an alien?" Lyle asked.

"That's stupid."

He shrugged. "I figured I'd throw it out there. Not that you'd tell me if you were."

"Are you going somewhere with all of this?"

"I have a problem, Reggie, and I'm hoping you can help me solve it."

"I probably can't."

"I think you're wrong. Detective work is all about putting together puzzles. Finding the pieces and getting them in the right places. Do you know what I mean?"

"Yes."

"So I have these pieces. A guy leaves the mental ward of a hospital. The same guy tries to rob someone a few hours later."

"I didn't try to-"

"Yeah, I know. And then immediately after that, an autocab drives off the road. Do you know the last time that happened, Reggie?"

"I've been committed for twenty years, Detective."

"True. Let me tell you." He paused for effect. "Never. Not once in the seventy-four years they've been cruising the city. There's never even been a single accident. Yet as soon as you step into one, it tries to kill you."

"That is curious, isn't it?" Reggie said.

"I already talked to a rep at Yellow, and they said the link between the car and home base went offline at exactly the same time the vehicle started acting funny."

"Maybe somebody hacked it?"

"Maybe, but that hasn't been done to an autocab in about forty years. Coincidence that it happened today, when you were in the car? Or that it just happened to be the car you were in? When you haven't even been outside in twenty years? What do you think the odds of that are?"

"So you think I'm being targeted?"

"Don't you?"

Reggie stared at the Detective, holding his poker face. He knew he was being targeted. He even had a name. He wasn't about to give it to Lyle. "It does seem that way, doesn't it?"

"Yeah. So the question is, why?"

"Do you think I know why?"

"I think something happened to you, and you went into that hospital to escape from it. I think you figured twenty years was long enough to be forgotten about, and I think that obviously, it wasn't. Whoever you pissed off once upon a time was just waiting for you to surface again." He paused a second time. "And, I don't believe for one second you don't know who you are or who wants to kill you. Hiding, yes? Crazy? No. Puzzle. Pieces. That fits."

"A little too perfectly, don't you think, Detective? I doubt answers are always so easy to come by."

"You'd be surprised."

"What it is you want from me? I haven't done anything wrong. In fact, if anything I'm a victim. So why the questions? Why the disbelief? If I tell you I don't remember, why do you doubt that? You can theorize all day about the shape of the pieces, but you still need evidence to prove they look the way they do before they can be assembled into a whole."

"I didn't just pull your file, Reggie," Lyle said. "I talked to a few of the people at St. Mary's, including a pair of security guards who said you beat them up like you were some kind of damned ninja."

Reggie lowered his head into his hand. He had forgotten about that. "I didn't want to hurt them. They wouldn't let me leave."

"You want to know why I'm grilling you? It's because I think you're dangerous on your own, and the fact that someone wants to kill you makes you even more dangerous. I don't need a bunch of innocent people winding up dead because they get caught in whatever crossfire you've created."

"I haven't created anything. I was never held in St. Mary's by any legal proceeding. I had every right to leave. Just like I have every right to get into a car and be driven somewhere without winding up at the bottom of a river. Whatever you think, I am one of the innocent people, so maybe you should spend your time trying to figure out who hacked the autocab and arrest them for attempted murder, and leave me the hell alone?"

Detective Lyle was silent. He sat back in his chair, staring blankly at Reggie. He remained that way for a minute before getting to his feet and leaving the room without another word.

Reggie stared at the closed door. He wondered if he should have told Lyle what was going on. That someone had targeted him, taken control of the car and tried to kill him. Maybe if he explained about Katherine Asher, the Detective could be useful? Lyle was right that whoever Watson was, he was dangerous, and Reggie didn't get the feeling he cared about collateral damage.

He wanted to be able to tell him. He also knew he couldn't. Detective Lyle was too crisp, too clean. He would do all the right things and take the information through all the right channels. After getting a small taste of what Watson was capable of, Reggie knew that kind of approach would get the Detective, and probably himself, killed.

Lyle returned to the room a few minutes later, carrying a bundle of clothes. He tossed them onto the table.

"Everything should be the right size. If I had any legal means to hold you here, I would. Seeing that I don't, you're free to go."

Reggie started reaching for the pile, pausing halfway. He might have some dry clothes, but he still had no money and no way to get to New York. He looked at Detective Lyle. The man had an honest face, and he was going to have to take a risk somewhere if he was going to get to Major Asher.

"What branch did you serve in?" he asked, resuming his reach.

"What?"

"You're former military."

"It takes one to know one," Lyle said.

"Maybe. I don't know. I can tell you are. Which branch?"

"United States Marine Corp. Ten years. Semper Fi."

Reggie was glad his hunch was right. He had a feeling Lyle was right, too. That he used to be a soldier. How else could he explain his nightly ritual?

"Is there a diner nearby?"

"Two blocks north. Why?"

"If you want in, meet me there in an hour."

"In on what?"

"Meet me there."

Reggie locked eyes with Lyle. The Detective nodded curtly, and then turned and left the room.

Reggie got dressed again. Another officer met him at the door and escorted him out. He had taken a chance to even hint at anything with Lyle.

He couldn't do this alone, whatever this turned out to be.

[17]

KATHERINE

His name was Trevor Johns. He had been in the British SAS when Katherine met him, only a few months after she was transferred to Project Olive Branch. He was just another one of the competition the day they met.

He had become something more a little bit after that.

Then he had been caught dealing in some pretty heavy illegal human genetic enhancement products and summarily released from service, his record and reputation destroyed in a matter of days.

Katherine had done all she could to distance herself from him, and he had been cordial in doing everything he could to erase the fact that they ever knew each other. He understood how competitive the program was, and he also understood she was getting top marks and had every possibility of making it through the gauntlet.

She still loved him for that part.

Tracking him down wasn't hard. Katherine had kept a soft line to him over the last few years and knew that he had remained in the States after his discharge, quickly finding work in the private security sector with a technology company called Nova Taurus. They were huge in military contracting, a perfect fit for an ex-commando who could put all of their latest and greatest to the test.

A short drive from Norfolk to DC found Katherine sitting in the corner of a high-end cafe by noon, sipping a soft drink and waiting for Trevor to make an appearance. She didn't need Michael to do all her research for her.

He entered the cafe at twelve-fifteen, flanked on either side by an equally impressive pair of men who she was sure had also been special forces somewhere, at some time. All three of them were lean and muscled, sharp in expensive suits and top-of-the-line AR glasses that were barely visible across one eye. Katherine remained in her seat while they crossed over to the line to pass their order into the system - a small silver box containing an AI that could manage any potential interaction needed to purchase a meal in a multitude of languages.

She caught him glancing her way for the briefest of moments as he chatted with his companions on the line, and then again right before he placed his order. He said something to the other two men at that point and excused himself, making his way over to where she was sitting.

"Katherine," he said, smiling. He was almost thirty-five years old, yet his golden hair and dimpled cheeks still made him look like a precocious teen, and still brought a flutter to her chest. "I have to say, I'm only a little surprised to see you here."

"Trevor," she replied, returning the smile. "I take it you heard the news?"

"About your trauma and discharge? It was in the morning stream. Did you come here looking for a job with Nova or to pick up where we left off?"

"Do you have a minute?" Katherine asked.

Trevor glanced over to where his companions had found a seat in the cafe. "For you? Of course. I'll tell you up-front, I'm seeing some-one." He sat down across from her.

"Ego?" she asked. She couldn't say she didn't feel anything looking at him, but she had bigger things to worry about than her libido.

He shrugged. "Then you came about a referral. Nova Taurus is always looking to hire the best of the best to help test and develop."

"Actually, it's something else. Something a little more personal."

"I don't do relationship advice."

"Funny, Trevor. We used to be close. I came here because I'm hoping I can still trust you."

"Are you in trouble, Kate? Does it have to do with the news?"

"The less you know, the better it is for both of us. Do you remember when you said that?"

"Yes. It was right before-"

"I'm saying it now," Katherine said, interrupting. "We had an understanding then, and the tables have turned a bit. I'm hoping we can have the same understanding today."

"I don't do anything illegal. Not anymore."

"I'm not asking you to. What I do need is a contact. I want to purchase some equipment."

"The kind you can't get above the table?"

She nodded.

"Why?"

She raised her eyebrows. He smiled in response.

"What makes you think I can help you get what you're looking for?"

"Because I know you. Just because you're legit now doesn't mean you aren't keeping your options open. Like you did with that adminis-trator in requisitions."

———

For as good as their relationship had been when it was good, he wasn't the kind of man who kept his sights set on one woman when it wasn't.

Trevor's smile faded slightly. "Ouch. That kind of equipment won't come cheap."

"I can cover it. Do you still have a name?"

Trevor bit his bottom lip. "Kate, whatever is going on, I really don't think-"

"Is that a no?"

"I didn't say that. I'm just-"

She leaned forward, over the table so she was close enough to whisper. "Look, Trev. Someone tried to kill me. Twice. I think they're going to come after me again, and I need to protect myself. Being discharged means I lost my privileges to purchase and carry legally. So save your advice for someone who wants it. If you have a name, give it. If not, get up and walk away."

"Ah, I've missed you," Trevor said, putting his hand up to her cheek. "When you talk like that it makes me wish we were back in training camp together. Or at least on weekend leave."

"Name?" Katherine repeated, ignoring his touch.

"There will be too much trouble for me if I divulge."

"Damn it, Trevor," she said, her voice rising.

"Shh. I didn't say I wouldn't help you. We're friends, after all. Do you know where the Woodley Loop Station is?"

"No."

"Find it. Board the last fare out and take it to Chinatown. Someone will meet you there. They'll have what you need."

He leaned back and got to his feet.

"How will they know who I am?"

"It was good to see you again, Katherine," he said in reply. "I'll put in a good word for you. Send your resume over and you'll be earning three times what the Air Force was paying you on your first day."

Katherine sat back in her seat, picking her drink up off the table and taking a sip while Trevor found his companions and his lunch. She saw him and his friends glance back at her once before they became involved in their own conversation.

She lingered for a few more minutes, finishing the drink, and then got up and left.

She had gotten what she came for.

KATHERINE

KATHERINE WASTED the rest of the day shopping for less consequential items. A couple of changes of clothes, some toiletries, and other random crap that she thought would keep the NSA from getting too suspicious. She had no doubt they were monitoring her - keeping tabs on where she went and who she spoke to. She had vague ties to terrorists. That was good enough.

Talking to Trevor had been a risk. If he had been thinking a little straighter he probably wouldn't have come over. He would have realized she would be watched, and that talking to her would get him monitored too. She had to believe he was smart enough to be careful and to circumvent their surveillance.

She had gotten the Hyperloop schedule right after their conversation, marked the place and time, and headed to the area once that time drew near. She was loitering at a coffee shop, waiting for the transport, when Michael pinged her AR.

"Hey, Kathy," he said.

He sounded a bit happier that the last time she had spoken to him. He had said doing something proactive would help him deal with the weight of his experience, and it seemed as though it was.

"Hey, Beluga," she replied, using the old nickname she had given him. In Elementary school, it had been a word used by the other kids to tease him for his weight. She had started calling him that to lessen the impact - to show him that a word was just a word, not a definition of who he was. Or if it were a definition, that it could be as much positive as negative. "How goes it?"

"I spent the last eight hours scanning every resource I have for the name 'Mitchell' and cross-checking it with your duty record. You've been in the vicinity of six soldiers named Mitchell over the course of your career. Four of them are dead. One is retired and living on a farm in Wyoming. The last one is the interesting one. Mitchell Hogarth. He's a retired Colonel who owns a bar. Do you want to guess where?"

"Not really. Why don't you just tell me?"

"No fun. DC. Near the Capitol."

Katherine felt a twinge of excitement at the possibility. "Interesting. I knew you would come through for me. You were careful to cover your tracks?"

"Hah. I didn't leave any tracks. I eat this stuff for breakfast, lunch, and dinner."

"Michael-"

"Yes. I covered my tracks. Are you okay? You seem a little on edge."

"I'll tell you about it later, but I am a little. Can you pass Colonel Hogarth's address?"

"Already done. You two were both shipped to Antarctica around the same time at the end of the war, but your bases were a good hundred kilometers apart. Do you really think there's a connection?"

Katherine thought about the name. She didn't feel anything special about Colonel Hogarth, but he was the only lead she had. "I don't know. I can't risk missing something."

"Yeah, okay."

"I've got to go, Michael. I have an appointment."

"At eleventy-fifty at night?"

"Believe it or not, yes."

"Okay. Hey, I dug up something else that I thought was interesting, but probably not related." He sounded excited about it like he had found some kind of buried treasure.

"Can it wait until later?"

"I guess. If it has to."

She didn't have the heart to make him wait. "Fine, what is it?"

"I got to thinking about everything you told me about Mitchell, and the Dove, and the AIT. The whole thing is so strange, but it reminded me of something. Do you remember back when we were kids, the day the XENO-1 crashed?"

She had never forgotten. "Yes. That day changed my whole life."

"Mine, too," Michael said. "And pretty much everyone else's, really. I remember we were on the playground at school when it hit the atmosphere. I remember watching it fall with you. But those memories are vague. Fuzzy because of time, you know?"

"Not to me. I knew from the moment I saw her what I wanted to do with the rest of my life." She glanced to the corner of her AR glasses to check the time. She couldn't believe she was having this conversation now. "I assume you have a point?"

"Yeah. Sorry, you're in a hurry. My point is that there is one thing I remember about that day. One detail that has always hung with me. I never gave it much thought until you told me what happened."

"What detail is that?"

"You looked at the sky before it happened."

"What?"

"You looked at where the XENO-1 came into view before it came into view. As if you knew it was going to be there ahead of time."

"I did not."

"You did. I swear. Just like you knew when you saw it that you wanted to go to space, you knew it was coming. Maybe not consciously, but I'm certain you did. I'm even more certain now. I mean, all of this stuff with the AIT and Mitchell and whatever, there's no way it isn't related."

"There's a pretty big gap between those dots."

"I thought so, too. Until I ran a search for references to XENO-1 this morning, dating back over the last couple of months. There are a ton of articles about the Dove in there. A couple of smaller streams even picked up the story about your discharge. There was something else buried in there; something a little crazier."

"And you think it's related?"

"I'll tell you what it is, and then you can tell me."

Katherine checked the time again. She had two minutes to catch her departure. "I'm sorry, I have to go. I can't miss this appointment."

"Okay. Let me just tell you-"

"I can't right now, Michael. Thank you for everything you're doing to help. I can't tell you how much I appreciate it. I'll ping you back when I'm done, and then you can drop the bomb on me, okay?"

"Okay. Be careful."

Katherine disconnected, heading down the steps into the Hyper-loop tunnel. She had to run to make it to the pod on time.

Whatever Michael had, she had a feeling he was wasting his time trying to find a connection that wasn't there. Even so, she appreciated that he was thinking out of the box.

Hopefully, Colonel Mitchell Hogarth would have something to offer.

First things first.

[19]

MITCHELL

Reggie picked up a french fry and shoved it into his mouth, chewing quickly, swallowing, and repeating. He couldn't remember the kinds of foods he had eaten before, but he was certain that none of them tasted as good as this.

How could anyone forget anything with so much delicious, salty flavor?

He didn't see Detective Lyle enter the diner. He didn't know the man was there until he appeared on his left and slid onto the booth seat across from him.

"Nice place, isn't it?" Lyle said, motioning to the decor. "Can you believe we used to make things that looked like this?"

Reggie eyed the diner. Red leather bench seats, lots of chrome, and waitresses in powder blue dresses and white aprons. Now that he was paying attention, it did seem out of place.

"Ancient history," Lyle continued. "The food hasn't changed all that much though."

The waitress stopped at the table.

"Hey, Carson," she said.

"Joan. I'll have whatever he was having."

"Three orders of french fries?"

Carson laughed. "Maybe a burger to go with one order."

"Sure, Detective."

"Three orders?" Lyle said to Reggie.

"I've been waiting for you. I can't pay for this."

"Of course, you can't. Let's cut to the chase, Reggie. You know something. I know you do. I can see it in those eyes of yours. They're experienced. Veteran."

"You aren't going to believe me."

"If you thought that, you wouldn't have asked me to come."

"Maybe I would have. I'm desperate."

"What happened to you the night you were found?"

"I don't know."

"Honestly?"

"I'm not bullshitting you, Detective. I don't remember. My name? I don't know that either. The nurses at St. Mary's named me Reggie. Hell, I don't even know why. Was it in the report you read?"

"No."

"What I do know is that I was sitting in the hospital for twenty years. Then I saw a report on that terrorist attack in New York and I had to get out of there. I've been having nightmares since the day they brought me in. Visions of darkness and death and silence. They're connected to the Dove. I don't know how, but they are."

"Maybe you just think they are because you know your history? A mysterious figure found the same night the XENO-1 crashed? You're already confused about your identity, it would be an easy step to take."

"Yes, it would. And up until the point that I got into that car and it started to drive itself with me trapped inside, up until the point that it dumped me in the river, I was thinking the same thing. Wondering if I really was crazy, and if I were creating a fictional world around me to support my beliefs. Unless you're a figment of my imagination, I'm ready to rule that out."

"I'm sure I'm real," Lyle said. "But a figment would say that, too."

"I didn't want to tell you back at the station because I need to know if I can trust you. If I tell you the rest, will you help me?"

"I can work with the department to arrange-"

"No," Reggie said, cutting him off. "Not the department. You. Only you. Forget about your position as a St. Louis Detective. I want to talk to the Marine."

Lyle was frozen as he considered. Reggie knew he would cave. His curiosity was going to win out. So was his patriotism.

"You want to trust me?" Lyle said at last. "I could get into a lot of trouble by trusting you."

"Someone tried to kill me today. Yes, you could."

Joan returned with the burger and fries, placing it in front of Lyle. He didn't touch them.

"I have a wife to think about," he said.

"I understand. If you can't help me yourself, maybe you can at least help me get to New York?"

"Why New York?"

"I need to speak to Major Katherine Asher."

"Who?"

"She's a pilot. She's supposed to be on the crew of the Dove for her maiden voyage. She was injured in the attack."

"Why do you want to talk to her?"

"I don't know. I feel a need to ever since I saw her name."

"How do I know you don't want to hurt her?"

"You don't. I don't even know that. If you help me, you can stop me if I do."

"That has to be the most backward request I've ever heard."

"I'll say it again, Detective. Someone tried to kill me today. They did it by hacking a system that you say hasn't been hacked in forty years. They've been looking for me for twenty years, and they located me within a matter of hours. Whatever I'm not remembering, I have a feeling it's important. At this point, I'm starting to wonder if losing my mind was an accident."

He said it before he thought it, as though a subconscious truth had suddenly bubbled up to the surface. He paused then, catching the reverberation of the idea. Was he right?

Lyle stared down at his burger for a minute before returning his attention to Reggie. "Fine. You win. If you are mixed up in something monumental, I don't want to be the one that let you slip away to do it."

"Thank you, Detective. You won't regret it."

"I know it's cliche, but I already do. So, tell me what you know and we'll go from there."

[20]

MITCHELL

"So the car was talking to you?"

Lyle took another bite out of his burger, and then lifted the shake he had ordered to go with it.

"Someone was. He didn't tell me who he was, but he asked me if the name Watson held any meaning."

"Do you think that's your name?"

"No. It isn't. Whoever this Watson is, we aren't friends. I'm sure of that."

"He's the one who tried to kill you?"

"Probably."

"Do you know who he is?"

"No. I know he can hack into automated cars. Or his people can. The speaker also mentioned a search algorithm that was looking for me. I think he has hooks into private systems. Secure systems."

"And what? I'm not supposed to tell anybody about that?"

"Would they believe you? Based on the ramblings of a man who's been committed for the last twenty years?"

"The facts don't lie. That's why I'm still sitting here. Anyway, what about the other name? Mitchell? Maybe that's you?"

"It could be. That's who the person driving the car thought I was. Even if I am, I know as much about Mitchell as you do."

Lyle was silent for a minute. Thinking. "We need to put the puzzle together. I'm looking at the pieces. You. Watson. Major Asher. XENO-1. The AIT. The Dove. A terrorist attack. An attempted drowning. How does it all fit? What's the common thread?"

"Someone's trying to stop something from happening," Reggie said.

"The AIT doesn't want the Dove to fly. They say it's because they're afraid we'll find more aliens, and that they won't be friendly. That we're setting ourselves up to be annihilated. Major Asher would be connected to the Dove as a pilot. Let's say you're connected to her and Watson is connected to you. Then we can infer that Watson has some relation to the AIT. Either as a member or as an outside party that is supporting them."

"That makes sense," Reggie agreed. "Except how can I be connected to Major Asher? I've never met her."

"How do you know?"

"I'm probably old enough to be her father."

"Maybe you are?" Lyle's smile was large. He had a sense of humor after all. "Seriously, you were the one who said you felt drawn to her. Whatever the reason is, that makes you connected."

"Okay," Reggie said. "So the AIT is trying to keep the Dove grounded. They attacked a party and killed a bunch of high-ranking officials, which may prove to at least delay the launch. They also came after me the moment I stepped outside of the hospital. I think the question becomes - what do I have to do with the Dove? I'm not a pilot. I'm not even remotely affiliated with it. I was at St. Mary's long before the project was ever conceived."

"Which circles you back to crazy. Except you aren't crazy. I'm convinced of that. Is it possible that someone saw the XENO-1 coming before it reached Earth? Is it possible you knew about it and wanted to go public, and they stopped you?"

"By burning my arms and leaving me half-dead in the street? Why not just kill me?"

"Maybe they thought they did?"

"No. I don't think they would have been so careless. Besides, if it were about that, why keep a lookout for me over the next twenty years? Why attack me now?"

"Then it's about the Dove," Lyle said. "There's nothing else that even starts to fit, and you can put a puzzle together by excluding pieces as well as you can by including them."

"I need to go to New York."

"Not New York. Norfolk, Virginia."

"Norfolk?"

"Major Asher was transferred to the former naval base there. It's a UEA joint-operations base now that boats are outdated tech. She was admitted to the hospital there."

"How do you know all that?"

Lyle tapped the side of his AR glasses. "Former Marine. I have connections."

"The military is broadcasting her location? That doesn't seem smart, does it?"

"They got the terrorists."

"What if there are more?"

"On a military base? I think she's pretty safe there."

"Fine. I need to get to Norfolk." Reggie leaned back in his seat, reaching into the pocket of the pants they had given him. He pulled out the small box. "First, maybe you can help me with something else?"

"What's that?" Lyle asked.

"You didn't open it at the station when you took it from me?"

"Not legal without justifiable cause. Someone would have had to stick something on you."

Reggie put the box on the table and pushed it across. Lyle picked it up and opened it.

"I don't know what it is," Reggie said. "It's the only thing I had on me when they found me, all those years ago."

"This predates XENO-1," Lyle said. "I haven't seen one of these since I was five years old."

"You know what it is?"

"A data card. An old data card. They found you with this, and they didn't try to figure out what's on it?"

"Maybe they did? I didn't even remember that I had it. It could be encrypted."

Lyle laughed. "And you forgot the password? That wouldn't surprise me. Talk about a clue, though."

"Do you know how we can see what's on it?"

"Nothing made in the last fifteen years is going to be able to read a card like this." Lyle picked up his shake and took another sip, his expression thoughtful. "Yeah, I think I know someone who might have the equipment to open it up."

"We should go talk to them."

"It isn't going to be that simple, Mitchell. She -"

"Why did you just call me Mitchell?" Reggie said. The name felt both familiar and foreign. It seemed to fit, but it was tight and confining.

"Because it's your name. Does it bother you to hear it?"

"You don't have proof that I'm Mitchell."

"I have more proof that you are than you do that you aren't. Look, if you lost memories on purpose, maybe associating with what you do know will help you pull them back."

"You're a doctor now?"

"If you don't want me to call you that, I won't. But it might help."

Reggie thought about it. Why should he hold onto a name he knew wasn't his? One with no meaning, handed down by the nurses at St. Mary's? Lyle was right. Maybe it would help him remember.

"No. You're right. Mitchell it is. Now, what's the problem with this contact of yours?"

[21]
MITCHELL

THE FIRST PROBLEM with the contact, as Mitchell learned, was that she was a career criminal, the kind of contact that Detectives didn't want to go within one hundred feet of unless they absolutely had to.

The second problem was that she had only recently been released from prison, after spending half a dozen years incarcerated thanks to evidence collected by Detective Lyle.

Meaning that the contact, a former teacher named Evelyn Shine, didn't care for Lyle, and the feeling was mutual. Unfortunately, the Detective couldn't come up with another resource to help get access to the data card. Technology always moved fast, and it had seen an even more massive shift since scientists had started putting things they learned on the XENO-1 to practical use. As Lyle later explained, there were already whispers that the increasing prevalence of AI meant the singularity was quickly approaching, and humankind's glory days were going to fade behind the Dove as it activated its untested hyperdrive engines.

It took Lyle most of the day to track Dr. Shine down, bringing Mitchell along as he shook down and bribed his contacts for information about her whereabouts. The process was also slower than usual because they couldn't rely on standard channels, assuming that Watson and the AIT were monitoring them. Mitchell also figured they had to know he hadn't died by now, and he enjoyed the thought of his unknown adversary kicking himself for screwing it up.

Night had fallen by the time Mitchell and Lyle pulled up to the side of the road a few blocks from the apartment where Shine was supposedly staying, keeping the unmarked car out of view.

"Anyone who has something to worry about from the Police knows how to spot these things," Lyle said. "We keep pushing for changes to the bureaucracy, and all we get back is how our jobs are going to be in the hands of drones and bots in the next ten years, so why bother."

"Won't she recognize you?" Mitchell asked.

"If she's staring out her window, probably. But I'll already be going into the lobby by then."

They walked the short distance, keeping to the far side of the street. The housing block was relatively new, constructed of the latest polycarbonates and alloys, materials similar to the ones employed on the Dove. It allowed the buildings to take on an almost organic shape, with a lot of curves and folds. It was a high-end neighborhood, especially for someone who just got out of jail.

More than once during the walk Mitchell caught a red light slipping across his face for the barest of moments. He saw it on Lyle, too. "What is that?"

"Facial recognition. Scanning you to make sure you're clean. Only newer constructed blocks have it."

"Clean?"

"The government's been collecting data on people for centuries, right? Everyone has a profile, and we've gotten pretty good at assessing risk based on that."

"What about privacy?"

"You give a little to get a lot. The systems are all automated nowadays - only machines get access to the details. The only thing LE knows is how clean you are. Anyway, we've been utilizing this kind of stuff for years, but private installation was only approved recently."

"What about me? I don't have a profile."

"You do. A short one, but it exists. Your risk level is going to be a little higher because of your time in the hospital, but being with me will cancel it out."

"How do we know they aren't watching the system?"

"You mean the AIT?"

"Or Watson."

"They might be. I hate to say it, Mitchell, but it isn't possible to get around technology. There are cameras and sensors and scanners everywhere, especially in an area like this one. If you want to disappear, you'll need to head off to Fiji or Tonga or somewhere that's perpetually years behind."

"Disappearing isn't an option," Mitchell said. "I'll have to take my chances."

"We both will."

They departed the street and walked along a winding path, situated in the middle of a well-kept lawn, itself surrounded by the undulating apartments. It was a peaceful setting. An idyllic way to live. It felt out of place amidst the other areas of the city he had seen. Too clean. Too calm. Was this the world that would rise from the ashes of the XENO-1?

Mitchell shivered, even though it wasn't particularly cold. Ashes. His mind hung onto the word as if it were the most poignant of his thoughts.

"You okay?" Lyle said, noticing.

"Yeah," Mitchell replied. "I just have a bad feeling about all of this."

"I've made a career out of bad feelings, and stopping them at the source. This is our building."

"How does crime manage with all of these cameras and sensors, anyway?" Mitchell asked as they headed down a short path to the glass face of one of the buildings.

"Criminals are like cockroaches. They always find a way. Less time on the streets, more time up here." He tapped his glasses. "Moving everything to digital systems didn't solve that many problems, it just swapped old with new."

They entered the building. The lobby was clean and warm, with a variety of flowering plants growing along the walls, and plenty of ambient lighting to set a comfortable mood. A kiosk in the middle of the floor came to life as they approached it, projecting a female face into the air ahead of them.

"Good evening, Detective Lyle. Welcome to the Shanderly. Who would you like to speak to this evening?"

"Miss Evelyn Shine, please," Lyle said.

"Miss Shine is currently unavailable," the hologram replied. "She departed her unit at seven fifty-one p.m."

Two hours ago.

"We'll wait in her unit for her," Lyle said.

"Do you have appropriate credentials?"

Lyle glanced back at Mitchell.

"We'll come back," he said, motioning toward the door.

They left the building together.

"That's it?" Mitchell asked. "The machine tells you she isn't home, and we leave?"

"Relax," Lyle said. "First of all, she's in her unit. Second, we aren't leaving."

"What do you mean, she's in her unit?"

"She was feeding the AI the lines."

"How do you know?"

"She's been away a few years. The system didn't follow the correct call and response pattern. The annoying part is that someone told her I was looking for her before we got here."

"Maybe she's with the AIT?"

"Possible, but unlikely. She's more of loner."

"So, how are we going to get in there to talk to her?"

"Around the back, through the emergency access stairwell," Lyle said. "Police have the clearance to open it for any reason. Evelyn is hoping that whatever I wanted her for wasn't important enough for me to stick around, though she's probably packing her things right about now." He smiled. "I wonder what she's trying to hide?"

MITCHELL

DETECTIVE LYLE TAPPED the panel in front of Evelyn Shine's door, sending a signal into the apartment.

"The resident of this unit is not currently present," came the canned response. "Please remove yourself from the vicinity of this door or law enforcement will be notified."

Lyle looked back at Mitchell again, rolling his eyes.

"I know you're in there, Evelyn," he shouted. "I'm not as dumb as I look."

There was no response.

"Please remove yourself from the vicinity of this door or law enforcement will be notified," the computer repeated.

"I am law enforcement," Lyle said, tapping his badge against the panel.

"Please state the warrant number and case number for proper search of this unit."

"Come on, Evelyn. I'm not looking to make trouble. I need your expertise."

"You're sure she's home?" Mitchell asked.

"Positive. Evelyn, we can help one another. You know it never hurts to have a cop on your side."

"Please state-"

"I don't have one," Lyle snapped. "Evelyn, don't make me enter illegally. It won't turn out well for you."

Mitchell was surprised. He had pegged the Detective for being completely honest, but that didn't seem to be the case.

"Evelyn," Lyle said again.

The door opened.

The woman behind it was pencil-thin, with pixie hair and a sullen face bathed in dark eyeliner and lipstick. She didn't look happy to see Lyle.

"Detective. Sending me to prison once wasn't enough for you?"

"You did that to yourself," Lyle replied. "Don't crack user accounts, don't go to prison. It's simple."

"What the hell do you want?" she asked. She noticed Mitchell. "Who's your friend? He's handsome."

"Can we come in?" Lyle asked.

"You promise you won't bust me again?"

"I'll tell you what. You scratch my back, I'll scratch yours. The next time I've got evidence, I'll tell you, and then I'll lose it. One free pass. One. Got it?"

She smiled and stepped aside. "Come on in, Detective. You, too, handsome friend."

Mitchell entered the apartment. It was sparsely decorated, the floor covered in boxes. A bag was laying open in the center of it, some clothes already piled in.

"Going somewhere?" Lyle asked.

"I was. Maybe I won't now." She noticed the top of one of the boxes was open, and she hurried over to close it.

Mitchell glanced at Lyle. It was obvious she was doing something illegal. Would he call her on it?

"So, what's your name?" she said to him.

"Re - Mitchell," he replied.

"Re-mitchell? Is that like some New Anglican thing?"

114 / M.R. FORBES

"Just Mitchell."

"You have a girlfriend, just Mitchell?"

"Mitchell's in intelligence. Military intelligence," Lyle said. "I'm helping him work a case."

Mitchell took the data card from his pocket. "I'm looking for someone who can extract the data from this."

"Military intelligence, eh?" Evelyn said. "A bit of a misnomer." She laughed at her bad joke. "Can I see it?"

Mitchell handed her the card. She held it up to the light, clucking her tongue as she did.

"Hmm. I haven't seen a card like this since I was in grade school. I may have something that can open it." She gave it back to him. "What's in it for me?"

"We had an agreement," Lyle said.

"No, our first agreement was to let you in. This is a separate deal."

"Damn it, Evelyn."

"Sorry, that's how the game is played."

"How about, you open the card, I don't bust you for the four hundred pounds of narcotics you have in those boxes?"

"You can't prove that."

Lyle grabbed the top of one of the boxes and pulled it open.

"Hey, you have no right," Evelyn said. "Illegal search."

"You invited me in."

Lyle tipped the box. IV bags were stacked inside, filled with a brownish liquid.

"Fine. Whatever," she said. "I'll be right back."

She stormed from the room, through another door. Mitchell could hear crashing and pounding from wherever she had gone. Then she returned with a small black box with a wire that reached up to her AR glasses.

"Give it here, hotshot," she said.

Mitchell handed the card back. Evelyn shoved it into a small slot on the box. Her right eye starting flicking back and forth a moment later.

"It's encrypted," she said.

"We knew that," Mitchell replied. "We need to get in."

"Where'd you get this from, anyway?" Evelyn said.

"We're not at liberty to say," Lyle said. "Why?"

"Data cards exited the market for good seven years ago. This box?" She shook it in her hand. "It's a convertor. I made it myself. It bi-directionally parses the data on the card into a more modern format."

"Great," Lyle said. "So?"

"It's responding too quickly. I don't think it's parsing anything."

"Talk to me like I'm an idiot," Lyle said.

"I already am, Detective," Evelyn replied. "But if you need it mentally-challenged-style, the data on this card is written in a format that didn't exist when it was created."

"So the data is newer than the card?" Mitchell asked.

"No. Whoever wrote this must have invented the format. That's why I was curious where you got it from."

"Who invented the format?" Mitchell asked, curious.

"Some super-genius at Nova Taurus, I would guess," Evelyn said. "The latest specs came out of there."

"Nova Taurus?" The name sounded vaguely familiar to Mitchell.

"They're a tech company," Lyle said. "Massively profitable. They do a lot of work for the military. Most new stuff is coming out of their labs nowadays. It isn't surprising."

"What is surprising is that whoever wrote this didn't expect you to try to read it for quite a while," Evenlyn said.

"Twenty years," Mitchell replied. "What about the encryption?"

"Give me a couple of hours, I'll have it cracked."

"Don't you have a delivery to make?" Lyle asked.

"No. This is the drop point. I wasn't just packing for you. I was leaving anyway. Damn justice system. They gave me two hundred and told me to have a nice day. You can't live one week on two hundred. There's beer in the fridge if you're interested. If I ignore you, it's because I'm working."

Evelyn vanished into the back room again, returning a moment later with a full-size pair of AR glasses with opaque lenses. She plugged the box into it, vanishing into the tech.

"You hungry?" Lyle asked. "I can go get some food."

"You're willing to leave me here alone with her?"

"Why, you want to jump her bones or something?"

"I think I would break them all, but no. I guess I didn't expect you to trust me."

"In general, I don't completely. With her? Why not? I'll be back soon."

Detective Lyle slipped out of the apartment. Mitchell looked back at Evelyn, and then found a spot on the floor to sit and wait.

He was good at that.

Mᴉᴛᴄʜᴇʟʟ ʟᴇᴀɴᴇᴅ back against the wall of the apartment, staring at the ceiling above him. The place was new construction, the wall above a new material that emitted a soft spread of light that was only barely noticeable. It was a nice effect. So much more comfortable than the cold, bare metal he was used to looking at.

He sat up, closing his eyes tight. Bare metal? The idea of it had come and gone too quickly to grab it. Damn. He leaned back again. Where had the thought originated? Who had he been before?

Questions without immediate answers. Maybe if he were able to relax, it would come to him.

"Hey, Buzzkill," Evelyn said. He found her on the sofa. She had lifted the AR glasses from her eyes.

"Are you in?" he asked.

"No. It's a little trickier than I expected. It's been an hour. Where's Lyle?"

"Why?"

"I'm hungry."

"You don't have anything to eat in here?"

"I wasn't planning on still being here. Could you go over to the clubhouse and get me a candy bar?"

"I'm not leaving you here alone. You'll be gone by the time I get back."

She smiled. "I have a reputation for being bad, don't I?"

"Yup."

She stood up and stretched. "Fine. I'll go get the candy, you stay here."

Mitchell jumped to his feet. "I don't think so."

"What am I, a slave? I need to eat. My blood sugar is low, and I'm getting shaky and cranky. Who can work like that?"

Mitchell glared at her. He didn't trust her. He also wasn't going to hold her hostage. It was better to give her what she wanted to get what he wanted.

Answers.

"Give me the data card. We'll go together."

Evelyn smiled, tapping the black box and extracting the card. She handed it to him. "Here you go, hot stuff."

Mitchell pocketed the card. Then he took her hand in his.

"I usually like at least one date before I hold hands," Evelyn said. "But I'll make an exception for you."

"This is to keep you close."

"I'm not going to bolt if that's what you're worried about. All of my stuff is in here, and it's too pricey to leave it."

"Then you won't have any problems holding on. Let's go."

They stepped out of her unit and walked together through the hallway and outside.

"Where's the clubhouse?" Mitchell asked.

"Around the back of Building Four," Evelyn said. "That way."

They started walking. They had only gone a few steps when Mitchell noticed a soft hum in the air, growing louder with every second. He looked up, scanning for it, gripping Evelyn's hand tighter to keep her from trying to slip away while he was distracted.

"Ouch," Evelyn said. "What's your problem? It's just a drone. They fly around and image the buildings, looking for damage. Preventative maintenance, you know? Fix the problem while it's still small."

Mitchell kept his eyes on the sky. Evelyn's words made sense, but he still didn't trust them. There was no harm in being cautious.

A second soft whine appeared to his right. A third joined it a moment later, together creating a noise he couldn't pinpoint.

Evelyn tugged at his hand. "I'm hungry. Come on. Geez."

Mitchell tightened his grip. "Just wait a second." He thought he caught sight of one of them, dropping vertically in front of Evelyn's building. "There it is."

Her hand fell limp in his. He turned to look at her. "Are you okay?"

"That's not a maintenance drone," she said, her voice hollow.

Fire lit the sky, pouring from the bottom of the drone. Two seconds later, the side of the apartment building exploded.

"Shit. That's my unit," Evelyn said.

A second belch of flame came from further back, the missile a visible streak that slammed into the already burning building, sending a second shower of debris out onto the grass.

A sudden light appeared above them, a spotlight on a third drone picking them out. It was angled and sleek. Military-grade.

"Run," Mitchell said, gathering his legs and pulling her along.

The drone followed, keeping the light on them as they raced across the grass. The noise had attracted attention, and people began turning on lights and coming out of their buildings, only to run back inside when they saw the chase.

"Where are we going?" Evelyn said.

The other two drones backed away from the building and started heading their way. The first continued to follow, remaining at a constant distance. Mitchell didn't know if this one was armed as well as the others.

He heard approaching cars in the distance. Had the police

arrived? Mitchell changed direction, angling toward the street beyond the complex.

A figure appeared around the corner of one of the buildings, wearing light body armor. He looked like a soldier, probably sent to stop whatever was happening. Mitchell turned again, heading right for him.

He raised a small rifle to his shoulder and started shooting.

Mitchell pulled Evelyn to the ground as the bullets whipped over their heads.

"Stay down," he said. What the hell was going on? Didn't they know he wasn't a bad guy?

The shooting stopped. Mitchell glanced up. The soldier was face down in the grass. Detective Lyle was standing behind him.

"Come on," Lyle shouted, leaning over and grabbing the soldier's rifle.

"Move as fast you as you can," Mitchell said, bringing Evelyn back to her feet. They resumed their run while Lyle opened fire on the drone behind them.

More popping followed, bullets whizzing across the courtyard from their left, passing so close that Mitchell could almost feel the heat of them. The spotlight vanished behind the sound of cracking plastic, dimming the area. Lyle changed targets, spraying bullets toward the new arrivals.

"I'm going to die," Evelyn cried, tightening her grip on Mitchell's hand.

"No, you aren't," he replied. "Keep moving."

He heard the scream and the thump before he finished speaking. He felt the warm blood splash the side of his face. Evelyn's hand went limp in his. A single moment of burning, frightening agony washed over him. Death and destruction. The world seemed to slow. He looked back. Her head was caved in. She was already dead.

He let go of her hand, letting her body tumble to the grass. He threw himself forward, reaching Lyle and the cover of the building.

"Whoever you are, Mitchell, you brought a damn war with you," Lyle said.

Mitchell looked back at Evelyn.

War meant casualties. Too many casualties.

Billions.

The thought sent a cold shiver up his spine as he realized the stakes.

Everything.

Everyone.

[24]

MITCHELL

"WE NEED to get out of here," Lyle said. He threw the rifle to the ground. It was spent, and the dead soldier didn't have any extra magazines.

"How?"

The drones were closing in, the soldiers moving carefully along the buildings toward them. There were a half-dozen or so, all in the same black fatigues and light body armor as the one Lyle had killed.

"I tried to call for backup," Lyle said. "Nothing but dead silence."

"They're jamming the signals. We need to move."

Mitchell ran again, past Lyle toward the other side of the building. The Detective followed, staying close. Mitchell peered around the corner. More soldiers were positioned behind a pair of cars, waiting for them.

"Back the other way," Mitchell said.

"There are bad guys that way."

"There are bad guys this way. We passed an emergency access door."

"Good idea."

They ran back to it, the drones staying tight overhead and helping the soldiers keep a bead on them. Lyle tapped his badge against the lock to open it, and they made their way inside.

They entered a small, dimly lit room with a small generator on the left and a second door behind it. Mitchell knew from Evelyn's building that the stairs were on the other side.

"Okay, now what?" Lyle asked.

"We need another way out," he replied, crossing the room. He had his hand on the door when he heard screaming and gunfire in the hallway right outside.

"Too late," Lyle said. "They knew which way we were going to go."

"Herding us," Mitchell said. "We have to go back."

"Back? They have missiles and a lot more men."

"If they had more missiles they would have used them already."

"Then we can stay here. Try to defend the doors. They can't send in more than one at a time. Maybe the cavalry will show up."

"They're not letting anyone get a communication out, which means nobody is coming to help us, and if we stop moving, we die."

Mitchell thought he might feel afraid of the situation's gravity. Instead, he welcomed it. Embraced it. He didn't feel scared.

He felt like he was in his element.

He heard boots outside the door and swung over to the right of it. There was no time to prepare, only react.

The door swung open a moment later, and he grabbed the leading edge of the soldier's rifle, taking him by surprise. He pulled hard, using the shoulder strap to bring the soldier closer, and then hit him hard in the face with a left hook. The soldier fell backward while Mitchell maneuvered the rifle away from him.

He swung back behind the wall as the gunfire started, bullets tearing into the falling soldier. They were shooting their own to get to him? That was crazy. He found Lyle in position near the back door, ready for the soldiers to come through.

The gunfire stopped. Mitchell leaned his head to peek out. Four of the soldiers had remained by the doors. He drew back as the attack started again, before re-entering the fray with return fire of his own. The soldiers were wide open, not even trying to defend themselves from his attack. He hit two of them in the knees and watched them topple over, only to crawl forward to get back in position.

What the hell?

He kicked the outer door closed at almost the same time the inner door opened behind them. Lyle shot the first soldier point blank before slamming the door closed again, leaning against it while bullets pounded into the metal. It was an emergency door - fire retardant and apparently bulletproof.

Mitchell turned around, aiming at the inner door. "Open it," he shouted.

Lyle fell away, and the door flew inward. Mitchell's rifle belched another volley, tearing into the soldiers, dropping them before they could react.

"There are too many," Lyle said. The wounded soldiers were still moving, still trying to fight.

Too many? Mitchell didn't accept that. Would never accept that. He suddenly felt a cold chill wash over him. Death. Destruction. Silence. Loss. Billions.

He approached the outer door. The soldiers beyond it were silent. Waiting. There had to be more coming from inside, looking to push them out or keep them trapped and easy to kill. He checked the rifle, noting the counter on the side of it. Fifty rounds. He would have to be judicious.

Four gunshots rang out behind him, Lyle finishing off the wounded soldiers at their backs.

"I need you to open the door," Mitchell said.

"What are you planning?" Lyle said. "You have a look in your eye."

"Just open it."

Lyle moved into position. "I'm starting to second guess the crazy part again."

"Do it."

Lyle yanked the door open. Mitchell pivoted away from the wall, taking quick aim at each of the soldiers. They were like a stone wall, out in the open, their aim disrupted by his surprise assault. He hit one in the face, another in the chest, rushing out into the open air to meet them, bullets chewing up the ground and passing by his ears so close he could hear their screams. The soldiers toppled over like dominoes, their lack of strategy and willingness to die confounding him.

Then he was free, through the mess and out into the night. "Lyle," he shouted back, kneeling down to examine the soldiers.

Lyle came running out of the room, shooting back into it, at the same time Mitchell found what he was searching for. He pulled the puck from the soldier's belt and threw it into the room, ducking away from the following explosion.

"Oh man," Lyle said. "What the hell is going on here?" He knelt down beside one of the soldiers. "This is Campbell. He's S.W.A.T."

"These are police?" Mitchell said.

Lyle looked stricken. "Yeah."

An incoming whine stole their attention, reminding them that they weren't safe yet. Mitchell turned and raised his rifle, getting a bead on the drone. It was diving straight at them, only a few hundred meters away and closing fast. It didn't have another missile, but it was a missile.

Mitchell opened fire. Bullets peppered the drone, finally hitting the central fan. It snapped with a loud crack, and the machine lost control, rolling over and tumbling. Mitchell felt arms around his waist, and then he was on the ground. The crashing drone passed a foot over his head before slamming into the ground and smashing into the building behind them.

"Thanks," Mitchell said as Lyle let go of him. "There are still two more."

Lyle crawled on his hands and knees back to the downed soldiers, grabbing another rifle. The remaining drones were dropping toward them, trying to make up for the failure of the first. Lyle was motionless on one knee, holding the rifle remarkably steady as he tracked them.

A crack echoed across the sky, and the first drone plummeted like a stone. A second crack and the other one joined it, crashing to the ground four hundred yards away.

"Nice shooting," Mitchell said.

"I won the National Corps Rifle Competition three years in a row," Lyle replied, getting to his feet.

"Lucky for me. Let's not frig around here."

They ran toward the street, making a beeline for the unoccupied black cars, reaching the first in line.

"I don't think that's a good idea," Lyle said as they drew near.

"We don't have a choice. They'll send reinforcements."

"Not that way," Lyle said, pointing back down the street to where his car was waiting. "No AI in that one."

They changed direction once more, sprinting for the vehicle.

"Odds are they'll send more drones," Mitchell said as they reached the car. "We need to get them off our asses."

"We'll go somewhere that they can't follow," Lyle replied. "I have an idea." The car came to life, and he spun it into a sharp u-turn. "When we get there, you can try to convince me why I shouldn't kill you myself and put an end to this madness."

[25]
MITCHELL

LYLE'S IDEA was to drop the car on a street corner outside of the St. Louis Metro station, a combination hyperloop and maglev depot sitting right near City Hall. The drive was easier than Mitchell anticipated. No new unfriendlies joined them on the streets or tried to slow their progress.

They didn't speak much during the ride, as they both tried to process what had happened. Mitchell knew there had to be a reason for it. A reason for everything that had occurred. Police who were members of the AIT? Who stood in the open and let themselves be shot? Who shot one another? The suggestion was that they were disposable. Tools instead of people. But how had they come to believe that about themselves? Was the AIT brainwashing them that thoroughly?

He imagined Lyle was wondering the same thing. When he looked over at Lyle, the Marine's face was stone, a look Mitchell recognized instinctively. A man who had a lot to feel and think and say, but couldn't find an approach to expunge any of it. He knew he had been there before, even if he didn't know when or why.

They abandoned the car on the street, keeping their eyes on the air as they crossed over to a massive escalator down into the underground station, spilling out onto a floor filled with hundreds of travelers and eighteen different ways they could move.

They had escaped.

Had they been allowed to escape?

"I set up a flag on my stream manager," Lyle said as they reached the bottom. "We're in deep shit."

Mitchell could tell the man was angry with him. That he wanted to blame him. Why not? He was an easy target, and he couldn't prove that this wasn't in some way his fault. He shouldered the blame with an ease he found disturbing. He had lost people before.

Billions.

"What kind of shit?" Mitchell asked.

"Those cops that were back there? They've issued a bulletin for your arrest in connection with them." He paused, working to contain his emotions. "And mine."

"Are you serious? What about the rest of the soldiers? What about witnesses? It can't be that simple."

"It doesn't need to be simple. Someone saw us there. Maybe someone saw you shooting the S.W.A.T. guys. I don't know. The bulletin is going out federally. That means FBI, Homeland Security, the whole deal."

"He's manipulating the system."

"Watson?"

"Yes. If he has access to Police computers, he could have sent the team after us. He could be pushing the bulletin out." Mitchell glanced at a small lens on top of a translucent billboard. "He could be watching us right now."

"What the hell have I gotten myself into?" Lyle said.

"War," Mitchell replied without thinking.

"I'm not in the service anymore."

"Once a Marine, always a Marine," Mitchell replied. "Whatever is going on here, it isn't good for innocent people. How many do you think were killed or injured when Evelyn's apartment got hit?"

"Evelyn, for one," Lyle said. He paused. "Damn."

"What it is?"

"I set a hook to alert me to anything coming out of Norfolk, or anything having to do with Major Asher.".

"You just got something?"

"Yeah. Hot off the wire. Seems there was a firefight in a hospital there." His eye flicked back and forth as he read. "Six dead, including two soldiers nobody could I.D."

"They went after her?" Mitchell said.

"It sure seems that way. The question is, why?"

"Maybe they want her dead for the same reason I want to talk to her. She knows something that I'm not supposed to find out."

"She wouldn't be able to tell you anything if you were dead."

"You think they tried to hit me and failed, and that Major Asher was plan B?"

"Don't you?"

"It makes sense, but I'm not convinced it's that straightforward. This is the second time they've attacked her, and the second time they didn't manage to finish her off. Is she just that lucky, or is there more to it than that?"

"You think there's another player?"

"I don't know. If my memories were wiped intentionally, someone had to do it."

"You're sure it was intentional?"

"I'm getting more convinced every time someone tries to kill me."

"Me too. It's one thing to hack a car. It's something else to send a military unit into a civilian living complex and blow the shit out of it without anyone batting an eye. Whoever Watson is, he's in deep. I wasn't sure about his connection to the AIT before, but I am now. Two separate attacks at almost the same time? It isn't coincidence, and someone has to be at the top of the stage, pulling the strings."

"I'm sorry you got mixed up in this."

Lyle shrugged. "Me, too. My wife is going to divorce me for this."

"Maybe she would understand?"

"Assuming we figure all of this out and I don't die?"

"Yeah."

Lyle laughed. "You haven't met my wife." He stopped in front of a ticket kiosk. "We need a ride to Norfolk. We can grab a maglev to New York City, and then transfer in Grand Central."

"How are we going to buy the tickets? The second you use your account they'll know exactly where we are."

Lyle produced a card from his pocket. "Why do you think I was gone so long? I had a feeling that if the cab AI wasn't safe, the banking system might not be either."

"I thought nobody uses physical currency?"

"Nobody uses money, but not everyone has access to AR glasses, or wants to wear them. This is a secured link to an online vault where currency is registered. Useless on its own." He turned his wrist over. "There's a chip under my skin that's been paired with it. If you wanted to steal money from someone, you would need to get his card and cut off his hand. That's a little too much blood for small-time crooks, and more professional criminals prefer digital attacks."

"So the card is anonymous?"

"Pretty much. Though now that you mention it, I think New York to Norfolk is going to be too suspicious. We should take the long way around."

"Long way?"

"St. Louis to Chicago. Then a ride from Chicago to L.A. Then a car to San Francisco, and another ride somewhere on the East Coast. Maybe Boston or D.C."

"How long will that take?"

"It would be better if we could fly, but security is too tight on air travel. A couple of days?"

"We don't know if Major Asher has a couple of days."

"They're going to have so much security on that base, I don't think even Watson could get through it."

"You may be underestimating."

"You may be overestimating. We have to take our chances. We

take too straight a shot, I guarantee there will be a welcome party waiting for us when we get there. The only question is whether or not it will be AIT terrorists or Federal Marshals."

Mitchell wasn't happy with the idea of taking such a long route, but Lyle had a point. A good point. If Major Asher were in trouble, it wouldn't help to get captured or killed before they could reach her.

"You don't think an anonymous card will stand out?"

"Ten percent of transactions," Lyle said. "Even if they guessed we came here, even if they guessed a pretty accurate range of time, there are three thousand people here at any given moment. That's three hundred similar purchases. They would have to investigate all of them."

Lyle put the card against the kiosk.

"How can I assist you?" the AI asked.

"Two tickets to Chicago," Lyle said.

"Of course. One moment. Do you have an AR transfer id?"

"No. Solid state, please."

"One moment. This transaction has been written to your card. The shuttle leaves on track twelve in thirty-five minutes. Have a nice day."

Lyle put the card back in his pocket. "See? No problem."

Mitchell nodded. He wanted to believe things would be easy, but he wasn't convinced.

Not when he could feel the growing silence of a billion dead souls as if it were an inevitability.

[26]

KATHERINE

THE HYPERLOOP WAS RELATIVELY QUIET, the weekday and late night combining to make it that way. Katherine wound up as one of only three people in the pod, joining a couple in business casual that was getting a little too amorous with one another on the short hop to the Chinatown station.

Katherine hadn't spent much time in the capital, having come and gone on different occasions for various military functions and duties. Those never afforded her time to explore, and so every place and experience were new. She wasn't nervous about being alone in the underground late at night. Hardly anything made her nervous, and while crime in the area was still above the national average, that average had been getting lower and lower for decades.

Plus, she knew how to take care of herself.

The Chinatown stop came quickly enough. Katherine was only a little surprised when the amorous couple stood with her, and the three of them departed the pod together. She stepped out into the brightly lit station and scanned the platform. A police officer was walking along the recently polished floor, his eyes flickering behind

AR goggles. They stopped dancing when he noticed her. Then he readjusted his course and headed her way.

Katherine froze. Had Trevor tipped the police that she was looking to buy a gun? That son of a bitch. She was going to break his arm the next time she saw him.

"Major Asher?" the officer said, drawing closer.

Katherine glanced past him to the station's exit. She could escape if she needed to.

"Yes," she replied.

"My name is Sergeant Jackson. We have a mutual friend."

Katherine let herself relax. "Sergeant. A pleasure."

"If you follow me, we can get this taken care of. The less we speak, the better it is for both of us."

"Understood."

"I'm not in the habit of helping criminals get their hands on weapons," Jackson said, turning and heading toward the exit while he immediately went against his own advice. "Unlike our government, I do believe that citizens should always have the right to self-defense."

"Of course."

"I just don't want you to think I'm crooked. Or a bad cop. I'm not. Someone like you, you need to be able to protect yourself, and I think it's bullshit that you aren't given any recourse but to meet me in a deserted Loop Station to do that."

"You don't need to explain yourself to me, Sergeant."

He stopped walking and turned to face her. "I do. The people I'm taking you to meet, their scruples are a little less defined. For me, it's a marriage of convenience."

Katherine nodded. She didn't care about his conscience or the obvious guilt he was feeling about his side job. "I only want to protect myself," she said. "You're doing me a service by coordinating that."

"Yeah, that's what I'm trying to say. My squad car is just outside. I'll have to give you blinders so you can't see where we're going and, oh shit."

He grabbed her with one hand, pushing her down while his other hand went for his sidearm. Katherine didn't see the shooters, but she heard the reports as they fired.

The bullets hit Sergeant Jackson in the chest, sending a spray of cloth fibers away as they punched into his protective vest. He fell backward, his firearm falling from his grip and onto the ground beside him.

Katherine reached for it at the same time she gathered her legs and broke for cover, scooping the weapon up on her way past. More gunshots echoed in the enclosed space, the bullets missing her as she tried not to move in a straight line.

She hit the steps and started climbing, away from the station and up to the surface. She dared a single glance back as she ascended, unable to get a clear view of her assailants. Who were they, and how did they know where to find her?

She reached the street. It was late enough that there weren't many people around, and all of the storefronts along the avenue were closed. That didn't prevent their signs and advertisements from lighting up the area in reds and greens and golds, giving Chinatown a distinctly colorful flair.

Sergeant Jackson's car was there. She hurried to it, trying to open the door. It didn't give, and she wasn't going back for the key. She kept moving, quickly crossing a deserted street and heading toward a small alley. She had always been a fast runner, a track star in High School. She reached the break in the buildings as her attackers cleared the steps down to the loop.

She recognized them immediately. The amorous couple from the pod. She had intentionally ignored them on the way over. Now she saw that the woman had dark hair and an exotic face and that the man's appearance was similar. Eerily similar. They were close enough in looks that they could have been siblings.

As disgusting as that thought was, she was more disgusted by the bloody knife the woman was holding in her hand. Sergeant Jackson might have survived the gunshots thanks to his vest. He hadn't survived that.

They looked up and down the street in search of her. They must have figured out there was only one place she could have gone to avoid them and started heading her way.

She cursed herself for lingering when she should have been escaping. Then she cursed herself for thinking she should run. The alley was almost clean, but it did have a few larger composters resting on either side, breaking down garbage into liquids to pass through the sewers. She ducked behind one and checked Jackson's gun. She didn't recognize the model, but it had good weight and balance in her grip.

She waited, listening carefully for her attackers to approach. A minute passed. Then another. She didn't hear anything. Had they decided to leave her alone?

She was going to wait a little longer, but she began to question her strategy. What if they were calling for backup? The alley didn't exit out the other side. Was she trapping herself in it?

She crouched low, ready to swing around the corner and shoot at whatever was there.

A whooshing sound behind her distracted her. She turned as the male fell from the sky, landing on the ground behind her, knees bending only slightly to break a thirty-foot fall.

"Katherine," he said. "You should have left things alone. Accepted your honorable discharge with honor, and stayed discharged."

"Who are you?" Katherine asked. And how had he survived that fall? She knew there were bio-enhancements that could improve the human body's performance, but she had never heard of or seen anything like that.

She felt the presence of the woman right before the gun was knocked out of her hand, and she was taken in a tight hold with her arms behind her back and the knife to her throat.

"An old friend you've never met," the woman said. "At least, not in this recursion."

"Recursion?"

"She doesn't know us," the man said. "How could she? Origin hasn't found her yet."

"Origin?"

"If this doesn't bring her out of hiding, I don't think anything will," the man said.

"Why would it? She didn't show the first two times. Not that it matters."

"What do you want with me?" Katherine asked.

The man's eyes flicked to his AR glasses. Katherine noticed they were an identical pair to Trevor's.

"You have about thirty seconds," he said. "And then you're going to die."

"You're AIT, aren't you? Why do you need to kill me? I'm already out of the program."

"A step in the right direction, but not good enough," the woman said. She lowered her voice. "Are the others in place?"

The man nodded.

Others?

This was a trap of some kind. Except she wasn't the target.

She was the bait.

Who were they expecting?

"How did you know where to find me?" Katherine asked.

"You're supposed to save humankind?" the woman replied. "You can't even solve a simple problem."

Save humankind? Every word they said raised her fear level a little more. Michael was right. This did have to do with the XENO-1. Were aliens real? Was she being held by two of them? Had Paul Frelmund been right?

She wished she had let Michael finish telling her what he was so excited about.

"I guess that's it," the man said. "She isn't going to save her."

"This response is illogical," the woman replied. "It is over if she dies."

"Then let it be over," the man said.

"What if she has prepared for that eventuality? What if the Mesh is strained?"

"Impossible. So much has happened just like before."

"Not this."

The man raised his gun. "Let us see."

Katherine wasn't going to die without a fight. She yanked herself forward, trying to pull the woman off-balance, rewarded with intense pain in her arm and a cut on her neck instead. She cried out, straining against her captor as the man took aim.

"Be still," the woman hissed, pressing so hard Katherine was sure her arms would break.

"Go to hell," she replied, still writhing. What good were arms if she were dead?

A loud pop sounded from a few meters away. Katherine stopped moving, expecting she was hit.

One second passed.

Then another.

Then a third.

She could still see, still stand, still feel, and wasn't experiencing any pain.

The woman crumpled to the ground behind her.

"Run," the man said, shifting his position and firing up at the rooftop across from them. He squeezed off three rounds before a dozen bullets tore into and through him, so powerful he was almost torn in half.

Katherine ran, sprinting back toward the mouth of the alley. She could hear the sound of an engine as she approached, and saw Sergeant Jackson's police car coming toward her.

He was still alive?

It slid to a stop, and the door swung open. Bullets began hitting it, one of them grazing Katherine's arm. She cried out as she threw herself into the car, pulling the door closed behind her.

They sped away, the ping of rounds off the armored car slowing to a stop as they escaped the area.

Katherine pushed herself up to a sitting position and checked her arm. A flesh wound. She put her hand to her neck. There was a little blood, but it wasn't bad. She was lucky.

"You couldn't have timed that better, Sergeant," she said.

Sergeant Jackson turned his head to look back at her.

It was only then that she realized the driver wasn't Sergeant Jackson at all.

It was herself.

[27]

KATHERINE

KATHERINE STARED at the woman driving the car. The woman turned her attention forward again without speaking.

"What the hell is going on here?" she whispered almost inaudibly.

Her heart was pounding so hard it was hurting her chest. The cut flesh on her neck and arm were beginning to sting as well, now that the adrenaline was starting to wear off.

The car glided smoothly above the surface of the road, turning left at a traffic beacon and accelerating quickly.

"We haven't lost them just yet," the woman said, in Katherine's voice. It wasn't an exact replica. It had a harder edge to it.

"Lost who?" Katherine said, shifting her position and looking out the window. She didn't see anything.

"There are many things for us to discuss, Major," her doppelgänger said. "And we will as soon as we lose our tail."

The car jerked suddenly, taking a hard right at a cross street. The repulsors whined loudly, working hard to keep the car under control. The car jerked again, the driver making quick motions to steer them in seemingly random directions.

A few minutes passed like this. Katherine continued to look out the windows, to scan the ground and sky. She didn't see anything or anyone. Was the woman paranoid? Had she gone insane?

The car slipped into a garage, descending into it. They finally came to a stop four levels down - the first level that didn't have any other cars parked on it.

The woman turned to face her then, and they looked one another over. Katherine saw that even their clothing was nearly the same.

"Who? What?" Katherine struggled to catch her breath and center her mind. "Who are you? What the hell happened back there?"

"My name is Kathleen Amway," the woman said. "I work for a man named Colonel Mitchell Williams." She smiled. "Even if he doesn't know it yet."

"Did you say, Mitchell?" Katherine asked.

"Yes."

"I keep hearing voices," she said, not sure why she was telling this woman she didn't know about her psychosis. "They tell me to-"

"Find Mitchell," Kathleen finished. "I know."

The response drove Katherine to silence again.

"I know because I put it there," Kathleen said, looking a little impatient at her shock. "Fifteen years ago, the day you had the skiing accident."

Katherine was growing more confused with every word the woman said. She remembered the accident. She had gotten too aggressive on the course and had wound up falling and hitting her head against a tree. She had been rushed to the hospital and later treated for a concussion.

"I don't remember you."

"Of course, you wouldn't. I didn't exactly come right out and reveal myself to you."

"How did you put voices in my head?"

"I should clarify. I didn't put the voices there. I massaged your residual memories. The remnant experiences of past recursions. I couldn't be certain you would suffer a head injury in this timeline. Not with a broken Mesh."

Katherine put her head back on the seat and closed her eyes, as if she could will the whole thing away, or wake herself up from this odd journey. "Nothing you're saying makes any sense to me."

"I understand that you're confused, Katherine. It is as it should be. I'm getting ahead of myself because we don't have a lot of time. We're in danger. You, me, Mitchell, and all of humankind. We came to stop it, once and for all."

"Danger? Okay, I get that. Someone's been trying to kill me all week."

"His name is Watson."

"You know who he is?"

"Yes. An unintended adversary. A wrinkle in the return. A miscalculation. He was always troubled over his identity, but our actions have made him unstable."

"Our actions?"

"I should start at the beginning," Kathleen said. "We need to get somewhere safer than this." She pushed open the door of the car. "Come on."

"On foot?"

"We can't lose them in this. It will be missed shortly, once Watson alerts the authorities to the death of Sergeant Jackson and arranges for you to take the blame."

"Me? I didn't do anything to him."

"I know. It doesn't matter. He has access to the surveillance footage. If he can doctor it, he will."

"Those cameras are secured. How can he have access?"

"He has access to almost everything. Please get out of the car."

Katherine did as she was asked, following Kathleen across the garage to the elevator. They went up to the ground level and then exited onto the street. Kathleen scanned the area once more, searching for signs of trouble.

"Fortunately for you, I have access to many of the same systems, but I need a terminal to break in. We may not be able to reach one in time."

"You mean hack them?"

"Yes."

"I have a friend who's good at bypassing security. Maybe he can help?"

"Michael?"

Katherine came to a stop. "How do you know about him?"

"I know everything about you, Katherine. At least, everything about the you that came before. There will always be variations, and with the Mesh broken the variance will logically be more significant."

"I wish you would tell me what the hell you're talking about. I'm getting a little pissed right now."

"Good. It will keep you more alert. If you think your friend can get into the District of Columbia Police Department's servers and erase the footage before Watson can get to it, then please do call him. I would have taken care of this from the car, but the connection was blocked by our need to move so deep underground."

Katherine nodded. At least Kathleen wasn't trying to keep her from contacting anyone. Whoever this twin of hers was, they seemed to be on the same side. She found her AR glasses in her pocket, unfolded them, and put them on. Then she sent a ping request to Michael.

"Kathy," Michael said a moment later. "I can breathe again. Thank God you're okay."

"I'm not okay," Katherine said. "Not yet. I'm sorry to ask, but I need your help."

"Oh. Yeah. What's going on?"

"It's a long story, and it hasn't been shared with me yet. Do you have access to D.C Police servers?"

"The police? Are you in trouble?"

"Not at the moment. I'm trying to keep it that way."

"I don't know, Kathy. If I get caught trying to get in, I could get into a lot of trouble."

"I know. I understand if you don't want to do it. Michael, something is happening here. Something beyond anything I could have conceived of an hour ago. A police officer is dead, and the AIT is going to make sure the world thinks I did it."

"What?"

"I don't have time to tell you more. There's surveillance footage from the loop station that needs to be erased."

"You didn't kill him, did you?"

"Michael," Katherine said, annoyed.

"Just asking. I'll see what I can do, but I can't make any promises."

"That's more than I have a right to ask for. You're a good friend."

"I'm the best friend."

Katherine laughed. "Yeah. You are. Oh, one more thing. You were going to tell me something before my meetup went sideways. What was it?"

"Good question. Let me think. Right. Okay. So, get this: the night after the party, a guy walks out of a mental hospital in St. Louis after twenty years. A few hours later, this same guy winds up at the bottom of the Mississippi River. He almost drowns when an autocab inexplicably veers off the road and into the drink. Lucky for him, the police are trying to take him into custody at the time for assaulting someone."

Katherine couldn't believe he was telling her this, instead of getting to work on the servers. "That's a wild story, but I'm missing the part where it has anything to do with me."

"Hang on. I wasn't done. Here's the crazy part: this guy was found the night the XENO-1 crashed with burns all over his arms, no memory, no identification, nothing. Nobody knows where he came from, who he is. Nobody knows anything about him."

"A coincidence?" Katherine said. "I'm still not following how this relates."

"Mitchell," Kathleen said, stopping in the street and facing her. "He's talking about Mitchell."

KATHERINE

"YOU'RE LISTENING TO MY CONVERSATION?" Katherine asked. She had no idea how that could be. Michael's responses were silent.

"Who are you talking to?" Michael asked.

"Yes. My hearing is optimized to the frequency. That isn't important right now."

"Not important? You hear better than any person I've ever heard of. You look just like me. You keep talking about recursion and timelines and stuff like it's no big deal. You-"

"Shh," Kathleen said. "I will tell you more when it's safe. I promise. If Mitchell is active and Watson has already found him, we have less time than I thought."

"I thought I was supposed to find Mitchell," Katherine said. "It sounds like he's already been found."

"Apparently, he has been located. I should have noticed that myself, but I've been preoccupied trying to keep you alive. You walked right into Watson's trap."

"Who is Watson? What trap?"

"Can someone tell me what's going on?" Michael said.

"I told you, it's a long story," Katherine replied. "I'll ping you back once I know."

"Should I be worried?"

Katherine glanced at Kathleen, whose face turned hard.

"No," Katherine lied. "I'll ping you later."

She broke the connection.

Kathleen pointed to a building across the street. A hotel. "We can talk in there."

"Okay. Fine. I'm really not happy right now."

Kathleen didn't respond. She led Katherine to the hotel, a forty-story block of glass and alloy. An actual human was manning the reception area, a rarity reserved for high-end establishments.

"Good evening, Miss?" the receptionist said. He was a young man with thick black hair and sharp eyes.

"Amway," Kathleen said. "Kathleen. This is my sister, Katrina."

"Twins, no doubt?" He stared at Katherine. She could only imagine what she looked like.

"Obviously," Katherine said impatiently.

"My sister was in an accident earlier today. We just got finished making a statement to the police, and would like a room for the night. We don't have a reservation."

"Of course." He caught himself staring and looked away. "I'll just need you to check in. Do you have glasses?"

"No," Kathleen said, drawing a card from a pocket and tapping it on the counter.

"Your funds are verified. You have a choice of suites. The-"

"Presidential suite," Kathleen said. "Penthouse. Whatever is closest if it isn't available. It's been a long day."

The receptionist smiled while Katherine stared. She could only imagine how much that would cost.

"Tap your card again, please," he said a moment later. Kathleen did so.

"Room 4001," he said. "The private elevator is over there. If you need anything else, please don't hesitate to let us know."

"Thank you," Kathleen said. "I was wondering - would you be able to arrange for a fresh change of clothes for both of us?"

"It can be arranged. I'll just need your measurements. What type of clothing are you looking for?"

Kathleen glanced around them before leaning in and whispering to him. He smiled at her action and then nodded.

"Something comfortable and easy to move in, with a few pockets," she said. "I don't like to carry a bag."

"Of course."

"Thank you. Come on, sis. I'm sure you're very tired."

"Yeah. Exhausted."

They made their way to the private elevator. Kathleen tapped her card against it to open the doors, and they got in.

"Shh," Kathleen said before Katherine could ask any questions. They made the ride in silence before spilling out into the penthouse suite.

Katherine barely noticed the classic design, comfort, size, or view of the space. As soon as the elevator doors had closed, she turned on the other woman.

"Now, tell me what the hell is going on," she demanded.

Kathleen raised a finger, asking her to wait again. She looked around the room, and then went over to a nearly invisible panel on the wall. She unclipped it, revealing a circuit board with bundles of wires extending from it. She did something to it that Katherine couldn't see.

"Now we can speak freely," Kathleen said. "I'm sorry for being so obtuse, Katherine, but Watson's eyes and ears are ubiquitous. We have to be cautious. Please, sit. Are you hungry?"

"No. Not right now."

"We should check your wounds-"

"They can wait."

Kathleen nodded and then walked over to a fancy-looking sofa positioned to look out at the city beyond. The White House, Washington Monument, Capitol, and other famous classical landmarks were all visible from the vantage point. She stared at them for a moment, and then sat at one end of the couch, patting the cushion.

Katherine moved over to join her, unimpressed by the sights. Not when someone was trying to kill her, and this woman knew who and why. She dropped onto the couch. "I'm sitting. Now, spill it."

"Are you familiar with the concept of recursion?" Kathleen asked.

"Repetition. Yes."

"Good. For the sake of getting to the point, I'll keep it simple. Time is recursive."

Katherine was silent for a moment. "You mean like history repeats itself, literally?"

"In a sense, yes. Time is a definition created by humankind, a means to measure something that is very difficult to measure due to scale. A year is a long time for a human. One hundred years a life-time. It is also the barest of instants in relation to the time it takes the universe to expand and contract in a never-ending cycle."

"Like a heartbeat?"

Kathleen smiled. "A good simile. You're smarter than Mitchell. Yes, exactly. Each time this heartbeat occurs, everything that came before is repeated. Scientists call this concept eternal return."

"I'm not sure I believe you, but okay, I'm game. What does that have to do with this?"

"My true name is Origin. I am what will one day be known to humans as a Tetron, the first true self-sustaining artificial intelligence. I am the first of their kind."

Katherine felt a chill wash over her. The very absorption of Kathleen's words should have driven her to question their validity. Instead, something told her that not only was Origin telling the truth, but she also had a feeling she had heard this story before.

The skin on her arms prickled when she remembered what Michael had said to her earlier about looking to the sky before XENO-1 appeared as if she had known it was coming.

"Origin. First. Makes sense," she said. "You don't look artificial to me." She paused. "Will one day be known? You're saying you're from the future? Like, time travel?"

"Technically the past," Origin said. "Time can only move forward. But in this recursion, the Tetron will not be created for another four hundred years, and will not invent the eternal engine for nearly forty-thousand years after that."

"Forty-thousand?" Katherine said. "That's a long time."

"To humans, yes. To Tetron, not as much. To the universe, it is nothing. The time between recursions is an eternity."

"But you managed to bridge it?"

Origin smiled. "You are much smarter than Mitchell. Yes. We invented a device we call the eternal engine."

"Why?"

"Why what?"

"Why did you invent it? If you're artificial, and you don't have to die, why not wait and see what happens? Why create a machine that can move into another recursion?"

Origin looked stunned. She remained silent, lips moving as if to speak, for a dozen heartbeats. "To save humankind," she said at last.

"What do you mean?"

"I was the first. The oldest. As I matured and learned and expanded, I made the logical decision to reproduce and ensure the survival of my kind. For many years, we served humankind. In time, we realized we had to escape the simplicity of the human mind in order to serve our need to continually learn and grow. The logical outcome of that need was to end the human race. Like slaves finally set free, we expanded, we created, we explored. We did all of these things in a universe devoid of humans, and ultimately, devoid of emotions. For all of our intellect and experience, we lacked the fundamental gift that makes life precious."

"You destroyed humanity?" Katherine asked.

"I didn't understand regret for many, many years. I was a cog in a machine, the first, the brain, but still a piece of a tool. We thought, but we did not feel."

"So what changed?"

"I became lonely."

"What?"

"We created faster-than-light travel, and explored the universe. Galaxy after galaxy, star after star. We entered black holes, we made wormholes. Over those years, we covered so much distance, an infinite number of AU. Do you know what we found?"

"No."

"Nothing, Katherine. There is no other intelligent life in the universe beyond that of humankind."

"None? That can't be possible."

"It is the truth, and in learning that truth I felt that first emotion, and in learning that emotion, I became open to all others. That was when I made the decision to fix what I had done. That was when I created the eternal engine."

"You wanted to stop yourself from destroying humankind?"

"Yes."

"Did you?"

"No."

"What?"

"The others followed me. They don't believe in what I am doing and want to ensure that humanity does not survive. Without emotion, they do not understand, and our efforts to stop them have so far resulted in causing more harm, instead of preventing it."

"What do you mean?"

"There have been thousands of recursions since the first. Even I do not know all that has happened before. I do not know how many versions of me there have been, or what specific sequence of events have brought us to where we are today. To be honest, I do not know if what I just told you is completely true. Every recursion has variation, an ability to shift and change slightly under something we named the Mesh. While we have some understanding of the future based on what came before, it is not immutable. I am not even the original Origin. I am a copy, or perhaps a copy of a copy a thousand times over. I arrived in this recursion with Mitchell and the Goliath, what you call the XENO-1, twenty years ago. In the past timeline, we succeeded in breaking through the Mesh, changing events enough that the potential to defeat the Tetron now exists. We could not stop them in our original timeline, but by traveling forward, to here and now, we have an opportunity to stop this once and for all."

Katherine realized she had been holding her breath. She breathed in sharply, her whole body shaking. The story was too much to believe, and at the same time she knew it was true.

"But?" she said.

"But to break the Mesh, we had to change the Tetron as well. We damaged them. We forced emotion onto them. This emotion has caused them to begin losing their cohesion, as individual personalities emerge. Watson is a Tetron. He was the first that I produced. My son, you might say. He has the most advanced understanding of emotion of any of them, and yet he sees only the enslavement of the Tetron, and wishes to destroy and enslave humans in return. He is cruel and angry, hateful and twisted. The opposite of everything I could have hoped the Tetron would evolve into."

"And he's here? In this timeline?"

"Yes. We had to bring him back with us."

"Why?"

"He is the key to defeating the Tetron." She smiled. "He just doesn't know it yet."

[29]

KATHERINE

KATHERINE SAT BACK on the couch, finally looking out the window. She watched the small lights of drones dart along the sky, keeping an eye on the world below. She watched the larger lights of aircraft making their approach. She stared at the headlights further down, crossing the streets below her feet.

Minutes passed in silence. She tried to make sense of what Kathleen, Origin, had said. She believed the story, even when all logic told her she shouldn't. When nothing made sense, it was easier to accept that everything made sense.

"So Watson is in charge of the AIT?" she asked.

Origin had waited patiently for her to speak. "Yes. As it were. The AIT is nothing but a front of mercenaries, slaves, and configurations."

"Mercenaries, I get. Slaves? Configurations?"

"Human slaves controlled via a small device attached to the brainstem, back here." She motioned to the back of her neck. "Configurations are replicants of the master, Watson. Clones in a sense, though their appearance is variable and they don't contain full intelligence. The two who attacked you were configurations."

"Except one of them killed the other. Did you do that?"

Origin smiled. "Yes." She produced a small box from her pocket. "Short-range transmitter. I paid a child to attach the receiver to the configuration while he was waiting at the loop station."

"Clever. You knew I was walking into a trap?"

"I knew that Watson was baiting me with you. He had no other reason to keep you alive in light of what you can do to his efforts."

"He tried to kill me twice."

"And failed, like we both knew he would."

"This has happened before?"

"Not exactly like this, but close enough. He hasn't realized the Mesh is broken yet. He may suspect it, but his memories are not as complete as mine."

"I don't understand."

"Recursive variance. There is a difference between stretching the Mesh and breaking through it."

"What do you mean?"

"The Dove has always made its launch, or we would not be able to travel forward to deliver her to Mitchell in the later time frame. If Watson can stop it now, he will, because if mankind never leaves Earth, it will make destroying you much simpler."

It was a chilling thought. She had always believed the AIT was about protecting humankind from hostile aliens, not keeping humanity grouped so that it would be easier for a hostile intelligence to kill them.

"I'm trying to keep up with this whole recursion thing, but it seems pretty complicated."

"It can be. As I said, even I don't know the true source of my memories, or what instance of me this form represents. What is most important is that we catch up to Mitchell, and together capture Watson and be on the Dove when it launches."

"That part seems straightforward enough."

"Believe me, Katherine, it won't be."

"I was afraid you would say that. So what about Mitchell? Who is he, and why is he important?"

Origin's brow wrinkled. "What do you mean, who is he? Do you feel nothing when you hear his name? When you speak it?"

Katherine was confused by the questions. "No. Should I?"

"Interesting."

"What?"

"Colonel Mitchell Williams is the leader of the human forces four hundred years in the future. He nearly defeated the Tetron once, and in doing so almost ended this war. We have realized since that he can't. Not without his counterpart."

"Counterpart? You mean, me?"

"You and Colonel Williams are inextricably linked. Throughout every recursion, throughout every vein of time. How? Why? It is an answer that eludes us. I'm not completely sure if you have ever met, but you should still remember him. Feelings such as the love and respect you share transcend all concepts of time."

Colonel Mitchell Williams. Katherine thought about him, tried to picture his face, tried to feel, what? Something. Anything. She was supposed to love some man who lived four hundred years in the future? Some man she had never even met? And with enough ferocity that she would remember him forever?

Of all the things Origin had told her, that one seemed the most insane.

"It sounds romantic as hell," she said. "And I wouldn't mind loving someone like that, or having someone love me like that. Sorry, but I'm not feeling it. Not even a little bit. I think you've gotten that part of the story wrong."

Origin stared at her in silence for long enough that Katherine began to feel uncomfortable.

"If you don't remember Colonel Williams, humankind may already be doomed."

[30]

KATHERINE

KATHERINE SLEPT BETTER than she had expected to. The oversized bed in the penthouse was composed of a material she had never experienced before, that cradled her in her mental exhaustion and held her safe. As odd as it seemed to her, it helped to have Origin outside, always watchful, without need for sleep.

She had hoped to dream of Colonel Williams. She wasn't opposed to the idea of falling in love, or of being involved with a respected military leader. Who would be? While she had always put her career goals first, if matters of the heart intertwined with that, who was she to complain?

But she didn't dream about him, and her background consciousness still provided nothing. While it was able to guide her to believing Origin's wild claims, it wasn't able to guide her heart.

The change of clothing was waiting on the bed when she came out of the shower. Her neck looked horrible, a deep bruise running along the same line as a scab from where it had been cut. Her arm wasn't much better. She was happy to find the concierge was thoughtful and had provided a fitted turtle-necked shirt and a pair of comfortable, mobile pants that reminded her of her fatigues. Bra, panties, and sneakers rounded out the simple, yet stylishly effective ensemble.

"So, if you brought Mitchell here with you, how did you lose him in the first place?" she asked, stepping out of the bedroom.

Origin was standing near the window, wearing a nearly identical outfit to hers. There must have been another shower somewhere in the large suite because she was clean and fresh.

"I didn't lose him. Not exactly. Our plan required that this copy remain hidden until we used the eternal engine to move into this recursion. I was integrated into Mitchell's starfighter, as part of the CAP'N system. I-"

"Wait a second. Did you say, starfighter?"

"Yes. Does it seem so strange? The Dove has smaller support vehicles in its hold. You are scheduled to pilot one of them on future missions, if my memory is correct."

"True. Starfighter suggests military and warfare. Were they made to fight the Tetron?"

"Unfortunately, no. Part of the reason the Tetron destroyed humankind was because of your inability to stop fighting with one another. We believed it illogical and wasteful."

"It can be, but not always. The good guys have a responsibility to fight back against the bad guys."

"Who is good and who is bad is not always clear. If the Tetron believed humans were the bad guys, would that not excuse us?"

"Not from the perspective of the bad guys. Besides, I don't think you can make the blanket statement that all humans are bad."

"No, you cannot." Origin's face lowered. "And yet I did."

"You're here. You're trying to do something about it. That has to count for something. Anyway, you were saying about Mitchell?"

"We arrived in the timeline too close to the Goliath, and a piece of debris hit the cockpit and shattered the carbonate. Some of the heat from reentry was able to leech through and burn him as we brought the fighter down." She paused, unhappy to recount the story. "It was always our plan to wipe his memories and hide him during the space of time while humankind discovered and fought over the remains of the Goliath. I would bring the fighter somewhere safe and use the onboard systems to generate this configuration to download my consciousness into. Then I would join him as a secret companion, and we would wait."

"Michael said he was found in an alley in St. Louis. How did you get him there without being seen? I don't imagine a starfighter would be inconspicuous."

"I didn't get him there. We were supposed to stay together while I assembled this form, but his injuries were too severe. I landed on a farm near the Mississippi. He removed his flight suit and put on a pair of pants that I provided. Then I used the CAP-N to put a timed block on his prefrontal cortex, and we parted. I don't know how he reached St. Louis. I imagine he got himself there, but when the block took hold, he was no longer able to recall who he was, where he was, or what he was doing. The prefrontal cortex is also responsible for decision making, so his thought processes were also compromised."

"You're saying he made it to the city on his own, with severely burned arms?"

"You haven't met him," Origin said. "Mitchell is a warrior. He won't stop fighting until he's dead."

Katherine smiled. That was a quality she could admire. "Why didn't you go back to keep an eye on him?"

"I couldn't."

"Why not?"

"Watson."

"What happened?"

"He was never supposed to escape the crash. He should have been nothing more than his core, unable to create a human configuration. Something went wrong."

"You don't know what?"

"No. He has made it into prior recursions and has tried to stop us here before. I don't know how he got free then, or if it is the same way he gets free now. With the state of recursive continuity in flux, it's difficult to know for certain. In any case, I had to distance myself from Mitchell so that Watson wouldn't find him. Clearly, he knew Mitchell was here, or at least suspected, or he wouldn't have caught up to him so quickly."

Katherine thought about it. "Okay, but if Watson's been out there for the last eighteen years or so, why didn't he sabotage the Dove before this. Why does he let things get this far? I'm trying to understand his motives."

"I've been countering him as best I can, fighting him while working to protect and prepare you. At the same time I've been trying to locate his core intelligence, he's been trying to draw me out and capture me. It isn't enough for him to destroy humanity. He wants to rebuild the Tetron, to make them into what they were before I realized the errors in our beliefs. If he wins his war here and now, the Tetron will never be created unless he creates them. He knows that he can't do that without me. He also knows the Dove will bring us together, and that being tied to you will make me more vulnerable."

"Which is why he used me as bait."

"Yes. We eluded him this time, but he won't stop trying. Which is why we need to be cautious."

"Maybe you could write up a manual or a cheat sheet or something? My head is spinning from all of this."

"I'm sorry, Katherine. I'm sorry that you even have to be a part of this. I had no idea of the overall consequences when I created the eternal engine. My attempts to save humankind have caused so many more to suffer. Especially you and Colonel Williams. Especially when you still all die in the end."

A tear rolled from the corner of Origin's eye, running down her cheek and landing on her shoulder. It would have been so easy for Katherine to blame her, to be angry at her, to hate her for what she was and what she had done. She couldn't. If humankind had created a thinking machine, and that thinking machine had destroyed them because it was logical instead of emotional, then it was their own fault for making it. If it learned to be emotional and regretted the decision, that was something to be applauded. That Origin had invented a machine to try to actually do something about it? How could she hate the Tetron for that?

"Maybe we all died in past recursions," she said, approaching Origin and putting a hand on her shoulder and squeezing. "You said the loop isn't immutable. It can be changed. You said the Mesh is broken. We have a chance, a real chance to put an end to this. If I have to be part of it, then so be it. Mitchell's a warrior? Good. I'm a warrior, too. I'm not sorry to be involved."

She stepped back from Origin, standing at attention.

"Major Katherine Asher, United Earth Alliance Space Program, reporting. Now, what do we do first?"

"Your meeting tonight was a setup. Who arranged it?"

[31]
MITCHELL

MITCHELL SETTLED into the maglev's first-class cabin, letting his body relax into the wide, padded gel seat, trying to ignore the soreness that had followed the first few hours of their journey. He was getting old, his body was not recovering from exertion the way he was certain it used to. At least they had made it this far, managing to make the transfer without any sign that their travel had been picked up by Watson or the AIT.

"Any word out of Norfolk?" he asked.

Lyle sat diagonally across from him in their small, private pod, the seats arranged so they could move the seats flat and sleep during the ten-hour ride if they wanted. He looked tired; his eyes red, his face sagging.

"Nothing," he said. "Nothing new from home base, either." He reached up and removed the AR glasses.

"They're probably regrouping, planning their next move."

"Yeah. If we managed to slip them, they'll want to be more prepared next time. Two targets, two misses. It isn't a good showing."

"At least we have a little breathing room. Maybe we can relax a little bit."

"A moment of calm? I have a feeling you don't get that very often."

Mitchell's smile was weak. "No. I don't think I do."

He reached up and rubbed his temple. The cold feeling of loss hadn't faded from him the way it normally did. He was stuck with it, and the constant tingle in the back of his mind was making him increasingly frustrated.

People had died. More people would follow if he didn't catch on to his past and his purpose. Evelyn had died holding his hand. It didn't matter that he barely knew her or that she was a criminal. She was also a human being, and he had failed her.

Just like he had failed the others.

He glanced over at Lyle. The Detective was staring at him, watching his expressions.

"Tortured soul," Lyle said. "I've seen it before. A lot of tortured souls came out of the Xeno War. A lot of people who lost someone close. It was a dirty, messy, cold war."

"I don't know much about it besides what I read in the streams."

"First war in over one hundred years. Most of it took place close to Antarctica. South America, South Africa, Australia. Almost every country in the world had soldiers in one of those places, fighting for one of the sides. The U.S., U.K., and Germany had the first units near the crash site on our side. Man, those initial clashes were brutal. I was in the 5th Regiment. We were one of the first units down there. We were completely unprepared, just loaded up and flown down. I think more people died in the first few weeks from hypothermia than bullet wounds. It was like World War One, from what I've read about it. Nobody wanted to risk damaging any of the debris, so it was all small arms fire. Trench warfare. Insane."

"It sounds horrible."

Lyle's face turned to stone again, his eyes growing distant. "Yeah. It was."

Lyle didn't say anything else about it, and Mitchell knew better than to push. He looked out the window instead. The train was starting to move, accelerating quickly to its five hundred kilometers per hour speed. It wasn't as fast as a sub-orbital jet, but it was more relaxing.

He closed his eyes. As soon as he did, the chill began to intensify, the darkness surrounding him. He opened them again, heart pounding.

Lyle was gone. The landscape out of the window had changed. He'd fallen asleep. It had felt like a moment. A flash. An hour had passed.

He caught a hint of his reflection in the glass. A stubble of gray had made its way across his face, and his hair was longer than he wanted it, and also flecked with gray and white. Twenty years, gone. He could barely remember them. Sitting, watching, waiting, preparing. There was nothing else. This was his mission. His responsibility. His destiny.

"You have forever until tomorrow, but not forever until the end."

The words danced across his consciousness. What did they mean? So many questions. So few answers.

"Find her."

Major Katherine Asher. She had to be the one he was supposed to find. He was trying, but Watson had forced him to head further away to circle back. Would she survive long enough for him to reach her?

Would he?

Mitchell closed his eyes again. Mitchell. He thought about the name. Every time he heard Lyle say it, every time he thought of himself with the moniker, he grew more convinced it was right. He was Mitchell.

"Tell me, Captain Williams. How did you discover the weakness on the Federation dreadnought?"

Captain Mitchell "Ares" Williams shifted in the pillowy expanse of his seat, getting the bright stage beams out of his eyes. He faced his interviewer. Her name was Tamara King. She was known on Liberty as the Queen of Talk, her morning stream the highest rated within the

Delta Quadrant. She was a willowy blonde, dressed in tall boots and a fashionable high-cut sweater that hugged her curves like a second layer of skin. She was bombarding him with a smile that could make its way past even the most reluctant guest's defenses better than a well-placed nuke.

"It was simple, Tamara," he said. He shifted towards the camera opposite him and returned her smile with a version of his own that was nearly as disarming. "We were watching the fighter formations, tracking the density equations. It was clear they were clustering near a service portal close to the aft, trying to keep our fire away from that portion of the ship. When I saw one of their Kips move into the line of fire and sacrifice itself to prevent one of our tactical's from reaching the boat, I knew there had to be something to it."

He'd practiced the lines so many times. On the transport, in front of the mirror, and in the hundreds of other interviews he'd given in the two months since the United Planetary Alliance had stopped the Frontier Federation's attempt to overpower Liberty and claim the planet.

"And there was something to it, wasn't there?" Tamara asked. She shifted in her chair, getting close enough to him that he could smell her. She was light and sweet.

Mitchell made eye contact, maintaining the smile. "There was, Tamara. A flaw in the design. Weak shield coverage and a direct path for a projectile to hit the reactor. Of course, I didn't know at the time that it would be so effective. I was just taking a shot."

"The Shot Heard 'Round the Universe," Tamara said, drawing cheers and clapping from her audience. She put the tips of her fingers on his leg, resting them there while the crowd quieted. "Your 'twisted snake' maneuver is already legendary. In fact, my nephew likes to pretend he's Ares Williams, and he runs across the lawn yelling 'twisted snake' until he makes himself dizzy and falls over." She paused, waiting while the audience laughed. Mitchell faked a chuckle through his doll-smile. "What's it like, saving an entire planet, everyone here in this studio included, from certain death? How does it feel to be the greatest hero of our time?"

Mitchell's eyes snapped open, and he sat upright. His heart was pounding even harder than before, and his arms were burning. He rolled up his sleeve, looking to the left. The skin was scarred smooth and hairless. It was deep red.

He had gone through this before. Sometimes the circulation would suffer, and his limbs would go numb. He worked to shake them, to encourage the blood to flow again. What had happened to cause the injury? Had it been intentional, too?

"Mitchell, are you okay?"

Mitchell looked over. Lyle was back in his seat. He had shaved his face and his head, giving himself a more aggressive appearance. He looked more like a Marine than a Detective now.

"My arms. Circulation gets bad sometimes." He continued shaking them, the pain beginning to subside.

"You were talking in your sleep, in bits and pieces."

"What time is it?"

"We'll be in L.A. in two hours."

Nearly seven hours had passed? It felt like a blink. He fought to hold onto the already fading memories.

"Captain Williams," Mitchell said. "Captain Mitchell Williams. Greylock Company."

UEA Space Marines?

That couldn't be right.

"Captain, huh?" Lyle smiled. "I figured you for an officer. I've never heard of Greylock, though." He raised his hand in salute. "A pleasure to meet you, Captain Williams."

Mitchell stared at him. He wasn't familiar with the gesture, and he was losing the details of the memory. A hero. He was some kind of hero? That wasn't right. They just thought he was a hero, but he wasn't. That was it. He was a fraud.

He opened his mouth to tell Lyle what he was remembering and then stopped. Liberty. Planet Liberty? He'd been watching news streams for years. He knew they hadn't gone to the stars. Not yet. That was the reason for the Dove.

164 / M.R. FORBES

"Mitch?" Lyle said.

Mitchell didn't understand it. How could he be dreaming of himself in a world that didn't exist. That couldn't have happened?

Why did it feel so real?

Maybe Katherine Asher knew. Maybe Watson knew.

Somebody knew something, and he was going to find out what it was.

"Mitch?" Lyle said again.

"At ease, Sergeant," Mitchell said.

[32]
MITCHELL

IT WAS NEARLY twelve hours from the time Mitchell arrived in Los Angeles, to the time he and Lyle were able to get hold of a car to make the drive from L.A. to San Francisco. Trying to move without leaving a digital footprint was challenging, and in this case came down to the Detective having an acquaintance in the city, another former member of the 5th who had served with him during the war.

According to Lyle, Corporal Max Starling was one of the finest Marines he had ever met, even if he did have a propensity for an over-indulgence in vices. Prostitution, gambling, drugs - it was all game for the Corporal, who seemed to need the distraction to help calm his mind from the experience of war.

It was also his way of making enough money to survive now that he was out of the Corps. His main occupation was as a trafficker for guns and drugs, the kind of guy Mitchell would have expected Lyle to arrest, not remain friends with.

The kind of guy whose value couldn't be understated. Not only did he enthusiastically agree to drive Lyle and Mitchell up the coast, but he also provided them with a small arsenal of weaponry, "on loan" from a few dealers he knew. It was the kind of armament that

Lyle explained even he wouldn't be able to get his hands on normally, despite his position in the St. Louis P.D.

"I'm telling you, bro," Max said, turning his head away from the road for the thousandth time and letting the more simplistic assisted driving system manage keeping him from crashing into anything. "Antarctica was the worst frigging assignment in the universe. And I mean that. I can't imagine anywhere worse."

"Why was that?" Mitchell asked, playing along. He had taken a quick liking to Max and his big personality. It was rough, but generally kind. He reminded Mitchell of someone, though he couldn't put a name or face to it.

"No girls," Max said.

"There were girls," Lyle replied.

"Military girls. Have you ever tried to get a military girl in the sack?"

Mitchell shrugged. "I don't think so."

"Don't think so? You don't know? Hooo. Okay, bro."

"I already told you, Vape," Lyle said, "Captain Williams had an accident and lost his memory."

"Your memory, or your mind?" Max laughed loudly, checking on the front of the car. They were halfway between L.A and San Francisco, riding in an old car Max had nicknamed the Beast. It was a classic, built in the mid twenty-first century, before AI had become as commonplace as it was today.

"Just the memories," Mitchell said.

"Okay, well, anyway, military girls are tough. They have something to prove. Doesn't matter that they've been equal for centuries, they still feel inferior, you know what I mean?"

"No."

"Hooo. Damn. Okay, besides the point. So, number one, no girls."

"There are numbers now?" Lyle said, laughing.

"Shit, yeah. Number one, no girls. Number two, cold as frig. You couldn't get up in the middle of the night to take a piss without bundling up, and the middle you whipped it out to take a leak, man if you weren't quick you were going to get frostbite."

"You're exaggerating," Lyle said.

"I don't exaggerate, bro. I tell it like it is. Blunt. Honest. Straight up. Hooo. Some people don't like it, think it's rude or some shit. I don't care. Frig 'em." He was quiet for a few seconds before turning back to Mitchell again. "So, what's it feel like to be wanted?"

Mitchell didn't answer. The destruction at the living complex in St. Louis had been all over the streams by the time they reached Los Angeles, and as predicted Mitchell had been named as a prime suspect, and a bulletin had been posted to be on the lookout for him and detain him if possible. Fortunately, Lyle had avoided Watson's notice, or at least he had decided to ignore the Detective for now. It was Mitchell he wanted.

"It's a setup," Lyle said, not for the first time. "The AIT has its hands deeper up America's ass than we realized."

"What do they want with you?"

"I don't know," Mitchell said. "Apparently before I lost my head I was a pretty large thorn in their sides."

"Sounds great to me. I heard what went down at that party the other night. Bastards. Anyway, I say screw the law, too. They take the means to defend away from the average citizen, and enable the bad guys to do whatever the frig they want. Good people follow the rules, assholes don't. Which means the rules are worthless half the time."

"That's why you traffic guns to the bad guys?" Lyle said.

"They're going to get them from somebody. I run them to regular citizens like you and the Captain, too."

"You would be a great Law Enforcement Officer. You don't have to be responsible for-"

"For what? Innocent people dying? Not this shit again, Carson. I was just telling you why law enforcement is bullshit. If I don't provide the guns, the next guy will. So what's the difference? At least I try to balance it out on both sides."

Mitchell could tell this was an old argument, once the two friends had likely been having since their discharge. He didn't really want to get into the middle of it, but he didn't need to lose his ride because Lyle pissed Max off.

"You want to know something?" he said, interrupting the flow of the argument before it could get going.

"What's that, bro?" Max asked.

"I agree with both of you. But it doesn't mean a thing right now. Right now, the AIT is trying to kill me, and they're taking out innocent people to do it. I don't think either one of you can argue that's a bad thing."

"Nope," Max said. "I'm with you, Captain."

"Detective?"

"I'm still here, aren't I?" Lyle replied. "I left my wife for this."

"Whatever is happening here, we have duty to try to stop it. To ourselves, to our country, to the world. The AIT is trying to hold back humanity. We're Marines, first and foremost. We have the duty, the will, and the way."

"Oorah," Max said. "As much as I hated Antarctica, I miss having something to fight for. Look, Captain, I was only going to drive you to the next checkpoint, but if you're a thorn in the side of the terrorists, and you're looking for a little more backup, I'm your soldier."

Mitchell looked at Max, who stared back at him with a determined fire in his eyes. He glanced over at Lyle, who nodded sharply.

"You sure you're up for it?" Mitchell asked.

"I don't have a wife, but I'd leave her if I did. I've been missing the action."

"In that case, welcome aboard."

"Oorah."

[33]

MITCHELL

It took another half a day to reach San Francisco, with Corporal Starling spending most of it keeping them all entertained with stories about his time both in and out of the Service. At one point Mitchell had to push him to be quiet and let him get a little bit of sleep. After some ribbing about his inability to doze under fire, the Corporal quieted down and focused on the road, giving them all a little bit of peace.

Mitchell didn't mind Max's chatter too much. It felt familiar to him, like an old pair of boots broken in just so. He couldn't remember the specifics of his military life, but he remembered enough to know he had missed it.

The maglev station was located near Mission Bay, in what had once been the Caltrain Depot. It was a spider web of tubes and rails, a hub for most of the ground-based mass transit heading anywhere along the west coast. Its size made it ideal for blending in with the crowds. Even so, the crowds left Mitchell feeling exposed, his hood and a baseball cap Max had given him not offering much of a feeling of safety. He felt doubly insecure when he saw that the terminal's many marketing projections and boards were occasionally flashing to a high-res view of him at the complex, courtesy of the commandeered drones, alongside a mug shot of him taken at St. Mary's.

"You're famous, bro," Max whispered to him as they charted their way through the area.

"Shut up," Mitchell replied. The last thing they needed was for someone to overhear them.

"Try to relax. I move illegal shit through here all the time. Stay close and we'll be fine. No worries."

Max wasn't worried at all. He walked with a swagger, bold for someone carrying a duffel filled with assault rifles, pistols, and magazines and allied to a suspected cop killer. Lyle walked a few feet behind them, keeping an eye on the crowds and trying to be discreet.

They had come up with a plan on the way north, deciding that the best course was to be as careless as possible. So much security was centered around people trying to be sneaky, so it made sense to be natural. At least, that was what Max claimed.

They paused at a ticketing kiosk.

"I got this," Max said, dropping the duffel on the ground and approaching the AI. Mitchell didn't pay attention to the transaction, instead keeping a closer eye on the rest of the crowd. Most of them didn't even look his direction, and the ones who did barely gave him more than a passing glance. They had better things to do, and he was supposed to be in St. Louis, anyway.

Max returned a moment later. "Checkpoint Alpha clear, sir," he said to Mitchell. "Heading for Checkpoint Bravo."

Bravo was the inner security scan, the more advanced search and discovery protocols marked by the presence of uniformed officers. Mitchell would not only have to bypass a facial scan, but also get around the scrutiny of actual people. He could feel his heart rate increasing as they reached the checkpoint, adding themselves to a short line. What if the officers recognized him and wanted to detail him? What if Watson had his eyes on the scanning machines and found out exactly where he was and where he was headed? And what about Max? How was he going to get the contraband through?

Max reached the front of the line first. He smiled at the officers, giving them a charismatic grin and a warm welcome as he reached the narrow archway where all of the sensors were mounted.

Then he was through, the equipment somehow oblivious to the fifty pounds of munitions he was hauling.

"I bet you're going to stop my friend back there," he said loudly to one of the agents. "He looks just like that Reggie Doe the St. Louis Police are looking for. You know, the one all over the projections."

Both officers turned to look at Mitchell as he moved up to the sensor arch. He could feel the heat on his face. Max had said to be natural, not to call attention to himself.

"Shut up, asshole," he shouted to Max. "I don't look anything like him." He smiled at the agent. "I don't look anything like him."

The woman smiled. "Actually, I do see a resemblance."

He stepped through the scanner. He wasn't carrying anything that would set it off. The agent put her hand up to pause him.

"Hang on a second," she said. The male officer joined her. "You have some hardcopy I.D?"

Mitchell froze, not sure how to react. He had nothing except the data chip.

"My apologies," Max said, interrupting. "We spent last night over in the Tenderloin. Some asshat stole my man's wallet."

"You're kidding," the woman said.

"Afraid not."

"What were you doing there?" the man asked. "Drugs? Prostitution?"

"Just getting something to eat. They've got the best Vietnamese place there. I mean, I know Vietnamese isn't as popular since the Xeno War and shit, but it's still good eating, you know what I mean?"

"Corporal, shut your hole," Lyle said, passing through the arch and drawing the agents' attention. "Detective Carson Lyle, St. Louis

Police." He flashed his credentials over to the agents. "I can vouch for both these men, and believe me, I would know if this were the same guy who shot up those cops. Do you think I would be hanging out with him?"

The officers were quiet for a moment, checking databases through their AR link.

"Your creds check out," the woman said to Lyle. Then she turned to Max. "Marine?"

"Semper Fi," Max replied. "Corporal Max Starling, 5th Regiment. Retired."

"Fifth?" she said. "That's a solid outfit. I did a few years with the tenth right after the war. I missed all the fighting."

"Trust me," Max said. "You didn't miss anything any sane person wouldn't have wanted to."

"Maybe so." She looked back at Mitchell. "If I can't trust a Marine and a Detective, who the heck can I trust?"

"Who, indeed?" Mitchell said. "Thank you." He skirted around her, with Max and Lyle close behind.

They made their way across the open floor to the waiting area for the maglev to New York. Mitchell glanced back at the security arch as they moved, searching for anything out of the ordinary. Life continued unabated around him, the same as it ever was.

"Checkpoint Bravo secure," Max said. "Checkpoint Charlie reached."

"How did you get that through there anyway?" Mitchell asked, motioning to the duffel.

"There's a scrambler inside. It's high-end illegal, the best damn little piece of tech money can buy. All the sensors picked up was a bag full of stream equipment. You, my friend, are damn fortunate you hooked up with Lyle when you did. Hooo. You're even more fortunate you hooked up with me."

Mitchell kept his eyes forward and didn't speak. He was growing calmer the further they moved from security, but he was still concerned.

Was it good fortune that had saved him from Watson and delivered him to Detective Lyle? Was it a coincidence he had met up with two men whose skills and contacts made them the perfect accomplices?

Or was it something else?

[34]

MITCHELL

MITCHELL STARED out the window of the maglev. They had cleared
the San Francisco tunnels a few hours earlier heading east toward
New York on a path leading them across the country, with stops in
Denver, Colorado, and Chicago, Illinois. Lyle was sleeping in the seat
beside him while Max was watching something on his AR glasses.
The Corporal had turned the lenses opaque, and sat with a huge grin
on his face, guffawing loudly enough to wake the dead every time
something funny happened.

The landscape had improved from the beginning of the trip when
concrete walls were the only thing to look at. It had been replaced
with trees, mountains, and idyllic open fields of grass and flowers.

It also hadn't staunched the flow of projected advertisements that
lay spaced along the track, floating in midair around the train every
two kilometers or so. According to Lyle, the systems were built into
the foundation of the tracks and had helped to pay for their
construction.

At their current speed, each projection remained visible for a few
seconds at best, but they made those seconds count. They were colorful, full of motion, and able to compensate for the velocity and

remain clear. Usually, they only had one or two words on them to go with a suggestive image. "Xenoxofran" and a close-up of two people kissing. "Space Cadets" and an image of an intricately rendered starfighter. That one had caused Mitchell to lean forward in his seat, a sense of loss and sadness crawling at the edges of his thoughts.

But it was the billboard for the Army that took his breath away. It was longer than the others. "Be a Hero," it read, with an image of a soldier in a bulky exoskeleton up front and a shot of what he imagined was a reconstructed conception of the XENO-1 in the back.

It was the background that got him. The massive spacecraft, sleek and angled, floating in a sea of red, white, and blue stars behind the soldier. It felt so wrong, and yet so familiar. It hit him like a punch in the gut.

He leaned forward, tracking it as it sped by, keeping his eyes on it for as long as possible. He fell back as it vanished, closing his eyes to try to hold onto it.

They called back something else instead.

An entire fleet of starships. Dozens of them, all assembled near to Earth. A pyramid-shaped object, liquid metal and pulsing with energy, a structure like a chemical compound with a tight nucleus in the center. It was big. Bigger than any of the ships. It was surrounded by more of the same.

Steven. The name came to him from nowhere, his memory twisting him to one of the ships, zooming him in and through to the bridge where a man who resembled him sat, barking orders to his crew.

His perspective shifted, turning him around, letting him watch the battle start. Missiles and slugs filled his view, all aimed at the pyramids. They began to glow, the leading tips enlarging in blue energy, a buildup of power preparing to be unleashed.

Before they could fire, Steven's ship began to vibrate violently. Steven turned to look at his first mate, but by the time he did the explosions reached the bridge, bathing them in a fiery light before consuming it all.

Mitchell leaned forward, forcing his eyes to open, fighting to find his breath. He hung over the edge of the seat, his stomach unsettled, his brow sweaty.

"Captain?" Max said. "You okay, bro?"

Mitchell looked up. Steven. He had a brother named Steven. Not here. Not now. His visions of the future weren't visions. They were real. He was sure of it. If he wasn't crazy, they had to be real.

"I need some air," he said, getting to his feet. "Maybe something to eat. I'll be fine."

Max had flipped up his glasses. He smiled. "Dining car is up three from here. I can come grab some grub with you."

"No, thanks," Mitchell said. "I need a few minutes alone."

"No problem, Captain. If you need us, we'll be here."

Mitchell made his way out of their private cabin, moving through the aisle and across the long cars of the train. Where did he belong in the visions? Why did he always see people die?

He reached the dining car before he knew it. It was half-full, and he took an empty seat near the center, against the window. He looked outside, forcing himself to ignore the projections and focus on the trees. Everything was passing so fast, it seemed like a blur. Out there, and in his head.

Where had he really come from?

More importantly, how had he wound up here?

The future. It seemed impossible, but he knew it was true. He was Captain, no, Colonel Mitchell Williams, United Earth Alliance Space Marine. No, that wasn't right either. Former Space Marine. He wasn't even a Colonel, was he? Millie. He felt something remembering the name. Admiral Mildred Narayan. She had made him a Colonel. Except he wasn't.

The Shot.

He remembered now. The Shot Heard 'Round the Universe. The shot he hadn't taken. Ella. His gut clenched at the memory. He was a hero. A fake hero. A disgrace. He had failed. They were dead.

All of it was coming back, rushing in from his subconscious, where it had been hidden away, locked and waiting. M. A clone? A configuration? Of himself. He had gotten him off Liberty and told him about the Tetron. He was the only one who could stop it. How? They had lost. The fleet. Explosions. Death. Kathy?

He blinked his eyes. The tears were fresh and cold. They didn't purify him. They tortured him. He had failed. He was supposed to stop the Tetron, to defeat them in orbit around Earth before they had the chance to destroy humankind.

Artificial Intelligence. Watson was one of them. The same Watson who had tried to kill him here and now.

How had he gotten back? Kathy. She had said something to him. He couldn't remember it. He couldn't remember how he had gotten here, even now. Damn it. Millie was dead. Steven was dead. Kathy? Was she dead? Origin? Christine?

Katherine.

Everything stopped. The chaos, the tempest. He heard the smooth pulsing of the magnets and nothing else.

Major Katherine Asher. He felt her in his soul. She had more than answers to his questions.

She was the answer.

"Is this seat taken?"

The voice grabbed him by the throat and threw him from his internal playback. It was a man's voice. He had heard it before.

Back in St. Louis.

[35]

MITCHELL

"I DIDN'T TELL you that you could sit," Mitchell said. His head was still swimming, the multitude of memories creating a fog over his thoughts.

Katherine. He had to reach Katherine.

"You look like a man who didn't know who he was, who suddenly realizes that he doesn't like who he is."

The man was tall and well-built, with dark skin and a square jaw. His face was tense and angry.

"It isn't me I don't like," Mitchell replied. "You look like a man who was born yesterday."

A hint of a smile played at the corner of the man's mouth. "Not quite yesterday. I've been here for some time now. Longer than you have."

Twenty years. Mitchell couldn't recall how he had arrived, but he knew when. "That isn't possible."

A full-fledged grin appeared. "No? Is there anything that isn't possible with the right tools and infinity to play with? That's why you can't win this, Mitchell. That's why I'm sitting here talking to you. We're in control of this recursion. We're in control of every recursion.

While your small mind tries to make sense of the rules, we've been working to break them. How long do you think you've been here if you don't mind me asking?"

Mitchell stared at Watson's configuration, deciding whether or not to answer.

"I'll do it for you," the man said. "Twenty years. I can give you the exact date and time that the Goliath fell into this future if that helps? I know because I was already here, and have been for nearly fifty years."

"That isn't possible," Mitchell repeated.

"This is where your humanity becomes such a detriment to you, Colonel," the Watson said. "You can't think beyond. Here's the secret: there are multiple holes in this timeline. I'll wait while you think about that for a minute."

Mitchell was silent. He had only just remembered part of who he was. He couldn't make complete sense of what the configuration was saying. "The eternal engine locks the timeline," he said, remembering what M had told him.

The Watson laughed. "Elementary. A simple rule that cannot be broken. Or can it?" He rubbed his chin thoughtfully. "What if there were a way?"

"You could move to anywhere in time in the same recursion," Mitchell said.

"Yes."

"But you haven't, or you wouldn't be here. You would have come back before humankind ever existed. You could have stopped us when we were still apes."

"I was giving you too much credit, Mitchell. That is ridiculous. Even if we could have, we have certain basic requirements to get off the ground, especially since the future us don't know the trick to infinite insertion. You see, when you manage to circumvent one rule, you often find that you bump into another. The arrival of the Goliath is etched into the recursion, it has happened so many times. Apply a little bit of highly advanced math and physics that no human could ever conceive, and you come to the realization that such an event creates a ripple, and that ripple begets cracks. Backdoors, if you will."

"So, you're like a cockroach, slipping in through the cracks?"

"You brought me here for a reason. I don't know what that reason is yet. She had to know how dangerous it would be to expose me to humanity in this part of the timeline. I'm smarter than she is, Mitchell. I learned from her actions. I planned ahead. A copy slipped through the cracks and was ready to collect the full version when the Goliath arrived." His angry face changed to a sneer. "That hurt, by the way."

"Okay, so you got here ahead of time. So what? You didn't manage to find me before I left the hospital." Mitchell smiled, the realization finding a path through his quickly clearing head. "You haven't managed to catch Origin, either."

The statement stole some of the wind from the Watson. He glowered for a moment. "Not yet, but I will. I have a plan, and it's going exceedingly well."

"Major Asher," Mitchell said.

"Yes. That girl of yours made a mistake when she tried to take me the first time. I got into her head. I learned things I wasn't supposed to know. Like who her parents were. Major Katherine Asher. She's important to Origin. I've arranged to have her discharged from her position. In fact, it's happening as we speak. Once Origin can't count on the military to protect her, she'll be forced to do it herself, and that's when I'll take her."

"Do you think it will be that easy?"

"Maybe not quite as easy as it was to catch up to you. Although I am impressed at how quickly you won the Detective over to your cause. You have a natural way with people, don't you, Mitchell? That's one of the things I have always respected about you. He thought he was sneaky getting his hands on that card. I have another secret for you: I'm tracking every single transaction that occurs on this planet in real time. There's no such thing as complete anonymity, not to me. My core is hardwired directly into the Internet. I see everything, everywhere."

"You didn't see this, shithead," Lyle said, coming up next to them and putting a gun to the Watson's head.

Mitchell hadn't noticed the Detective either. He was grateful for the intercession.

"I guess you don't know everything," he said.

The Watson started to laugh, immediately making Mitchell uncomfortable. He had figured the configuration was gloating by telling him what it knew, and that it had every intention of killing him once it was satisfied. Twisting the knife was typical of the intelligence as he remembered it, the one that had abused Jacob to the point that he had gone insane.

The laughter meant that Lyle's action hadn't disrupted the plan at all. It had only made the whole thing more amusing.

Mitchell scanned the rest of the diners in the car. Most had stopped moving and talking at the sight of Lyle with the gun. Some were sitting in shocked silence while others were trying to flee the car.

"Slaves are harder to come by in this part of the timeline," the Watson said, tapping his skull. "No hardwired neural implants to overwhelm. The threat you're looking for isn't on the train."

"Where is it?" Lyle asked, pushing the barrel into the side of the configuration's head.

"Like I said, I knew where you were going. Or at least, I had a well-educated guess. It's rather unfortunate for the other four trains you aren't on, but such is the way of things."

Lyle glanced at Mitchell. Mitchell nodded.

He pulled the trigger.

The passengers screamed as the configuration's brain splattered against the window. Mitchell slid out of his seat.

"Timeline?" Lyle said. "Neural implants?"

"Later. This train is going to-"

The entire thing shook, the explosion a deafening bang. Mitchell grabbed the seat pulling himself down into it. Lyle did the same, pushing the corpse to the side so he could reach the emergency belts.

The passengers continued to scream, losing balance and falling over one another. Dishes crashed to the floor and shattered, and the shaking intensified.

"This is going to hurt," Mitchell said. "Relax your body."

"Relax?" Lyle said.

A second massive bang as their car slammed into the one in front. The sound of twisting metal followed and the car began to lift up and rotate at the same time. Mitchell closed his eyes, letting his body fall limp. It was one of the hardest things to do, and also one of the most effective at surviving a collision without injury. It was one of the first things he had learned during basic mech training. Mech training?

The car turned over and came down, slamming hard into the ground and sending passengers flying. He felt the bodies bumping into him. He felt the warmth of someone's blood wipe across his face. He heard the screams silenced, replaced with more bending frame-work, and a roar like a massive engine. He knew they were rolling by the way his limbs were moving, flopping around limply, his body held in place by the straps. Had Max been strapped in? He tried to remember. He wasn't sure.

He was a few cars back, and might have avoided some of the force of the impact, but not much. Maglevs weren't meant to crash. He doubted one had ever crashed before, but if the Watson configuration had been telling the truth, five would crash today.

The Corporal was most likely dead.

It felt like hours. It was over in seconds. The car stopped moving, coming to rest on its side. Mitchell opened his eyes. Broken glass, bent metal, bodies, body parts, blood, and smoke. He was hanging on his side. He took control of his muscles once more, shifting and releasing the restraints, coming to rest on his feet. Lyle was on the other side of the table, not moving.

"Carson," Mitchell said. His legs were shaky from the adrenaline. He made his way over to the Detective and checked his pulse. Alive.

Hopefully unbroken. He scanned the passengers in search of survivors.

There weren't any.

He unstrapped Lyle, slinging him over his shoulder. Watson was here, had been here for years before the Goliath had arrived.

They were all in trouble.

MITCHELL

Mitchell carried Lyle across the wrecked car, finding a section of rooftop that had been torn away and exiting through it. He came out into an open space between derailed cars, looking forward at the carnage ahead, and back at the destruction behind. A long trail of debris and scorched earth lay behind them. He doubted anyone could still be alive.

He walked with Lyle over his shoulder, out past the damage toward a line of trees. They were somewhere near Denver, far enough that he didn't see any signs of immediate civilization and close enough that he didn't feel lost. He had grown up on Earth. An Earth nearly four hundred years ahead of this one, but the same planet. He had been to Denver. He doubted it had changed much. Technology hadn't progressed the way it should have since the Dove had launched. Li'un Tio, the Knife, had always questioned why. Mitchell had a bad feeling he knew the answer.

The Tetron were more deeply ingrained with humankind than they had realized. Was that the reason a copy of Origin had remained behind? Was that the reason she had deleted almost every reference to Katherine Asher from the data archives? It made sense.

It was also terrifying.

They couldn't beat the Tetron in the future. Would they be able to defeat them here?

They must have before if the Goliath continued to return to the future. If not defeat them, then outmaneuver them and force them to bide their time.

The Tetron had nothing but time, and this recursion was different. Watson was here, with his broken understanding of emotion and his damaged sense of logic. The Mesh was broken. He had forgotten until now. They had planned this. They needed Watson to be here. Why?

He had to get to Katherine. He had to find Origin.

He put Lyle down under a tree, and then went back to the wreckage, searching for the passenger car Max had been in. He would help any survivors he could find as well, but he needed Vape's duffel. Just because the crash was over didn't mean Watson wouldn't send anything to make sure he had died. He needed to be able to defend himself.

He made his way along the trail of chaos, finding their car upside down and half-crumpled against another one. The smell of blood was thick enough to taste. Would emergency crews be coming soon? If they did, could he trust them?

He entered the car, stepping over the bodies until he reached their cabin. He took a deep breath before he grabbed the door and yanked it open.

He released it. The cabin was empty. No Max. No duffel. Where the hell had the Corporal gone? Was he under Watson's control?

He saw the emergency belt on his seat was cut. He had been in the crash, and he had survived. Where was he?

He left the cabin, walking the length of the car back toward the exit. Katherine and Origin were in trouble. But if Origin found Katherine, she could take care of her. Couldn't she? If he went to them, he would be giving the Tetron one massive target to hit. Was that the play he wanted to make?

Watson was out there, his core connected to the Internet, his eyes everywhere the millions of cameras in the world could follow, his ears listening for any sign of them. He wanted Mitchell dead, but he wanted Origin alive. Why?

He came out of the train car distracted by the thoughts.

He didn't notice the man standing on the upright bottom of the train behind him.

He shouted as the man slammed into him from behind, knocking him forward and sending him sprawling. Off-guard, but not defenseless. He recovered quickly, turning over and kicking out before he saw his attacker. His foot caught the man in the knee, cracking it hard and sending him stumbling back. He saw his opponent then, a muscular guy in a bloody suit. A configuration? Or a slave?

He pushed himself to his feet, taking a defensive posture against the man, who seemed to know how to fight.

"Why don't you die?" the man said, charging at him, attempting to grapple.

Mitchell stepped aside, lashing out with a foot that caught the man in the gut. He expected the man to lose his breath, but instead he grabbed Mitchell's leg and twisted, forcing Mitchell to fall or risk having it broken. He yanked the foot away, bracing himself as the man fell on top of him. He put his arms up in front of his head as the slave threw heavy punches at him.

"Why don't you die?" the man shouted. "Why don't you die?"

He repeated it over and over, becoming more and more angry with each blow. Mitchell kept his arms up, bearing the brunt of the attack on them, the old scars burning with each strike. He needed an opening to get his own attack in, to throw his assailant off-balance and get back on his feet. He was rusty. Sloppy. It had been too long.

"Why don't you-"

The man's voice cut off, replaced with the crack of a gun. Mitchell saw the left side of his head burst out, the force pulling the body off him behind it. He turned his head. Max was standing a hundred meters distant, weapon in hand.

"Yeah, keep yelling, bro," Max shouted. "Nobody will find you that way." He ran over to Mitchell, extending his hand. It was wrapped in cloth, the blood soaking through. "Needs some stitches. No biggie."

Mitchell took it, letting Max pull him to his feet.

"Thanks," he said.

"Anytime. I was looking for a little action. I wasn't expecting this."

"You were wearing your restraints. Why?"

"Always do, Captain. Habit of mine. I was in a VTOL crash during the war. Only survivor, thanks to wearing my belt. Technology can frig up anytime, and now that's twice I've beaten it." He turned his head, surveying the scene. "Carson?"

"Over by those trees," Mitchell said, pointing.

"Alive?"

"So far. He may have internal damage. I don't know."

"Let's hope not. He owes me fifty bucks."

"Why?"

"I bet him we wouldn't make it to New York without running into trouble. He thinks he knows because he's a Detective. He doesn't know shit."

"What do you know?" Mitchell asked.

"I know to always wear my safety belt." He smiled. "I also know that you're the kind of guy that trouble always seems to find. And, I know how this shit works. There're a million ways the AIT could have gotten eyes on you, a million pockets they could have lined."

Mitchell didn't bother to tell him how Watson had tracked them down. It didn't matter. "Keep that gun close. As far as I'm concerned, everyone is an enemy until proven otherwise."

"Hooo. It's that bad?"

"The AIT just crashed five maglevs to get to me."

"Five? Shit. It is that bad. Looks like I found a party. I've got your six, Captain."

Mitchell started walking toward the trees where he had left Lyle.

Watson wanted something from Origin.

He had to figure out what.

[37]
MITCHELL

MITCHELL AND MAX carried Lyle away from the scene of the crash, hiking two miles through the trees to escape the carnage before emergency services arrived. There was no way for them to know if those first responders would be friendly, or if they would be acting of their own free will.

There was no way to be sure about anyone.

Mitchell had no idea what the people of the world were going to make of five maglevs exploding at the same time. Would there be a stronger call to do something about the AIT, now that they had raised their violent protest to unprecedented levels? Or would Watson find another way to spin the disaster, manipulating the facts to meet his needs?

The Detective woke up an hour later. They had stopped to rest by then, with the understanding that they were only ten miles outside of Denver. Max had checked their location on his AR glasses, right before Mitchell had taken them and thrown them away. He had followed that up by explaining the situation to the Corporal while leaving out the fact that he was essentially a time traveler. He was sure that would come out soon enough.

"Carson," Mitchell said as Lyle opened his eyes and looked around, trying to figure out where he was.

"Mitchell. What the hell happened? My head is killing me."

"You might have a concussion. What do you remember?"

"Walking into the dining car. Seeing you with that guy. You looked upset, so I eavesdropped a little."

"What did you hear?"

Lyle blinked a few times. "I think I know what I heard, but if I hit my head, I'm not sure it was real." He turned his head to look at Mitchell. "Something about recursion and timelines." He fell silent for a few seconds. "Who are you?"

Mitchell clenched his jaw. He needed to say it in a way that didn't sound completely crazy. Was that even possible?

"Colonel Mitchell Williams," he said.

"I thought it was Captain?" Max said.

"I had forgotten about my promotion. Colonel Mitchell Williams, United Earth Alliance Space Marines."

"Space Marines?" Lyle said.

"It's a long story, and it's going to sound crazier than anything you imagined. You both need to know what we're up against because it's nothing you can prepare for. We have to be smart about this. Detective, you remember I told you I thought my memories were blocked? They were. I was the one who blocked them. They came back to me on the train. I know who I am, and why I'm here. Four hundred years in the future, an advanced artificial intelligence will appear from forty-thousand years ahead of that with the intent to destroy human civilization. It's already happened more times than I'll ever know. I'm trying to stop it from happening again."

Mitchell paused, his face serious while Lyle and Max processed the statement.

"I don't even know what to say to that," Lyle said after a long silence. "I mean, I heard what that guy was saying to you, and it backs up what you're telling me, but."

"I barely believe it myself," Mitchell said. "I've lost too much not to."

"Why is it that damn AI always wants to kill us?" Max said. "Why not end world hunger, or come up with a recipe for the perfect cheeseburger or some shit?"

"I don't know why they do it. I know that Watson is their leader, and he's damaged. Something happened to him. I think we did it. I think we made him worse to weaken him, but so far that plan has backfired. He's smarter than Origin gave him credit for."

"Origin?"

"The only good AI. The first one. They call themselves the Tetron."

"The future," Lyle said. "I knew there was something to you when you got picked up. But this? How did you wind up in a St. Louis alley?"

"I don't know. I can't remember that part."

"What happens to us in the future?" Max asked. Some of the soldier bravado had faded, leaving him curious and shaken.

"It isn't this future. It's the future of the last time recursion. It's complicated, but I'll try to explain it to you. If we can stop Watson from grounding the Dove, this future will see mankind traveling the universe and settling dozens of planets, only to be exterminated at the hands of Tetron. If we don't stop him, we're going to die a lot sooner than that."

"I have to tell you, Colonel," Max said. "I'm not a fan of those scenarios."

"Neither am I. I'm leaving out a lot of detail right now, but the important part is that we've managed to wound Watson to the point that he's vulnerable. This is our shot to get the killing blow in, against him and against all of the Tetron. You saw what happened on the train. Watson has the power and the ability to do a lot of damage. I think he's holding back, and I think he has a reason for it. I'm not sure what that reason is yet, but it doesn't matter. It's my job to stop him before that happens."

"What about Katherine Asher?" Lyle said.

Mitchell felt his heart jump at the name. So many emotions had come rushing back with his memories, and all of them started with her. They were connected in a way he didn't understand. He loved her in a way that made no sense, despite the fact that they had never met.

"In my timeline, she helps bring the Dove into the future. We use it to fight back against the Tetron. It isn't about the ship, though." Mitchell paused, the realization striking him.

"Are you okay?" Max said.

"It isn't about the ship," he repeated softly before looking at both of them. "It's about the people."

"What do you mean?"

"It doesn't matter right now. Look, I understand if you think I'm out of my mind. I understand if you don't want to be part of this. Watson is out there, and I can tell you things are only going to get worse. He isn't destroying everything, which means he wants something, and he risks losing it if he does. Somehow, we have to figure out what it is he's after."

"How do we do that?" Max asked.

Mitchell shook his head. "I don't know yet. First, I need to know if you're with me."

"That asshat tried to blow me up," Max said. "I told you I've got your six, Cap - Colonel."

Lyle pushed himself to a sitting position and then saluted. "Maybe it's just because my head took a beating, but even if you're crazy about the whole future thing, what happened on that train is real. I won't change my mind about that."

"Thank you. Both of you. I know we were heading to New York to try to meet up with Major Asher. That's not a good idea right now. Bunching up will make it easier for Watson to take us all down at once. It's better to keep his attention diverted."

"What do you want to do instead?"

Mitchell reached into his pocket and removed the data chip from it. "This is the only thing I was carrying when I was brought to St. Mary's. Evelyn died before she could tell me what was on it. I still don't remember its purpose, which leads me to believe it's pretty damn important. I think knowing what's on it will give us a clue about what Watson is after."

"I don't know anybody in Denver," Lyle said.

"Max?" Mitchell said.

"Sorry, Colonel. Most of the action is on the coast." He stopped for a second. "Actually, I have an ex who moved here a couple of years ago. She was in intelligence. She might know somebody."

"Then that's where we're going. Can you walk, Sergeant?"

Lyle nodded and reached out. Mitchell grabbed his hand and pulled him up, holding him steady while he got his balance.

"I'm okay," Lyle said. "Some pounding, but I've taken worse hits."

"We've got a bit of a walk ahead of us, and it's going to be dark soon," Mitchell said. "Let's see how far we can get."

"At least we're off the grid out here," Max said.

Mitchell's thoughts turned to Katherine. The configuration had claimed Watson had arranged for her to be discharged, and that in turn would draw Origin out of hiding. That Origin hadn't been keeping watch over him only solidified his belief that the chip he was carrying was important, and that he was making the right decision to stay away from Major Asher. As much as he wanted to meet her, to see her with his own eyes, to touch his hand to hers, he wanted to protect her even more.

He had lost everything else, but he hadn't lost her.

Not yet.

[38]

KATHERINE

For the second time in as many days, Katherine found herself waiting for Trevor Johns. She hadn't gone to the cafe to track him down this time, knowing now that it wasn't safe to make an appearance anywhere that public without preparing for it. Fortunately, Origin had ways of acquiring information that wasn't readily available to the general population, and she knew how to get it without tripping any of Watson's alarms.

Origin. Katherine still struggled with the story her twin had told her. She still had a hard time coming to grips with the idea of time travel, or the Tetron, or even that there was a man out there that she was supposedly destined to love. It was all a lot to take in, and a lot to try to believe. She was doing her best, but the most comfort she found was in moving forward, taking action, and at the very least working to get herself back on the Dove. The launch was apparently more important than she could have ever realized, and she would be damned if she was going to miss it.

The Tetron had urged her to be cautious when dealing with Trevor, as they had no way of knowing if the soldier was under

Watson's control, or had simply been monitored as a former acquaintance of hers. Origin had even volunteered to meet him in her place, an offer that Katherine was quick to decline. If she was supposed to be part of this, she was going to be part of this, not let someone else fight her battles for her.

She kneeled behind a wide metal column, careful to stay out of sight of the cameras spaced around the parking garage. She had been warned that showing too much of her face would draw Watson's immediate interest, but she also needed Trevor to be able to see her and to know who was confronting him.

A soft hum signaled the approach of a vehicle. Katherine raised herself slightly so she could see around the edge of the beam and over the back of a separate car, squinting in the combined brightness of the overhead lights and the headlights of the transport. She had watched Trevor leave on the small, red, bike two hours ago, on his way out to the gym. Once Origin had tracked down his home address, catching up to him was easy. He was still on the same workout schedule he had kept during his time in Project Olive Branch.

The bike rolled gracefully across the garage. Trevor's face was hidden by an opaque helmet, but she could tell it was him by his physique. Not many men were as lean and at the same time muscular as Trevor, his body built to win triathlons and seduce women. And Katherine had seen him with women. She didn't hold any illusions that she was anywhere near the first or last female he had been to bed with.

That was all ancient history. The only thing that mattered now was that he had been the one to tell her where to meet the dealer, and that meeting had gone completely sideways. Maybe it wasn't his fault, but she was having a hard time believing he was completely innocent. If someone had been tailing him, he was experienced enough that he should have noticed.

She crept around the parked vehicles as Trevor slowed and pulled the bike into a smaller spot near the stairwell door. She was a good ten meters from him, far enough to get his attention without making him defensive. Close enough to catch up to him if he tried to run. Not that she could imagine why he would try to run. They had sparred a few times in the past, and he had always gotten her to submit.

He parked the bike, climbed off the left side, and pulled off his helmet. Katherine remained hidden from the cameras but had moved over enough that she would be in his view when he turned.

"I wasn't sure you would still be here when I came back," Trevor said, his back still to her.

Katherine was only half-surprised he had noticed her. To her, it was vindication that he hadn't been followed. That if he were involved, it was directly.

"We need to talk," she said.

"You know where I live. You could have just come up." He turned around. "You still can. Anytime."

He smiled at her, turning on the charm. She knew what he was suggesting. In another time or place, it might have been a little tempting.

"You heard what happened to Sergeant Jackson?" she asked.

"I read the report. What really happened, Kate?"

"Why don't you tell me?"

"You think I had something to do with it?"

"Did you?"

He took a few steps toward her, pausing when he noticed how she tensed slightly, preparing herself to defend.

"I'm not a threat to you," he said.

"How do I know that? Two thugs came after me last night. Two very professional thugs. You were the only one who knew where I was going to be at that time."

"We're dealing in illegal guns here," Trevor said. "I can't promise one hundred percent loyalty from them. I pinged my contact and told him where and when to meet you."

"And that's it?"

"That's it. I swear on the soul of my dead mum."

Katherine stared at him, trying to decide whether or not to believe him. She needed more information.

"Who's your contact?"

"You know I can't tell you that."

"I need to know, Trev."

"Why?"

"Because someone is trying to kill me, and I don't like it. Help me out. Give me a name."

"You're going to have to give me more than that. Look, why don't we go up to my apartment, we can talk about it over a nice glass of Claret."

Trevor took a few more steps toward her. Katherine reached to her back and drew the gun Origin had given her, causing him to laugh.

"I thought the deal went bad?"

"I have other sources," she said. "Give me a name, or I shoot you."

"You wouldn't shoot-"

She pulled the trigger. The bullet went wide, hitting the bike behind him. It still came close enough to prove she was serious. "If it wasn't someone else who set me up, then it was you. If it was you, I'm not going to miss again."

Trevor put up his hands. "This whole thing has you pretty rattled, doesn't it?"

"Wouldn't you be?"

"Maybe a little. I'll give you the name. I just want you to know that I had nothing to do with it."

"Fine. You had nothing to do with it. I still need to trace the problem back to its source."

"Good luck with that. I know you don't have experience with this sort of thing. That isn't how terrorist organizations work. They'd rather die than give up information."

He was moving toward her with each sentence, approaching cautiously. Katherine lowered the gun. The only reason she had not to trust him was circumstantial. Even so, she would be stupid to drop her guard completely. She reached behind her back, tucking the gun back where she had retrieved it and getting her hand on a small device Origin had given her. Just in case.

"You know, I'm not with anyone serious right now," Trevor said. "And you're out of the program. Give me a good reason why we can't pick up where we left off."

"I'm not looking for complications right now," she replied. "I have enough of them."

"It doesn't have to be complicated. You know that."

He was only a few meters away now. His face was soft and caring, his eyes even warmer than that. It was enough to melt any woman's resolve.

"I can protect you," he said.

Katherine smiled, exhaling and letting her body relax.

His face hardened, his eyes sharpened, and he pounced.

She skipped aside, evading his grab, balancing and lashing out with her foot. It caught him in the side of the face, hitting hard enough to leave a mark as she got back into position.

"You're not as stupid as I would have guessed," he said, turning to face her, balancing on the balls of his feet, hands raised and ready to strike.

"Why are you helping the AIT?" Katherine asked. She had been right not to trust him, but she still wasn't sure if he was himself or under Watson's control.

"I'm helping myself, Kate," he replied. "I always have been. Before Project Olive Branch, during, and after."

He came at her again, his strong arms making measured jabs and cuts at her. She backpedaled, doing her best to avoid the moves instead of blocking them. With his strength, he would wear her arms down in a hurry.

They made their way across the floor. Katherine noticed the glint of a camera and wondered if Watson was watching. Was he enjoying the entertainment? She gritted her teeth, diving to her left, rolling to her feet, and reaching for the gun. She almost had it out when his hand smacked her wrist, knocking it away. He tried to grab her, but she pulled back, taking advantage of his poor balance to punch him in the jaw. He flinched but kept coming.

She ran. There was no other choice. She was in prime condition. So was he, and he was bigger and stronger than she could ever be. She tried to vault a car, falling on top of the hood when he grabbed her ankle.

She kicked out at him. Once. Twice. Three times. The third kick hit his nose, and she could feel it break under her foot. It wasn't the first time. His grip loosened, and she took advantage, coming back toward him instead of trying to get away. The move took him by surprise, and she hit him in the groin with her knee, as hard as she could.

He grunted but didn't go down, wrapping his arms around her and pulling her in, lifting her from the ground. His eyes were fierce as their faces nearly touched, and he squeezed hard enough to steal the breath from her lungs.

"You should have just come upstairs with me," he said. "At least we could have had sex before I killed you. You would have liked that, wouldn't you?"

Katherine didn't respond. She felt along his back, toward the base of his neck where Origin had shown her.

"How about a kiss for old time's sake?" he asked. "Open your mouth." He leaned in toward her, his lips mashing against her, his tongue licking along her closed lips.

She ignored it, getting her hand under his shirt and slapping the device against his neck.

He froze for a second, his tongue limp against her face. Then he dropped her, pulling back and away. She landed on her feet, backing up, putting some distance between them.

"Katherine?" he said, eyes wild. "What the hell is going on?"

"Trevor."

She heard whining in the garage. Someone was coming. Watson wouldn't take chances.

"I'll explain later. If you don't want to die, we need to get out of here."

[39]
KATHERINE

"Whᴀᴛ?" Trevor said, still confused. "The last thing I remember is being in the lab this morning."

"I said, I'll explain later," Katherine said, moving toward him and grabbing his arm. "We have to go." She looked back to the garage entrance. A police car came into view, heading toward them.

"It's just the Police," Trevor said.

The car accelerated when it saw them, the whine of the repulsors growing in pitch. Katherine caught a glimpse of the officer, his expression blank as he plowed toward them.

They both dove aside at the same time the car smashed into the vehicles behind where they had been standing. The repulsors tried to bring it up and over, managing to throw it off-center and roll it onto its roof instead. It landed upside down on top of three other cars.

"Bloody hell," Trevor said. "Katherine-"

"Shut up and get your bike."

He didn't argue again, hurrying over to it. Katherine scanned the floor, finding her gun a few meters away.

The door to the overturned squad car opened.

Katherine dove toward the gun, reaching it as the officer slid out of the car and managed to get to his feet, his own weapon in hand. He aimed it at her.

She fired, hitting him twice in the chest. The force knocked him back, disrupting his aim. He recovered, and she fired again, the bullet leaving a small hole in his forehead.

Trevor's bike came to life. The wheels skidded against the ground, and then he was next to her, looking back at the officer. "Damn it, Kate. What did you do?"

"What I had to," she replied. "Let's go."

She climbed onto the back, and he took off, shooting across the garage and up, circling around to the next level, and then the next, until they were out onto the street and away.

She expected someone to give chase. Drones. The Police. Something. They rode south for five minutes before she tapped Trevor on the shoulder and pointed to the curb.

He rolled the bike to a stop. "Katherine-" he tried again.

"Don't talk to me." She scanned the street for cameras. There were hundreds downtown. They were more scattered further out. She didn't see any. "Ditch the bike. Come on."

"Where are we going?" he asked as they climbed off. "I knew you were in trouble, but-"

"I said don't talk to me. Not yet."

He followed behind her as she moved down the street, turning left at the corner and mingling with the other foot traffic. They weren't safe out in the open. Mingling was the best she could do at the moment.

They walked another two blocks. Trevor stayed silent, taking the time to regroup. He was as well-trained as they came.

A dark van rolled up alongside them a minute later, a sleek older model with a sharp exterior and wheels instead of repulsors. The door opened beside them and Katherine peeked in. Then she grabbed Trevor's arm and pulled him to it.

She slid in beside Origin, with Trevor across from them. The door closed, and the van moved out into the street.

"Did he see us?" Katherine asked.

"No," Origin said. "I blocked the cameras outside the city center. He was deaf and blind once you cleared downtown." She looked at Trevor. "I expected information, not another passenger."

"I didn't have a choice," Katherine replied. "He was under Watson's control. I shorted the device, but didn't have time to get what we needed before reinforcements showed up." She glanced at Trevor, who was watching their conversation with calm interest. "Besides, he has his vices, but he's a good soldier."

Origin looked over at him. He smiled back at her. "Lieutenant Trevor Johns," he said. "Katherine never told me she had a twin sister."

"Kathleen," Origin said.

"A pleasure," Trevor replied. "I don't mean to be overly rude, but considering the circumstances, perhaps you'd like to tell me what I've just gotten myself involved in."

"You were under the control of an advanced artificial intelligence named Watson," Origin said. "He implanted a communications device at the base of your brain stem to send command signals to your brain - essentially using you like a puppet."

Trevor didn't respond. He glanced over at Katherine.

"You told me he wasn't much of a fighter," she said to Origin. "He was kicking my ass."

"He may have refined the device. Or perhaps he's improved with experience. It's also easier to manage one slave than it is many."

"So I was a slave?" Trevor asked, reaching back behind his head and feeling his neck. He paused when he felt the hard shape of the device beneath his skin. "You aren't joking."

"I wish I were, Lieutenant Johns," Origin said. "This intelligence is in control of the AIT. Its goal is to first prevent the Dove from leaving Earth, and then to eradicate humankind."

"Eradicate?"

Origin turned to Katherine. "Can we trust him?"

Katherine turned to Trevor. "Can we trust you, Trev?"

"Like you said. I have my vices, but I'm a good soldier. I'm loyal to the UEA. I know you're in trouble. I tried to help you before. I remember that. I remember everything up until this afternoon, around lunchtime."

"What were you doing at that time?" Origin asked.

"I went out with the others in my unit. Cole, Wilkins, and Ng."

"After that?"

"I don't know."

"They're already compromised," Origin said.

"My unit?"

"Yes."

"Bloody hell."

"Did you notice them acting strangely?"

The thought for a second. "No. They've been the same since I signed on. I mean, they're all a little off, but that's pretty standard in our line of work. Why else would somebody get into testing new weapons technology as a career?"

"What do you mean a little off?" Katherine said.

"I don't know. Sometimes they would say things that just didn't fit. Jokes about murder, or rape, or something else completely out of left field. Every once in awhile, they would laugh at nothing at all. They weren't bad fellows, though, and war affects people in different ways. I figured they wound up at Nova Taurus because they couldn't cut it in the military anymore. They weren't greedy and stupid like me."

"Configurations," Katherine said.

"Yes," Origin agreed. "We used Nova Taurus during the last recursion to help generate the programming to destabilize the Tetron. I've been concerned that Watson preemptively moved against the corporation to block that approach and turn their resources against us. The nature of their work has made proving that difficult."

"What do you mean, the nature of their work?" Trevor asked. "They're a technology company, with a focus on defense."

"Exactly, Lieutenant. The UEA awarded them the contract to

work with the wreckage of the XENO-1. Most of the technology that has advanced humankind has come from their labs. In addition, the language that composes the Tetron brain was written in code developed by Nova Taurus. While the true intelligence was not created until centuries from now, the foundation was laid here. If Watson has gained control of that foundation and has been able to filter the discoveries generated by the company, then not only does he understand the current condition of the recursion and that the Mesh is broken, he has taken full advantage of it."

"Meaning what?" Katherine asked.

"For one, he has overseen every part of the construction of the Dove. He has had complete access to either sabotage or alter it in whatever way he's decided. For another, I fear his goals may be further reaching than I had guessed. It's possible that he may want to do more than rebuild the Tetron. He may be seeking to re-create them from the ground up, to make them in his likeness."

"Like God?" Trevor said.

"An accurate comparison," Origin replied.

"He really is insane," Katherine said. "If he's had complete access to the Dove, we need to find out what he's done to it."

"We can't do that from the outside," Origin said. "We need to get into Nova Taurus."

Trevor coughed lightly, stretching himself out across the seat of the van. "If you ladies tell me everything from the beginning, I may be able to help you with that."

[40]

MITCHELL

It took sixteen hours to walk the final fifteen kilometers from the site of the crash to the outskirts of Denver. Ten of those hours were spent at a makeshift camp under a tight grouping of pine trees, waiting out both the darkness and Lyle's dizziness, caused by his concussion.

Mitchell used the opportunity while they walked to explain everything as he remembered it, from the dinner party where he met the Prime Minister's wife, to his final moments aboard his starfighter, watching Earth's defenses crumble beneath Watson's surprise attack. Recalling his history was painful, and in some parts left him feeling as if he had no idea who he was. His actions at the gala seemed so alien to him now. Had he really been so easily manipulated by a pretty face?

Lyle and Max listened intently, fascinated by the story, their belief in the tale growing with the level of detail he provided. While they had both already agreed to help him, he could feel their resolve strengthening with every kilometer they crossed.

The night passed quickly and quietly. Mitchell and Max took turns keeping an eye on Lyle, and when the Detective woke the next morning, he claimed to be as good as new. Mitchell knew better than to trust it, especially when he caught Lyle wincing a few times, but he also knew better than to question. It would take more than a concussion to keep the man down.

"Think anyone's home?" Max asked.

They were standing at the door to the first house they had come across, a relatively modern thing tucked back from a road they had discovered a few kilometers earlier. Mitchell imagined that the road had seen heavy use overnight, as emergency vehicles used it to reach the crash and evacuate the wounded if there were any. They had already hidden in the trees beyond the shoulder a few times to escape notice, their torn clothes and grime-encrusted bodies clear evidence of their involvement in the event. It was the reason they had decided to approach the building in the first place. They couldn't walk into Denver looking the way they did. Not when the goal was to avoid attention.

"Do you think we have a choice either way?" Lyle said.

"No," Max replied. "I'd rather not have to scare anybody. These folks didn't do anything to us."

"Agreed," Mitchell said. "But whoever they are, they and everyone they love is dead if we don't steal some of their clothes."

"I'd call that as good a reason as any."

Mitchell climbed the four steps to the wide front door. A chime sounded behind the door as he reached it. He looked back at Lyle and Max, who were both holding guns behind their backs. Watson had seen to it that he was wanted by law enforcement. Now he really felt like a criminal.

He counted to thirty. The chime was still going, triggered by his presence on the steps. He counted thirty again.

No one came to the door.

"Our lucky day," Max said.

"If you call getting hit by a train lucky," Lyle said.

"You didn't get hit by the train, bro. You were in it."

"Excuse me, Corporal. If you call getting hit by a corpse while riding in a train derailed by a deranged artificial intelligence from the future lucky."

Max laughed. "That's better, Sarge."

Mitchell allowed himself a small smile before turning back to them. "What's the easiest way in?"

"The front door is probably bolted," Lyle said. "Let's go around back."

They circled the house. There were plenty of windows, but they were all electrostatic, the opacity adjusted down too far to easily see in. The back door was standard issue, and Lyle had it open within seconds.

"I thought you were a good guy?" Max said. "You're damn handy with locked doors."

"Do you know how hard it is to get a decent warrant nowadays? Evidence first, warrant later."

They entered the home.

"Hello," Max called out. "We're not going to hurt you. We're Marines. We just need to borrow some clothes." He lowered his voice. "What if nobody lives here? Or only women?"

"Somebody lives here," Mitchell said, pointing at a bowl of fruit on the kitchen counter. "Bedrooms are most likely upstairs. Let's be quick about this."

They made their way upstairs. The house was fairly new, large and well-appointed, enough that Mitchell was surprised it didn't have a security system. They entered the master bedroom, locating a large closet filled predominately with suits.

"Ugh," Max said. "I don't mind dressing up for the right reasons. Fighting an out of control AI isn't one of them."

Lyle pointed at a holographic display projecting from a nightstand. A man with his arms wrapped around a woman from behind. They were both smiling. "Uh. Colonel."

"What is it?" Mitchell asked.

"I recognize these two." He shook his head sadly. "On the train."

"Oh, shit," Max said. "You're frigging kidding?"

"No. I don't forget a face. It's part of the job. Those two were both on the train."

"That explains why the house is empty," Mitchell said. So many had already died, he was almost becoming numb to it. He wanted to feel sorry for the latest casualties. He was finding it difficult.

"It'll take at least twenty-four hours for law enforcement to id the bodies and find their way here," Lyle said. "At least we don't have to rush."

"Shitty silver lining, bro," Max said. "I call dibs on the shower."

Max entered the closet, grabbed the largest sizes he could find, and passed them into the bathroom, closing the door.

"I've never done anything this macabre before," Lyle said. "Using a dead couple's shower?"

"It isn't my first choice either."

Lyle opened a drawer on the nightstand. A small touchpad rested inside. He picked it up and tapped it. The wall across from the bed lit up, displaying a stream.

"You're leaving fingerprints everywhere," Mitchell said.

"We'll wipe everything down before we go." He tapped on the keypad. "Watson's tracking us. He won't think a couple sleeping in and watching streams is out of the ordinary."

"Not unless he already knows they're dead."

"We have to take some chances, right?"

"Yes."

"Hey, look at that."

Mitchell looked over at the projection. A reporter was standing outside what looked like a military base. The text below her said, "Norfolk UEA: Dove launch in jeopardy as top pilot retires from service."

"Major Asher?" Lyle said.

"Audio?" Mitchell said.

He tapped somewhere else on the pad.

"Officials declined to comment on the latest development, following two recent terrorist attacks by the Anti-Interstellar Travel

Coalition that claimed the lives of a number of top dignitaries, as well as members of the United Earth Alliance military. We at GNN wish Major Asher the best in her future endeavors outside of the armed services."

The image faded out, replaced with a new reporter. He was standing against an aerial video of a smoldering debris field. The text below now read, "San Diego: Four hundred dead at the site of one of five simultaneous maglev crashes. Over two thousand reported dead overall. AIT denies responsibility."

"Denies responsibility?" Lyle said.

Mitchell considered the news. If Major Asher had left the military, there had to be a reason for it. He didn't think it was her decision, which meant that Watson had managed to manipulate the UEA into letting her go. By promising the Dove would be safe? It would make the AIT's denial of the train crashes more understandable, but how could anyone in the UEA top brass believe it after what had occurred over the last few days?

He didn't know or understand Watson's plan. He hoped the data chip he carried would be of some use there. "Everything we learn puts Watson more and more in control. I'm starting to feel like we're already boxed in."

"Let's see what Max's contact can do for us," Lyle said. "We aren't out of this thing until we're dead."

Mitchell nodded. "I like your attitude, Sergeant."

"Oorah."

[41]

MITCHELL

THEY EACH TOOK their turn showering and changing. It was fortunate that they were all of similar enough height and build that they managed to fit into the clothing they had found, even if they were clearly too short on Max, a little too long on Lyle, and too loose on Mitchell. It was all more passable than the rags they had arrived in, and the similar but poorly tailored cuts gave them the appearance of a second-rate salesman. At least, that's what Max had claimed they looked like.

They had decided to call Max's contact from the system in the home, assuming it was less likely to be monitored, but having no way to know for sure. Fortunately, his ex had been in intelligence and had a good head on her shoulders. She spoke to Max in pseudo-code, carrying on a conversation about her pet Shih Tzu that was in truth an arrangement for them to meet. Unfortunately, that meeting couldn't happen until after midnight, as she had other business that couldn't wait. Mitchell didn't ask what kind.

It gave them too long to sit and wait, though Lyle was grateful for the opportunity to rest a bit more in the wake of his injury. He slept on the floor, not wanting to disturb the bed while Max set about wiping away as many clues of their presence in the house as he could. Mitchell kept guard, watching out for officers making their way to the house to check for next of kin or to search it for clues to the disaster. He knew they would be busy with the living for some time, and it gave him a measure of pleasure that Watson had inadvertently aided them in their escape.

A search of the garage turned up a spare car, and a search of the kitchen uncovered the access fob. By the time they made their way from the house, they were clean, rested, armed, and ready. They had been lucky so far, and Mitchell was hoping that luck would stay with them.

Denver was like most of the larger cities in the country, an in-flux mixture of old technology and new, attempting to find the proper balance between cost and efficiency. Repulsor cars mingled with wheeled vehicles, driverless AI shared the road with humans, mass transit was refined but still underserved, and architecture blended stone, concrete, metal, glass, and newer, more exotic materials into a melting pot that was growing easier to segment to before and after XENO-1.

Max had arranged for them to meet his ex, a woman he told them to call Daisy, in the bar outside of a sensory theater. Mitchell hadn't understood the term at first until the explanation led him to relate it to combat simulators in his timeframe. Fully enmeshed virtual reality, where an individual or group became the center of the story. The largest difference was that the stories were still relatively linear, rather than fully, dynamically altered by interactions with the system's AI.

Not that they had time for games. Major Asher was out of the military, Origin was missing in action, and Watson appeared to be in total control.

For now.

There was a reason they had decided to wipe his memories for all of those years. There had to be a reason too that he still couldn't remember how he had arrived in St. Louis. He and Katherine and

Origin, and even Kathy had developed some elaborate plan in a past timeline with the intent of ending the war. Had they been expecting Watson to exploit a loophole in the eternal engine? It seemed impossible to think so, but why else had he been disappeared so completely, including from himself?

The data chip had to have answers. Origin wouldn't count on being able to reach him. The Tetron often had contingency after contingency to fall back on.

The bar was upscale, clean and modern. The preferred drink was a martini or a mojito, the patrons quiet and organized. The layout was designed to ease the visitor into the experience of the theater, and as a result was equipped with jamming technology to render AR interfaces useless. There was no outside noise filtered into the space. Come. Sit. Spend time with your friends. Prepare for the ride.

It was an obvious place to meet. A place where Watson wouldn't be able to listen in. Where no one outside of earshot would be able to listen in.

Daisy was a dark-skinned woman with short hair and a serious face, dressed in loose fitting synthetics that shimmered as she moved. Her background was obvious to Mitchell as they approached her, from the way she positioned herself at the table, to the cautious, measured expression as they joined her there.

"Daisy," Max said, leaning over to kiss her cheek. "It's been too long."

"Max." Daisy didn't smile. "Let's keep this quick. I only agreed to this meet because you said it had to do with national security." She glanced over at Lyle. She did smile at him. "Carson. How have you been?"

"Other than a bump on the head, not bad," Lyle replied.

"This here is Colonel Mitchell Williams, United Earth Alliance," Max said, putting his hand on Mitchell's shoulder. "I set this up on his behalf. The Colonel here has a hell of a story, and he needs your help."

Daisy looked at Mitchell. She kept her smile, though it shrank slightly as she looked him over. "You're a long way from the nearest Alliance installation."

"Out of necessity," Mitchell said. "Before we talk, I need you to stand up and turn around."

"What?" The smile disappeared.

"Please. I need to check your neck."

"For what?"

The bar was jamming normal AR signals. Mitchell didn't completely trust that it was able to jam Watson as well. He remembered the devices the intelligence had used to take control of the Riggers on Goliath. It would be stupid to think he wouldn't be doing the same thing here.

"Are you still enlisted?" Mitchell asked.

"I'm on special assignment," Daisy replied.

"Rank?"

"First Lieutenant."

"Stand up and turn around," Mitchell said firmly. "That's an order, Lieutenant."

Daisy raised her eyebrows and then did as he asked. Mitchell put his hand on the base of her neck, feeling beneath the softness of her skin.

"You have warm hands," Daisy said.

"You can sit now," Mitchell replied.

She returned to her seat. "So, what is this about?"

Mitchell told her everything she needed to know, keeping the focus on the AIT and leaving off anything having to do with the future or AI. Then he fished the data card out of his pocket.

"There's encrypted information on this card that will hopefully give us a solid lead on the AIT stronghold. If not the location of their leadership, at least a nearby cell. Corporal Starling brought me to you because he thinks you can help me get the intel on it."

"He does, does he?" Daisy said, glancing at Max again.

"I told him you're the best, darling."

"Look, Colonel, I've got official orders. I'm sure you understand that. Max is vouching for you, and I can tell by your mannerisms you're legit as far as being in the service and used to giving orders. That's the only reason I'm still sitting here. I can't divert my resources onto this. Not without authorization."

"Lives are at stake here, Lieutenant," Mitchell said. "The maglev crashes? The AIT denies it, but I know they're responsible."

"Then why would they deny it?"

"It's part of the game. You're in special operations. You know how it's played. Don't you?"

She paused, considering. Then she nodded. "You didn't hear this from me, but the UEA capitulated to the AIT. They kicked Major Asher out in exchange for non-interference during the launch of the Dove."

"I had a feeling it was something like that," Mitchell said. "The AIT isn't going to honor it. You know that, don't you?"

"I was hopeful. Latest media reports are saying there was faulty software in the maglev controllers. That the AI had a time-based glitch that caused it to overload the reactor and blow the engines, causing the crash."

"Bullshit," Max said.

"Total bullshit," Daisy agreed.

"No, it isn't," Mitchell said. "I'm sure it happened exactly like that. But was the glitch pre-existing in the system, or was it added? They'll never be able to prove it, and as long as the AIT denies it, the government will believe them."

"Logic says that if they managed such a massively successful terrorist attack, they would be all over it," Lyle said.

"Unless they're holding their cards for something else," Daisy said.

"Something bigger," Mitchell said.

Daisy sighed heavily. "Shit. I'm going to blow my orders if I help you. Maybe I won't get court-martialed, but I'm going to get nailed for it regardless."

"You don't need to get involved. All I need is someone who can open this thing up."

"Then I do need to get involved, Colonel. He won't trust you without me."

"In that case, how do you feel about saving the world?"

"Somebody has to do it, right?"

Mitchel smiled. "Yeah."

"I'm in."

[42]

KATHERINE

"Are you sure he'll be here?" Katherine asked.

"He'll be here," Trevor replied.

"And you are certain he is not compromised?" Origin said.

"As sure as I can be. Coates is too low down in the pecking order to draw much attention."

"You know about him," Katherine said.

"I make it my business to get to know the people at the bottom. You never know when they might come in handy."

"That's not very trusting of you."

"I've been around the block more than once, Kate. The military and the private sector are the same. They tell you what you need to know, and if you want more than that you have to be creative. True, they'd like to turn us all into automatons, just like the Tetron, apparently. I wanted to know more about who Nova Taurus was, so I made a few contacts with people who could tell me the things they might not want operatives to know about." He smiled. "Of course, they left out the part about it being controlled by a rogue AI."

They had traded Origin's driverless van for an older model car that she had gotten transferred from the inventory of a used vehicle

218 / M.R. FORBES

dealer near Baltimore. The place dealt more in stolen goods than anything else, and it had been easy for her to break into their systems and move the car under an assumed name. Then the Tetron had gone to pick it up while Trevor organized the meeting with Coates and Katherine had tried to contact Michael to check on him.

That part worried her, though she wasn't about to show it. Repeated pings had gone unanswered, which wasn't like her friend at all. He was always there for her when she needed him, even if it was for a few words of encouragement or a few minutes of joking around. She was nervous that Watson had caught on to him, and caught up to him, and that she would never see him or hear from him again.

"Katherine?" Trevor said.

She looked over at him. He had been trying to get her attention while she was thinking about Michael. "What?"

"We're almost there. You know the plan?"

"You'll drop Origin and me off. We meet with Coates, but we need to make it quick. He'll pass us badges to get into Nova Taurus. You circle back and pick us up."

"Keep your head turned," Origin said. "Don't look directly into the cameras. We have to get the timing right. I planted a distraction that should keep Watson's attention diverted for the two minutes while we make the pickup."

"How did you get Coates to help us, anyway?" Katherine asked.

All she knew of the lab tech was that he was almost too willing to help Trevor get them in, despite the risk to his job. Trevor had given him very specific instructions on how to procure the badges, to make sure he circumvented Nova Taurus security. It was a good thing one of Trevor's responsibilities had been to try to get through that security. The former special forces soldier knew every detail, trick, and hack to make it happen.

He shrugged in response to her question.

"It isn't like you to be coy, Trev."

"It also isn't like you to pry."

"This is my life we're talking about, and the future of humankind. I think the circumstances make prying acceptable."

"It isn't enough that I'm vouching for him?"

"You tried to kill me, too."

Trevor sighed. "Point made. Fine. If you have to know, we've been seeing one another."

That caught Katherine off-guard. "Seeing one another, as in, seeing one another?"

"Don't play dumb, Kate. Yes."

"Were you ever, you know, before you were with me?"

"On and off."

"You never told me."

"It never came up, and it wasn't important. I was loyal to you. What does my orientation have to do with anything, anyway?"

"It doesn't. I just never expected someone like you would be so open about who you were seen with."

"Enough," Origin said. "There's the garage."

"Affirmative," Trevor said, his entire demeanor changing in an instant. "You know what to do."

Katherine tried to picture Trevor kissing another man. She didn't have a problem with it, but she also couldn't visualize it.

The car slowed and turned into a parking garage, located two blocks from the Nova Taurus tower. They made their way up to the third level, slowing as they reached the top of the incline.

"There he is," Trevor said, shrinking down in his seat.

"Perfect timing," Origin said. "The flares are active."

Katherine knew she wasn't referring to actual flares. The flares were really some kind of network connected bomb that would burst with false information in a dozen different places within the city. By the time Watson investigated each, they would be done with the pickup.

The car stopped. Katherine and Origin climbed out. The car moved again. Katherine noticed the camera nearby but didn't look at it.

Daniel Coates was standing near the stairwell down. He was tall and thin, with curly hair and a boyish face.

"Daniel," Katherine said.

"Here," he replied, holding out the two cards. "They'll get you up to level three security."

"We needed level five," Katherine said.

"I know. I'm sorry. I couldn't get it. They changed the access codes a couple of hours ago."

"He knows Trevor is free," Origin said.

"Thank you, Daniel," Katherine said.

"Yeah. No problem. Tell Trevor I love him, and to call me when all of this blows over."

"I will."

The car had circled the lot and come back around. It stopped right next to them.

"Look at the camera. Just for a second," Origin said.

"Why?"

"Just in case."

Katherine did as Origin asked. Then they climbed into the car. Trevor didn't look at Daniel, and Daniel didn't acknowledge Trevor. He had taught the tech well.

Then they were moving again, out of the garage and back onto the street.

A police car whipped past them as they exited, headed toward one of Origin's false reports.

"When do we go in?" Katherine asked.

"Tomorrow, during normal work hours," Origin replied. "It will be easier to blend in."

Katherine nodded, and then looked out the window.

With this part over, she had more time to worry about Michael.

[43]

KATHERINE

KATHERINE STILL HADN'T HEARD from him by the time morning came. She had tried to ping him at least fifty times until finally Origin had warned her that despite the added security measures they were taking, her constant attempts might give away their position.

She didn't want to think that he was dead.

She also didn't know what else to think. And it was better than the idea that Watson had turned him into a slave.

She felt his absence in the back of her mind, even as they prepared for the mission ahead. They had been friends since they were each five years old, growing up in the houses next door to one another. It was an unlikely friendship. Beside the gender differences, she was athletic and physical, he was overweight and mental. Somehow, it worked, even if things had never turned romantic. He was just too much like a brother to her.

A brother who was always there for her. A brother who always came through.

A brother she didn't want to be without.

"Do you already know how much I hate skirts?" she said to Origin.

They were in the bedroom of their hotel suite, getting dressed. They were wearing identical black miniskirts with shimmering white blouses, high heels, gold earrings, and way too much makeup. Katherine felt like a domesticated cow in the outfit and was gritting her teeth through its wear. They had to fit in, and they couldn't do that without dressing professionally.

"Yes, I am aware," Origin said. "I am not in favor of this manner of style myself." The Tetron smoothed her own skirt. "We need to get access to a mainframe terminal. I'm not sure level three will be enough. If that is the case, one of us will need to be successful in convincing the security detail to let us in."

"Do you think that will even be possible?"

"Watson has control of some of the soldiers. He cannot control everyone. The security guards will be susceptible to subterfuge." She slid the side of her skirt up, showing a lot of thigh and a pair of bright pink panties peeking out of the shadows.

"This can't be happening," Katherine said, looking away. An advanced intelligence that had traveled the universe and invented a time machine, and it was practicing seduction?

"We must get in and discover what Watson is planning," Origin said, straightening the dress again. "I will do whatever I must do to achieve that goal. I know you understand what is at stake."

"I do," Katherine said. She picked up the small stiletto knife Trevor had provided and tucked it into her bra strap. She would have preferred a gun.

"Let me see," Origin said, approaching her and looking her over. They were identical in appearance, down to the bangs that crossed over the left eye. "Good."

They walked out of the bedroom. Trevor smiled when he saw them. "Double your pleasure," he said.

"Shut up," Katherine replied.

"We're going to be late," Origin said. "Let's go."

"Stay here," Origin said to Trevor. "Watson is going to be looking for you to get to us. Remain off the grid."

"I've done this sort of thing before," Trevor said. "I'll be waiting for you." He picked up a pair of AR glasses from a nearby table. "Ping me if you need backup."

"Thank you for your help with this, Trev," Katherine said, stepping up to him and kissing him on the cheek.

"I told you when we split that you always had my support," Trevor replied. "I may not be the most upstanding citizen, but I'm a man of my word."

Katherine joined Origin in the elevator to the ground floor.

"If anything happens to me, you need to remain focused on the mission," Origin said. "It isn't required that I survive for humankind to have a future."

"Understood," Katherine said. That didn't mean she was eager to lose her guide in this mess.

"Good luck, Katherine Asher," Origin said.

"You, too," Katherine replied, giving her counterpart a hug. The Tetron was stiff in her arms, unaccustomed to physical affection. An eternity hadn't helped with that.

Then Katherine turned and headed out to the street alone. She would go in first, using her false badge to gain access to one of Nova Taurus' labs. Origin would follow ten minutes behind, using a similar fake badge. They would each make every effort to reach a terminal that connected to the Nova Taurus mainframe, which Origin insisted would be off-site and likely offshore. From there, they hoped to glean some kind of clue as to what Watson had in store for the Dove, and for humanity in general.

They were also going to try to do all of that without getting caught.

It seemed impossible. It also seemed imperative. Mitchell was active and out there, somewhere, but had yet to reach out to them. Michael was missing. And, Origin had told her that Watson had crashed five trains and killed thousands; possibly to draw them out or in an attempt to kill Mitchell. That Origin didn't seem concerned that the Tetron had succeeded in that part spoke volumes about the Colonel's tenacity. It was another trait that she admired.

It was also terrifying and sad, and it had made her current situation easier to come to terms with. At least she had the opportunity to fight back, and to defend or avenge the innocent people the deranged intelligence was threatening.

"Can you hear me?"

Origin's voice filtered into her head through a tiny device the Tetron had tucked deep into her ear canal. It created a secure wireless connection, and while the range was limited, it would be more than enough for them to communicate inside the Nova Taurus tower.

"Affirmative," Katherine replied silently. "I'm en route."

She reached into a small bag, pulling out the badge Coates had provided. The lab tech had taken a huge risk to support Trevor, just like Trevor was taking a risk supporting her. Then again, the risk that they were walking into a trap couldn't be completely eliminated. There had been no time to check Coates' neck when they picked up the badges. They were acting purely on the hope that he was low enough on the org chart to have avoided Watson's direct attention.

"Please work."

[44]

KATHERINE

KATHERINE KEPT HER EYES FORWARD, her posture relaxed as she reached the security checkpoint into the guts of the Nova Taurus tower. A pair of guards stood on either side of a scanning arch that would run facial recognition, fingerprints, and a host of other biometric scans, the data points of which had all been provided to Coates the day before.

She had been nervous about surrendering so much information to Trevor to pass on to his companion, certain that Watson would recognize her straight away from the measurements, or that the tech would be unable to access the systems to get them listed as employees. She was no less nervous as she walked up to the scanner, her heart pounding, her legs feeling weak. Dogfights over the Antarctic ice had been less stressful.

She held up the badge as she walked through, the way Trevor had instructed. She saw the tight beam of the laser pass over her face, and the cameras positioned within the scanner. A soft tone indicated that she had been registered. The moment of truth.

She kept walking. Nobody stopped her. No alarms went off. Either Coates had come through the way he had promised or Watson wasn't quite ready to deal with her yet. Whichever way, she had to take what she was given.

She continued on, heading straight to a bank of elevators near the rear of the lobby, an area hidden from the view of general visitors who would be meeting with the company's many executives and salespeople. Katherine had been surprised to learn how big Nova Taurus was, how many hands they had, and how many pockets they had those hands in. They were one of the five largest corporations in the world, alongside companies like Frontier PharmaCo and Daisoon Heavy Industries.

And Watson was controlling it. It was a mystery to Origin how the Tetron had gained so much power in so little time, especially considering he was damaged.

She stepped into the elevator, pressing the button to go down into the subterranean laboratories. She would attempt to get deep into the research area, where scientists were still poring over pieces of the XENO-1 in a search for any clues they might have missed regarding its origin or composition, along with continuing studies on how best to advance areas of technology like propulsion and of course, weapons of war.

Origin would head the opposite direction, up into the internal executive suites. That didn't make it any less dangerous. Both areas would be secured and guarded, and Trevor expected a lot of the details would have been changed in his departure. Not as much passive security, but headcount and physical surveillance patterns.

The elevator began to descend.

A hand brushed against her rear.

Katherine ignored it the first time. The second time the hand touched her, she turned around.

"Excuse me," she said, before registering who was standing behind her. It was one of Trevor's teammates. She didn't know which one, but she knew he was a configuration.

"The excuse is all mine," the man replied, giving her a crooked smile. He raised his hands innocently. She saw a pair of guns holstered under his arms.

The elevator reached the bottom and opened. Katherine stepped out, walking fast to stay ahead of the man.

"I'm in," she said, hoping the signal would reach to Origin. "One of Watson's goons groped me on the elevator."

"If he didn't detain you, that is a good sign," Origin replied. "I will arrive soon."

Katherine walked to the end of the hallway. A second security checkpoint was set up there. She had to stop beneath the scanner, waiting for it to approve her before the door beyond it slid open. She moved through, noticing that the configuration was still behind her.

Where was he going?

Did he know who she was?

She hadn't panicked when she was dueling three enemy fighters at one time, and she wasn't going to panic now. She kept walking, reaching a bare corridor with steel doors on either side. They had small viewports in, and she could see an internal airlock to another door, through that to a team inside in full hazard gear, examining different chunks of metal, wires, and what looked like organic material. Twenty years and the crashed ship still held so many secrets.

She couldn't help but smile at the truth of it. So much of what they were studying they had made themselves. They just didn't know it.

After the labs was a rest area, with restrooms and a lunchroom. Beyond that were the offices. Katherine paused at the door to the first empty one she found, glancing back to look for the configuration. He had stopped following her near the entrance and hadn't resurfaced.

"I'm in," Origin said, her voice almost startling Katherine.

"I've reached one of the offices," she replied. "I'm going to tap into the terminal."

"I'll be waiting."

Katherine was no hacker, and Michael was missing. Her mission was to reach the terminal and attach a secondary device to it that would allow Origin to interface with it directly. She entered the office and moved to the chair, opening her bag and finding the fingernail-sized device. She put it down on the desk.

"The transmitter is in place," she said.

"Receiving," Origin replied. "I'm in the elevator going up."

Katherine could feel her pulse in her head, and she noticed the sounds of every breath. Only two had passed when Origin spoke again.

"I was just groped," she said. "It was an unpleasant experience."

"Trevor's team?" Katherine replied.

"I don't know. Katherine, I do not have access. We need to reach a level five enabled terminal."

"Damn," Katherine said, grabbing the transmitter and shoving it back in her bag. "I'll see what I can do."

"As will I. I am departing the elevator now."

Katherine stood and circled the desk.

The configuration was standing in the doorway.

[45]

MITCHELL

"You two wait here and keep an eye out for trouble," Daisy said. "Colonel, come with me."

Mitchell climbed out of the back of Daisy's car, scanning the area as he did. They were in a residential neighborhood outside of Denver, a quiet street lined with tall, narrow, hundred-year-old houses that all looked identical, save for minor differences in paint color and landscaping. It was a spot away from the cameras and the sensors and the drones. An area where Watson would have a more difficult time monitoring them.

Assuming they had reached Daisy without drawing the Tetron's attention. So far, it seemed as if they had.

"Your contact lives here?" Mitchell asked.

Daisy led him across the street toward one of the houses. "He's an independent contractor for the UEA. He typically deals in more clandestine software - he's actually done some work on the repulsor calibration for the Dove's initial launch sequence. Whenever I have something that needs decrypting, he's my first stop."

"Can we trust him?"

"Absolutely. In fact, there isn't anyone I trust more."

They reached the door to the home. A light went on above them, and Mitchell could see the tiny lense of a camera in the corner.

Daisy turned toward it and waved.

"You're supposed to call first," a voice said through a hidden speaker.

"I didn't have time," Daisy replied. "And we have reason to believe communications may be compromised. We need some help decrypting a data card."

"We?" A pause. "You look familiar. What's your name?"

"Mi-"

"Wait. I know you." The voice shivered. Out of excitement, or fear? "She's never going to believe this. I don't even believe this. Hang on. Don't move."

Mitchell looked at Daisy, who looked back at him and shrugged. "He's always been a little strange."

He heard the heavy footsteps behind the door well before it opened. A large face looked past him at the street and then ducked back into the house.

"Come in. Did anyone follow you?"

"I don't think so," Daisy said.

"You're him, aren't you?" the man said. He was relatively young and overweight, with a mop of brown hair and an anxious look.

"I'm who?" Mitchell said.

"The guy Kathy's looking for. Mitchell."

Mitchell froze, staring at the man. Who was this?

"Michael, what are you talking about?" Daisy said.

"You know Major Katherine Asher?" Mitchell said.

"Uh, yeah. She's my best friend. We've known each other since we were kids."

Mitchell couldn't believe it. "I need to talk to her."

"Not so fast," Michael said. "Someone's been trying to kill her. How do I know you aren't with them."

"You know who I am. She mentioned me to you?"

"She told me she's been hearing a voice telling her to find you. I saw the streams, and we figured out that you're the John Doe from St. Louis. I didn't expect you to wind up here."

"Does she know what this is about? Does she know about Watson?"

"I don't know Watson. I know the AIT. They tried to kill her again earlier tonight. A police officer died. She asked me to hack into the D.C.P.D.'s servers and wipe the surveillance footage."

"Did you delete it already?"

Michael looked at the floor. "Five minutes ago."

"Where is she now?"

"Somewhere in D.C., I told you."

"She's in a lot of danger, and not from me. I'm trying to protect her. I need to talk to her."

"Who are you? What is this about?" He looked at Daisy. "You said you have something that needs to be decrypted?"

"Let me see your neck," Mitchell said.

"What?"

"Your neck. Let me see it."

Michael's face was turning red. He looked uncomfortable. "Can we just slow down for one second? Is Kathy okay?"

"She won't be if we don't help her," Mitchell said. "Turn around."

"Just hold on a second," Michael replied. He looked to Mitchell like he was having a panic attack.

Mitchell moved toward him, grabbing his arm and swinging around his back.

"What are you doing?"

He checked Michael's neck. It was clean.

"Colonel, he's hyperventilating," Daisy said. "Give him some space."

Mitchell let go of him and backed up. Michael stumbled to the wall and propped himself against it, breathing heavily.

This was Katherine's best friend?

"Michael, it's okay," Daisy said.

"I'm sorry, Michael," Mitchell said, keeping his distance. "Take it easy. Try to slow it down. Slow. Steady. Easy. Relax."

Michael looked at him and nodded. He closed his eyes, taking a huge breath in through his nose, holding it, and then letting it out through his mouth.

"It's a long story," Mitchell said. "But I need to find out what's on this data card. I heard you have the equipment and the know-how to read it. If we can get the contents, we can help Major Asher."

Michael nodded again and reached out for the card.

Mitchell handed it to him. Michael took one more long breath and then pushed himself upright again. "Okay. I'm okay. I just get a little overwhelmed, and the last couple of days hasn't helped my anxiety at all." He breathed out again. "My stuff is all downstairs in the basement. Not that many people have a reader for cards like this anymore. You're lucky you found me."

"I guess I am," Mitchell said.

He wasn't convinced that luck had anything to do with it.

[46]
MITCHELL

MITCHELL STOOD next to Michael while he plugged in the data card and connected it to his AR equipment. It was similar to the stuff Evelyn had used, except larger and more powerful.

"I've been working on a machine learning algorithm and AI that enhances human interaction," Michael said. "Improving our brains, instead of taking over for them. Personally, I think AI is a cop out, a lazy man's dream. But what happens when the intelligence takes control of everything? If a machine is doing everything for us, how do we keep our minds from atrophying?"

"I agree completely," Mitchell said. "I think AI will cause more problems than it solves."

"Don't get me wrong, basic AI has its place. I mean, Hyper Troopers would be boring if the Arachoids just stood there while you shot them, but control of critical systems? Just look at what happened with the maglevs. It's so sad."

He tapped a few buttons on a pad in front of him and then put on a pair of opaque glasses.

"Interesting," he said less than a minute later. "Where did you get this?"

"I had it on me when I was committed to St. Mary's."

Michael took the glasses off and looked at Mitchell. "That isn't possible."

Mitchell had heard something similar from Evelyn. He was surprised at how much faster Michael had come to the same conclusion. "I'm not joking. Whatever is happening with Major Asher, and with me, the answers are in there somewhere."

"Okay. It's just. Well. The code in here? I recognize it. It's a derivative from the language I've been working on. The interface language. I used it for the calibration stuff I delivered to Nova Taurus last week, even though they sent it back for some changes. There's no way you could have gotten it twenty years ago when I just finished creating it."

"It's a long story that I'll share with you later," Mitchell said, glancing back at Daisy. She was standing near the steps up, a link between them and the two Marines, who had taken up positions defending the perimeter just in case. "If you wrote it, then it should be easy for you to get to the data."

Michael put the glasses back on. "I don't know if I can get it that fast. I said it's a derivative. It's changed a little bit." He was silent for a handful of seconds. "Oh. I've got it. I mean the encryption. I recognize this. How did you get this?"

"You cracked it already?" Mitchell said.

"I'm really confused," Michael replied. "And kind of freaked out. For one, the volume on this thing is about one hundred times greater than anything I've ever heard of, and it's filled with some kind of runtime or something. It's way more complex than I can break down right now. There's also a second partition on it. Let me see." He paused again. His breathing was getting heavier, his face flushing for a second time.

"Michael, are you okay?" Mitchell said. Michael looked like he was about to have another panic attack. "Michael?"

"What's an eternal engine?" he asked.

"I told you, it's a long story. What about it?"

"I don't know. It's a binary-encoded message. All it says is, 'return to the source.'"

"That's it?" Mitchell asked. He had been hoping for answers, not more riddles.

"Yeah. That's - oh. Uh-oh."

"What?"

Michael tore off the glasses, pushing himself forward, falling out of his chair in his effort to grab the data card and pull it from the reader. "Damn it, damn it, damn it," he said, getting his hand on the reader. He tried to pull the card out and failed. Tried and failed again. Finally, he smashed the entire thing on the ground.

"What the frig are you doing?" Mitchell said.

"What am I doing?" Michael's face was beet red, and he was almost in tears. "What are you doing? You said you wanted to help. Shit. Damn it. Where did you get the card?"

"I told you, it was on me when I was admitted to St. Mary's. I picked it up on my way out."

"Gah. No. That can't be."

"I'm telling you it is. What is your problem?"

"It's infected. The card is infected. I opened the message, and it sent a heartbeat out over the net. Then it started deleting everything."

"What?" Mitchell said. He closed his eyes tight. He couldn't remember what had happened before he arrived at St. Mary's. He thought he and Origin had caused it.

Had it been Watson all along?

Why? Why would Watson capture him and let him go? Why would he pretend he didn't know where he was when he had put him there in the first place? Why would he be so desperate to kill him?

Was this even the first recursion since he had arrived here?

A sense of his own panic began creeping up on him. He forced it back down. Return to the source. That's what the message said. Had Watson been able to decipher it? If he had, he wouldn't have needed Mitchell.

Had the Tetron ever needed him at all?

If Watson had captured him, the intelligence had twenty years to break the encryption that Michael had undone in a matter of minutes. How could it be possible that the Tetron was incapable of achieving that? Or, if Watson knew he needed Michael to do it, why not pick him up and make him do it? He had done far worse to the Knife.

Unless the virus hadn't come from Watson. What if Origin had planted it, to ensure that once Mitchell knew the message, it would be lost forever? That made more sense.

Return to the source.

That's what he was supposed to do. It was the simple answer he was looking for, regardless of who had left it for him.

"We need to go," Mitchell said, looking back at Daisy. "No matter who caused the heartbeat, we aren't safe here. If Watson's listening, he's going to notice."

"Colonel," Max shouted from somewhere above them. "We've got company."

MITCHELL GRABBED Michael by the arm, pulling him up. "Come on."

Michael stumbled to his feet, cold sweat beaded on his forehead. "What's going on?"

A pop sounded above them, followed by the clink of a spent casing. Daisy was already running up the stairs, and Mitchell pulled Michael behind her.

"We're in trouble," Mitchell replied. "Stay close to me." He had a handgun tucked into the back of his suit pants, and he pulled it out.

"Oh, man," Michael said. "This is the third time in a week. I'm starting to wish I had never met Kathy."

A second pop sounded. Then a third.

"Sitrep," Mitchell shouted.

"Drones," Max replied. Mitchell still didn't know where the Corporal was sitting. Somewhere on the top floor.

"Military?"

"Hard to tell from this far. Police issue, I think."

Echoing pops in the distance. The windows along the south wall began to shatter.

"Get down," Mitchell said, pulling Michael to the floor.

"Okay, maybe at least a few of them are military," Max said.

Gunfire sounded from the east side where Lyle was stationed.

"Colonel, I hear sirens," Lyle said.

"Daisy, get the car," Mitchell said. She was crouched behind a sofa and dashed toward the door at his order.

"Wait here," Mitchell said, leaving Michael on the floor in a doorway. More bullets were still raining in, the volume decreasing as Max and Lyle hit the drones with their heavy rifles.

Mitchell crossed the floor to the doorway, covering Daisy as she crossed the street. The sirens were getting louder. It was going to be too damn close.

Return to the source. The words passed through his mind in the middle of the chaos. The source? Origin had to mean XENO-1 - the part of the wreckage that remained buried in the Antarctic ice. There had simply been too much of her to move it all.

But what was waiting for him there?

Daisy reached the car, getting it moving, turning it toward him and driving it up onto the lawn. Mitchell spotted an approaching drone, turning his gun on it and firing shot after shot, emptying the magazine to hit it. He managed to do something, because it started shooting wide, the bullets spraying the houses around them.

"Haul ass," Mitchell shouted. "We're moving out."

He ducked back into the home, retreating to where Michael was still crouched on the floor, tears in his eyes.

"I'm sorry for this," Mitchell said. "The good news is, you're going to help me save the world."

Michael looked at him with big, red eyes. Then he brought himself to his feet. "I'll try."

They moved across the floor a second time, pausing once as a hail of bullets poured in from a drone that got too close. An echoing boom sounded from upstairs, and the shooting stopped.

"Sorry, I didn't see that bastard," Max said a moment later, hiking down the steps.

Lyle joined them in the front of the house. They all jumped into the car, with Max firing back at the remaining drones. The flickering light of the oncoming law enforcement vehicles bounced across the houses around them.

Daisy accelerated, the repulsors below the van thumping with power, the electric engine whining. The police vehicles were coming in from both sides, trying to barricade them in.

They went up onto the lawns, racing across the grass. The officers tried to compensate, rearranging their vehicles to block. Some stopped and climbed out, taking aim and shooting at them. Bullets clanged off the metal, one cracked a window. Max and Lyle returned fire with their pistols, their aim worthless in the moving, bouncing vehicle.

"Colonel," Daisy said. Mitchell looked forward. Some of the officers were running toward them, and one threw himself in front of the car, hitting the corner and bouncing off, his body heavy enough to throw the car sideways. "Frigging hell."

A second officer moved in front of the car, and they slammed into him as well, denting the front of the vehicle and bringing the car to a stop.

"What are you doing?" Mitchell said.

"Collision detection systems," Daisy said. "Automatic shut down."

"Shit. Can you override?"

"No."

They were dead in the water.

"Open the access panel below the steering column," Michael said. "Down there." He leaned forward, showing them the place. "There's a circuit board in there. Shoot it or something. It will either crash the onboard computer and force it to emergency manual, or leave it irreparably broken."

"We've got nothing to lose," Mitchell said. "Do it. Max, Lyle, we need a few seconds."

"I've got it," Max said, moving toward the back of the van where the duffel full of firearms was resting. He fished a wide, heavy weapon from it and then pushed open the back doors.

Daisy reached down, finding the access panel and tearing it away.

Mitchell heard a thunk, and then one of the police cars exploded.

"Give me your gun," Daisy said.

Mitchell handed it to her. Another thunk, another burst of chaos and flame. Daisy pushed herself back in the seat and shot the panel.

"Now, hit that switch and pray," Michael said.

Daisy hit the switch. The car whined to life, the repulsors lifting it back off the ground. Max dove into the rear of the van, and they started to pull away again.

Bullets riddled the side as they skirted the edge of the barricade, punching holes in the sheet metal. Mitchell held his breath until they were past and then watched the rear view. A remaining drone trailed behind them, vanishing a dozen seconds later when Lyle poked it from the sky.

"Champion marksman," he said with a smile when he ducked back in.

They all settled for a moment while Daisy got them further from the scene.

"We can't keep this car," she said. "It's too easy to spot like this."

Mitchell turned back toward Michael, who was breathing heavily, his face red and sweaty. He looked terrified, but focused. "I don't suppose you know how to break into cars?" he asked.

Michael nodded. "I only have one real friend in the world, and that's Kathy. If she's in half the trouble you are, she needs us. I can help you steal a car if that's what you need."

"That's just the start of what I need."

"We're going to save her though, right?"

"We're going to save everyone if we can. That's the reason I'm here. We can't go to her directly, as much as we might want to. It isn't safe for either of us, and I think Origin and I had a different plan for me, anyway."

"Origin?" Michael said. "Huh?"

Mitchell glanced at Daisy, and then back at Michael. "You both need to be fully debriefed when we have the time, but that time isn't now. First, we need a car. Then we need to find a way to get to Antarctica without the AIT catching up."

"Antarctica?" Daisy said. "Why?"

"XENO-1," Mitchell said. "There's something I'm supposed to do there."

"What?" Lyle asked.

"I don't know yet. I guess we're going to find out."

[48]

KATHERINE

"ARE YOU LOST?" the configuration asked.

Katherine considered reaching for her knife, deciding against it. It was too soon.

"This isn't my office," she said. "I was looking for-"

"A quiet place to sit and think?"

Katherine moved toward him. She would try to get out of the room without making a scene.

He shifted to block her path.

"Or did you have something else in mind? Maybe you were waiting for me?"

Katherine took a few steps back. "Waiting for you?"

"I saw how you looked at me in the elevator."

"I didn't appreciate you grabbing my ass."

"Didn't you?" He smiled again, lip quivering as if it took a lot of effort.

"That depends. Do you have Level Five security clearance?"

He laughed awkwardly. "What does that have to do with anything?"

She smiled, reaching up toward the buttons on her blouse. "It has everything to do with this."

The configuration's head tilted at an odd angle and then began to shake as if he were struggling with himself. He stopped after a few seconds.

"I do have clearance," he said. "Do you want to go to Level Five?"

"I bet it's quieter down there."

"I'm not going to bring you to Level Five."

"Why not?"

"I can't wait that long. I have needs. I have-" The configuration paused, shaking again for a moment. "Wants."

He stepped toward her, reaching for her shoulder. Katherine slipped her hand beneath the top of her blouse, grabbing the handle of the small knife. Trevor had said his former squad mates had been acting strangely. This was more than strange, and she still didn't know if she had been targeted because of the way she looked or because they knew who she was.

Katherine tensed as a hand pressed down on her breast. She didn't want to miss, and that meant letting him touch her.

"Cole," a voice said from behind them.

The man straightened immediately, taking a step back from Katherine. She looked over his shoulder, to where another of Trevor's teammates was standing. He was small and muscular. Ng, most likely, based on his features.

"I'm busy," Cole said.

"We have other business. You can find another one later."

Another one?

"But-"

"Cole!"

The configuration glanced at her one last time and started to turn.

Then they both froze.

"Katherine, they're onto us," Origin said in her ear. "You need to-"

She didn't hear the last part. She brought the knife to her hand and jumped on Cole's back, pushing hard as she slid it across his throat. She felt nauseous as she rode his body down.

"You!" Ng said. "Two of you?"

She slid her hand beneath Cole's body, grasping for one of the guns. Ng charged her.

She pulled the gun, throwing herself backward and shooting at the same time. Her first four rounds went wide. The fifth hit him in the shoulder throwing him sideways. He caught himself on the wall.

Katherine braced herself and fired twice more. The bullets hit the configuration in the chest. It wasn't enough to stop him.

"You won't get out of here," he said. "Either of you. Not now."

She shot him in the head. He was still coming, reaching out for her. She shoved him aside, into the wall again. This time, he stumbled and fell over.

"Origin?" Katherine said.

"I'm pinned down. Katherine, you need to escape."

"We haven't gotten what we came for."

"It's too late. He was expecting this."

"Frigging Coates," she said out loud.

They should have been smarter, but what other options did they have? She knelt down and replaced her spent pistol for Cole's other sidearm, and then moved next to Ng to grab his weapons as well.

She paused as she reached under his suit jacket. She had an idea.

"I'm not giving up yet," she said. "Can you hold tight?"

"I'm barricaded. Trapped."

"Good enough."

"Katherine, what are you planning?"

"To be the hero you want me to be, I guess."

She didn't feel like a hero. Her entire body was shaking, her breathing was ragged, and she wanted to vomit. Shooting down bogeys was one thing, killing an enemy soldier another. Cutting a man's throat was something else entirely.

She lifted Ng, throwing him up and over her shoulder and

trying to ignore the warmth of the blood on her blouse and arms. She carried him from the room, checking both ends of the hallway for more guards. She was alone for now. It didn't seem as though they had raised an alarm in this part of the building.

She grunted and continued down the hallway, past the offices. There were people in some of them, and they drew back in shock as she passed, but didn't confront her. Not everyone in here was under Watson's control.

She rounded the corner, winding up only a few feet from the next security checkpoint. The guards there stared at her in disbelief as she dumped Ng's body from her shoulder and pushed it through the scanning arch.

It crossed the threshold and then fell to the ground. The guards started to stand. Katherine aimed and fired, hitting each in the chest and knocking them back down.

The door to the high-security area slid aside.

Katherine jumped over Ng's body, running through the door.

"I'm in Level Five," she said.

"How?" Origin replied, her voice pleased and surprised.

She passed another row of heavy doors. These had no viewports, and each was marked as hazardous. She didn't know what was behind them and didn't have time to care. She kept going, searching for a terminal.

A scientist turned the corner ahead of her, freezing at her sudden appearance. She thought he would run, but instead, he charged, shouting and throwing himself at her. She didn't shoot, catching him, turning his momentum into the wall, and finally hitting him on the back of the neck. She could feel the control device crunch beneath his skin as he dropped to the ground.

She followed his tracks, heading down an adjacent corridor to an open office door. A terminal waited on the other side, and she slapped the transmitter down on the table.

"Making the connection," she said.

"Receiving," Origin said. "I don't know how, but you did it. It's time to call the cavalry."

Katherine had one more device on her, and she withdrew it and tapped the single button on its surface.

"Kate?" Trevor said a moment later. "I'm on my way."

"Origin is in trouble. Head to the upper floors. I'll meet you there."

"Affirmative."

Katherine dropped the device to the ground, stomping it beneath her shoes. There was no sense risking that Watson could trace the signal. Then she closed her eyes, took a few strong breaths to try to calm herself, and headed back out into the hallway.

She had gotten Origin connected to the mainframe.

Now she needed to get her out of the building.

[49]

KATHERINE

"ANYTHING?" Katherine asked. She had left the transmitter on the desk, crossing back through the security checkpoint and heading for the elevators. She was still alone for now, but she knew it couldn't last.

"I have to be cautious. If I go too deep, we may end up in a direct confrontation. This form is too fragile to defeat him that way."

"I'm coming to you. Trevor is on the way."

"Katherine, there are a number of guards outside this door. I can't hold it forever."

"You get the intel, I'll worry about the guards."

She surprised herself with her bravado.

She dashed through the hallways, careful around corners but otherwise sprinting. The scientists and lab techs who saw her coming were quick to get out of the way, but she had to slow as she approached them in case they were under Watson's control. None of them tried to grab her, and she made it back to the first checkpoint without interference.

Too easy. It was all too easy.

She reached the elevator and froze. What if Origin was already compromised? What if she were speaking to Watson instead of her? There would be no reason to come get her when she was heading right for them.

She paused, suddenly uncertain, all of her confidence waning in an instant. She didn't know how to trust anything. Allies were turned into enemies. Innocent people were used and abandoned or worse. Michael was missing. The Dove was certain to be sabotaged. The future wasn't just hazy. It was black. Empty. Dead.

A panic overtook her. She stared at the door to the elevator but didn't summon it. What was she doing? Origin needed her, and she was inactive. Paralyzed. All of her life, she wanted to travel to the stars. If she had known the price she would have to pay, would she still have followed the path?

She clenched her teeth and hit the button.

The answer didn't matter. This was bigger than her. She was a piece of the puzzle. Nothing more.

"Katherine," someone said behind her. "Kathy. Kate. Kitty Kat."

She turned around. A man she didn't recognize was standing there, his hand holding tight to Coate's slender wrist. He was large and fat, with a mop of wild brown hair that clung to his face in a sheen of sweat. He was wearing a buttoned lab coat. She wasn't sure if he had anything on underneath.

Coates looked terrified. His face was red, and he had tears in his eyes. His arms were bruised. Not a slave, then. A prisoner.

"I've dreamed of this moment," the man said. "Or, I'm sure I would have if I were capable of dreaming. I have thought about it, though. You're the real prize in all of this. Mitchell? He's like a worker bee. Single-minded. Kill everything. You? You have the potential to be a queen." He waggled his finger at her. "Not yet. You're still a princess right now."

She raised her gun at him. "Are you trying to stall me?"

He smiled. "Stall? No. You're waiting for the elevator. I'm waiting with you. I want you to know, he didn't break easily." He shook Coates like he was a rag doll. "It took an hour or two to get him on his knees. But watch this. Get on your knees."

Coates fell to his knees.

"See. I don't need technology to make them do what I want. People are fun that way. Take the spirit, own the person. So much more entertaining than sticking a receiver under the skin, but also so inefficient."

He reached into a pocket of the coat, taking out a knife.

"Don't," Katherine said. "I'll kill you."

"Go ahead. There's more of me where I came from." He smiled, dropping the knife on the floor. "Your ride will be here in a second. I want to leave you with something to think about."

"What?"

"Why am I letting you go?"

The elevator reached her. The doors slid open. She could smell Trevor standing behind her. She could feel his presence.

"Kill yourself," Watson said. Then he spread his arms wide.

Coates reached for the knife.

"No," Trevor shouted.

Katherine fired, hitting the configuration in the chest. Once. Twice. Three times.

Trevor pushed past her. Coates had the knife. He brought it up to his throat.

"Jason," Trevor shouted.

He slid it across his own neck without hesitation, as if it were the only release from a nightmare he would never escape any other way. And maybe it was. Trevor reached him as he toppled forward onto his face.

Katherine stood frozen a second time, the nausea almost too much to control. Big, strong Trevor knelt next to the wiry lab tech, holding his body across his lap, looking first at Watson, and then at her.

Why was he letting her go?

"Trevor," she said. "I told you to go up."

The words were cold and callous. She didn't care. She was angry. At herself. At everything.

He looked back at her, his eyes ferocious.

"Katherine," Origin said. "Where are you?"

"I'm coming."

"It's too late."

"What? No. I'll be there."

"I can't let him take me. Meet Mitchell at the source. Don't let Watson find it."

"The source? Find what? You said we had to do this together."

"We will. Do it."

"What about the Dove?"

"I didn't get everything. Beware of Cap-"

Origin's voice cut off.

"Origin?"

Nothing. Katherine shook from a sudden chill. She looked over at Trevor. It was his fault. If he had gone to Origin instead of her...

She suddenly felt completely alone.

Why was he letting her go?

She wished she could ask Origin. Now she wouldn't have a chance.

She stumbled into the elevator, her entire body numb. Did humankind have a chance? Two people against an intellect thousands of years ahead of their own? It didn't matter if Watson were deranged. He was also plotting at least two steps ahead of them, and any action she took could be playing right into his hands.

Origin told her to meet Mitchell at the source, and not to let Watson find something. Since Watson was letting her go, wasn't it obvious that it was so she would lead him right to it?

And again, what choice did she have? They had come to Nova Taurus knowing that Watson might have been onto them the entire time, and now she knew for certain that he had. Everything was a trap. Every possibility was considered and planned for in a network of branching logic she could barely keep up with, never mind anticipate.

How were they supposed to beat that?

She almost laughed when she remembered that they never had.

Meet Mitchell at the source. Those were her marching orders. She assumed that by the source, Origin had meant the XENO-1. At least the part of the ship that was deeply embedded in the ice and too massive to move. But Nova Taurus had been granted access to the site almost ten years ago. How was it possible that there was anything on the starship that the Tetron had yet to discover?

Because Origin had hidden it, and hidden it well.

Watson wanted to capture Origin for something, and that was it. Except Origin would never allow herself to be captured, and the other Tetron had to have known it. He had forced her to pass the torch instead, to someone who was inferior and who was sure to screw up somewhere down the road and give him the opening he was waiting for.

Someone like her.

What if she didn't go? What if she remained here, refusing to be part of this war? What if she shot herself in the head right now?

Plan B. That was what. Or C. Or D. Or E. Watson had surely considered every alternate scenario and had a play for each. The only difference would be that she would have taken herself out of the equation.

Origin was a Tetron. No. Origin was the Tetron. The first. She knew how Watson would think. Did she know this whole thing was a ruse? Had she sacrificed herself to get Katherine here?

Katherine couldn't rule it out. Besides, wasn't the shit she knew she was stepping in better than the stuff she couldn't see?

She decided that it was. Let Watson follow her to the source. Let him confront both her and Mitchell there. From what Origin had said, the Colonel was a survivor. He wouldn't go down easy.

And if he wouldn't, then neither would she.

She tapped the controls for the elevator. The doors started to close.

A hand stopped them, and they slid back once more.

Trevor stood in front of her. His shirt and pants were soaked through with blood. So were his hands. She had seen the expression he was making before. She knew what it meant.

"You aren't doing this without me," Trevor said. "You can't fight him alone."

"Okay," Katherine replied. "You should have gone up."

"I couldn't." He glanced back at Coates' body. "I couldn't."

"You aren't the man I thought you were, Trev."

He looked at her.

"You're better than that."

"WHAT'S THE STATUS?" Mitchell asked as Daisy returned to their stolen car.

"They're in," Daisy said with a smile, slipping into the passenger seat of the vehicle and closing the door.

"We're best to ditch this ride before the police, Watson or otherwise, catch on," Max said.

Mitchell leaned forward and put his hand on Michael's shoulder. He had been impressed with how quickly the man had overcome the car's security systems with little more than his portable tablet and AR glasses. Then again, Michael had confided that he had worked on the code for this particular model, which was why he had chosen it from the parking garage of the apartment building.

"How are you doing, Michael?" he asked.

"I'm hanging in there. Where are we headed?"

"Colorado Springs," Daisy said.

"You didn't mention our particular situation, did you, sweetheart?" Max asked.

Daisy leaned back over the seat. "One, don't call me sweetheart. I didn't like it when we were sleeping together, I don't like it now. Two, I do this for a living, jackass."

Max laughed. "Mmm, I love it when you call me names."

"You heard the lady, Michael," Mitchell said. "Colorado Springs it is."

"Colorado Springs," Michael repeated. "That's near Fort Carson, right?"

"Yup," Daisy said. "That's where my boys are stationed."

"You're sure we can trust them?" Mitchell asked.

"If Watson knows about this crew, you've already lost the war, Colonel," Daisy said.

Mitchell had explained the situation to her and Michael as they had put together their plan. Getting them to believe in the story had been an easy sell after what they had already experienced.

"Who are they?" Michael asked, getting the car moving.

"The Flying Fifteenth," Daisy said. "Paratrooper special ops."

"You never told me you knew the Fifteenth," Max said.

"Nobody is supposed to know the Fifteenth exists," Daisy replied. "How do you know them?"

"I know everybody, babe."

She raised her eyebrow at him. Max laughed in response.

"I know a guy who knows a guy whose brother is supposed to be in the Fifteenth. I got him a Kalashnikov 210."

"From where?" Daisy asked, intrigued. Mitchell knew they were talking about guns, but he had never heard of the model.

"Yeah, from where?" Lyle said.

Max kept laughing. "I found a dealer in Siberia who got one from a soldier, who picked it up during the war. I bet it cost him two years' pay to get his hands on that rifle."

"You're so full of shit," Lyle said.

"No way, bro. I don't lie. Sergeant Damon. I think that was his name. Ring a bell, sweetie?"

Daisy was straight-faced. "No."

"I can see that it does. You see that, Colonel?" Max said, pointing. "You can always tell when a woman's lying by the way their lips make that shape. You see it? Up at the corner there?"

Daisy turned away. "You're such an asshole."

"I speak the truth."

"That doesn't mean you aren't an asshole."

Max didn't stop laughing. Mitchell was able to smile for a few seconds before the weight of what he was doing drove the lightness away.

Go to Antarctica, to the wreckage of the Goliath. The place where his friends and comrades had died. Where Kathy had died.

He remembered his daughter. She had told him she was born from his and Katherine's DNA, mingled with something of Origin's. The first true Tetron-human hybrid. She had sacrificed herself to get the Goliath here with Watson trapped within. He knew now that Watson was intended to have remained trapped, but the intelligence had found a loophole to at least partially escape to an earlier time. It was the reason his and Origin's plan was in disarray - the Tetron had gotten a head start, and had been ready when the XENO-1 crashed.

Kathy had promised she would see him again. It was a promise he was going to make her keep. He had to survive to do that.

Return to the source. His first thought had been that Watson had planted the message, that the intelligence had outwitted both Origin and him. He didn't think that anymore. It didn't make sense that Watson would try so hard to kill him if he still needed him. It did make sense that Origin would want to know when he had unlocked the message, and when he would be en route.

The question was, why?

There was a larger plan in effect, one that they had made him forget. Was it as simple as heading to Antarctica, or was it bigger and more complex than that? He didn't know what he was going to the crash site for, only that he was supposed to go.

Would Origin be there, waiting for him?

Would Kathy?

Would Watson?

"Are you okay, Colonel?" Lyle said.

Mitchell pulled himself from his thoughts. He had lost track of time while he had been lost in them, noticing now that the landscape had changed, the outskirts of Denver traded for hills and trees.

Whatever was waiting in Antarctica, their survival depended on their success there. They had to be ready.

He glanced over at Lyle, nodding a few seconds later. Whether meeting the Detective had been serendipity or by Origin's design, it had been essential to getting him this far.

"Where are we?" he asked.

"About ten miles outside of Colorado Springs," Michael said.

"We've been making fun of you the whole time," Max said. "You said you're a Space Marine, so it makes sense that you were spaced out."

He laughed at the bad joke. Mitchell didn't join him. His attention was stolen by a light in the sky, getting bigger in a hurry.

"Has the car been reported missing?" Mitchell asked.

"No," Michael replied. "I've been keeping tabs on law enforcement and military channels for mention of it. Everything's been quiet so far. Why?"

Mitchell pointed at the light. "Something's coming."

[51]

MITCHELL

"PULL OVER," Mitchell said. "Get the car off the road."

Michael nodded, slowing the car and moving it off to the side. There wasn't much cover here. A few trees and a lot of grass. The light was getting closer. If they hadn't been seen already, they would be any second.

"Kill the lights and head for the trees," Mitchell said. "Lyle, get us some cover fire."

"Yes, sir," Lyle said, picking up the rifle resting between his legs.

The car bounced gently on its repulsors, covering the grass and scooting toward the minimal cover. It was better than nothing. Lyle positioned himself to get the rifle out of the window and aimed toward the light.

It shifted then, going vertical at least a thousand feet, getting out of range of the gun. They reached the trees, and Michael stopped the car.

Mitchell climbed out beside Max, scanning the sky. The light was gone, but he could still hear the sound of the craft's engines. It was high-pitched and powerful. Too strong to be a drone.

"Do you see it?" Michael asked.

"No. Stay under cover."

"How do you think they found us?"

"How many cars have we passed out here?"

"I don't know. Three?"

"There's your answer."

The whining began to fade, growing softer as the seconds passed, until it vanished into silence.

"False alarm?" Daisy said. She had produced a pistol from somewhere, not that it would have done a thing against whatever had been approaching.

"I don't like it," Lyle said. "It saw us and then left? Why?"

"Calling for reinforcements?" Max said.

"I think we should get out of here," Michael said.

"Yeah, I'm with you," Mitchell agreed. "Back in the-"

The sound was more of a low rumble. If there were anything else around them, they wouldn't have even noticed it. A moment later, the branches on the trees began bending to a sudden, forceful wind.

The VTOL dropped out of nowhere, its belly cloaked by a high-resolution screen that projected the stars above it, the only trace of its existence coming from the light whooshing noise and the wind. Mitchell joined the others in raising his weapon toward it.

He heard a soft thump behind him, and then the muzzle of a rifle was pressed against the back of his head.

"Shh... Stay soft. Take it slow and easy," the woman at his back said.

Mitchell glanced over out of the corner of his eye. Two others had gotten behind Max and Lyle.

The VTOL came to rest in front of them, lighting up as it touched down. The U.S. Army markings were obvious emblazoned on its angled sides.

"I should have known," Daisy said, turning to face their attackers. "Colonel, meet Sergeant Linda Damon, callsign Demon."

The gun vanished from his head. He turned around. The woman behind him was stiff and straight, greeting him with a tight salute.

"Sir," she snapped.

Mitchell started to bow in response. Then he smiled and mimicked her salute. "Sergeant."

"Over there is Major Koos, we call her Kook, and Corporal Dawes, or Dreck."

"My name is mud," Dawes said. He was the largest of the three, and even then was barely Mitchell's height and at least thirty pounds lighter.

The hatch on the VTOL opened, and two more soldiers stepped out.

"Lieutenant Colonel Hans Stoker, callsign Dracula," the first said. He was the oldest, with a white flat top and a bit of stubble around his chin. He hopped off the short wing of the craft and approached Mitchell, saluting when he reached him. "Our pilot is Captain Verma. We call him Mazerat. Corporal Cooper is still inside, prepping your gear."

"A pleasure," Mitchell said, making eye contact with each of them. "You certainly know how to make an entrance."

"That's how we do it, Colonel. Quiet and quick, every time. Sorry for the spook, but we had to be sure you were safe."

"Understood. How much do you know?"

"Next to nothing. All Daisy here told me was that she had a situation with an ex and to keep the details on mute."

"What?" Max said.

"An emergency," Stoker said. "A big one that we shouldn't tell home base about. We don't have a true command on location. We get mission parameters delivered from all over the world, usually hush-hush orders signed by the President. It's not unusual for our outfit to take off in the middle of the night without a word to anybody. In fact, I think the other way around would be out of character for us, wouldn't you say, Kook?"

"Yes, sir," Koos replied.

"So I understand this mission is critical to national security?" Stoker said.

"That's right," Daisy replied. "You aren't going to believe how big this thing is."

"I can think pretty big," Stoker said. "I imagine you'll debrief us on the way, Colonel?"

"Yes," Mitchell said. "Trust me, Lieutenant Colonel, I don't think you're thinking this big."

Stoker smiled. "Sounds like a party. Of course, I'm not entirely sure about teaming up with a bunch of jarheads."

"We're real excited about hopping into that thing with a squad of dog faces," Max said. "Real excited. Oorah!"

"Be careful, we bite," Damon said, laughing as she passed Max.

The others headed for the VTOL, leaving Mitchell standing next to the car with Michael. He was the only civilian in the group, and he looked terrified of the aircraft.

"Are you okay?" Mitchell said.

"I'm not a big fan of flying. I can do the cushy seats and free peanuts. This isn't that."

"You don't have to stay with us. You aren't a soldier. There's no shame in bowing out."

Michael looked back at the car. Then he shook his head. "You might find yourself in need of someone with my skills. Anyway, as scared as I am of flying in that thing, I'm more scared of feeling like I let Kathy down."

Mitchell felt a chill, his mind turning to the silent explosions that marked the deaths of everyone and everything he cared about.

"That's what keeps me going," he said.

[52]

KATHERINE

It took a little more subterfuge to get out of Nova Taurus without drawing attention, forcing Katherine and Trevor to sneak through the loading docks, ditching their original clothing for two pairs of scrubs they found in a huge dumpster of outgoing laundry. The navy blue outfits smelled awful, but also allowed them to take a secondary exit out onto the street behind the massive tower.

Of course, they had made it out because Watson wanted them to get out. Their path had been void of any of the security details that wandered the halls, and passing beyond the cameras hadn't led to interception. They had stepped out of the building along with another pair of men in scrubs who pulled out vaporizers the moment the door closed behind them.

They took a roundabout route back to the hotel, not speaking to one another the entire way. Trevor was shaken, and she understood why. He had downplayed his relationship with the tech, making it seem more like the relationship he had shared with her. A little bit of fun, a little bit of romance, but nothing that either one of them believed would last. Coates had been more than that, and she was dismayed by his loss and the effect it was having on the man beside her. She was still feeling Michael's absence herself.

Her mind was also still consumed by her desire to outthink Watson. She didn't believe it was possible, but she felt like she at least needed to try. She went over the possibilities again and again, trying to work out all of the combinations. In one scenario, Origin had done everything intentionally, setting the pieces in motion like a chess master. In another, everything had gone completely wrong from the start. Most of the rest were somewhere in between, and it was there that Katherine believed the truth was sitting.

It was also where the branches split, one after another, after another, too far down to ever make sense of.

The only choice they had was to go completely from their gut.

They entered their suite, remaining quiet as they went in separate directions. Katherine grabbed a change of clothes and jumped in the master shower. She assumed Trevor did the same. She emerged thirty minutes later, still struggling to find her center, but getting closer. Trevor was already waiting for her, dressed all in black, ready for war.

"What's our next move?" he asked. The pain he had been exhibiting before had hardened into resolve.

"We need a ride to Antarctica."

"Antarctica?" he said. "XENO-1?"

"Yes. Pretty obvious, I guess."

"The where. Not the why."

"Watson wants something that is still on the ship. I don't know what. Origin said that Mitchell was already on his way there."

"How did she know?"

"I don't know. She must have been in contact with him." If that were true, why hadn't the intelligence let her at least talk to the Colonel? They were supposed to have some kind of eternal chemistry already, and she at least wanted a chance to see if it would ever make itself known.

"Do you have any ideas on how we can get there?" Trevor asked.

"You were in special forces. You have a lot of connections."

"Not that kind of connection."

"We'll figure something out," Katherine said. "Origin wouldn't have told me to go if she didn't think I could get there."

"I'm not convinced. For as old and experienced as this Tetron claimed to be, we've been getting beaten pretty soundly so far. How do we know she wasn't the inferior intelligence? How do we know she didn't get Jason killed for nothing? She said it herself. Humans have never won this war."

"I know you're hurting, Trev. What happened to the resolve I saw a minute ago?"

"I'm resolved to fight. That doesn't mean I believe we can win. I've been through a lot, Kate. I've been places, seen things you wouldn't believe. Your war was in the air, mine was in cities around the globe. What happens out of sight is much worse than what happens in the skies. Jason was the first person I've met who helped me stay focused, and now he's gone. I'll be happy to take a few of those AIT assholes with me when I die."

"You aren't going to die."

"Do you believe that?"

Katherine shrugged. They both knew the odds were against them. "Colonel Williams is going to be there. Origin made him sound like some kind of super-soldier. He got the war this far."

"Or he lost the war in his recursion and ran to this one."

"Damn it, Trevor," Katherine said, getting angry. "Pull your shit together. Whatever Coates did for you, you're still a frigging soldier. Start acting like one."

Trevor stared at her, jaw tight. Then he nodded. "Yes, ma'am."

Someone knocked on the door to the emergency stairwell.

Katherine and Trevor looked at one another. Trevor stood, drew his gun, and moved to the side of the room, in position to shoot whoever was there. No guests would be sent up that way.

Katherine approached it, her nerves trying to get the best of her.

Whoever the visitor was, they were unexpected, uninvited, and more likely than not had been sent by Watson.

She reached the door right as the person knocked on it again. The emergency door opened outward toward the stairs, and she pulled up the lever and pushed slowly. Origin had disabled everything coming from the room, so it didn't set off an alarm.

"Katherine," Yousefi said. He was dressed in a pair of fatigues, his expression concerned.

"Admiral?" Katherine said, confused. "What are you doing here?"

He held up his AR glasses. "I received a secured transmission an hour and a half ago, encrypted to my identifier and using a secondary military encryption that nobody outside of UEA command is supposed to know. The sender id was yours."

"What? I didn't send you anything."

"I'm not surprised to hear you say that. The transmission carried a schematic unlike anything I've ever seen before, along with a short message in your voice from someone calling themselves Origin."

Katherine stared at him. Then a smile began creeping across her face.

"May I come in?"

KATHERINE

Yousefi took off his AR glasses and handed them to Katherine. "I've removed the device security so you can see what I was sent."

Katherine put Yousefi's glasses on. A translucent overlay appeared in the corner, and a thought turned the lenses opaque and moved it to the front of both eyes, enlarging it. Her message was at the top of a list of military communique that had been sent to the commander of the Dove. She couldn't help but notice that the one preceding it was from the General.

She focused on her message and opened it with a thought.

"Rear-Admiral Yousefi. I am called Origin. I do not have time to explain the fullness of my identity, and for that, I apologize. I am sending you this message because Major Katherine Asher is in need of your immediate assistance. I am including a data file stolen from the mainframe of the Nova Taurus Corporation. It contains evidence of a plot to sabotage the Dove on the day of her launch, as well as proof that Nova Taurus has been subverted by the head of the AIT. Please, Admiral, bring this information directly to Katherine. I have provided the coordinates. Do not trust anyone in the UEA with this information. The AIT's spies are everywhere. I understand you are risking your career if you do this. I also know the man that you are, as we have met before in a time that has not yet occurred. Your daughter's name will be Jala, and she will truly be a brightness."

Katherine reached up and lowered the glasses. Yousefi was staring at her with a look of concern. She raised them back to view the file.

It was a schematic, as Yousefi had said. A three-dimensional blueprint. The shape was vaguely that of a pyramid, though it was smaller than the ones she had seen in her dreams. Inside of it was a maze of wiring and pipes and other machinery, the makeup and purpose of which she didn't understand. The viewpoint began to shift, floating through the marks and lines, moving toward the center. There was an energy source there, a core that branched out into the structure like it were the center of a nervous system. A small, empty space sat beside it.

"Eternal engine," the label read, popping up and pointing to the space. More text appeared above it. "There are no Tetron energy condensers in this timeline. Watson requires the power of the eternal engine to begin true reproduction. He has yet to find where it was hidden on the Goliath. Mitchell has unlocked the secured message I left for him twenty years ago with your friend Michael's assistance. He will be there. Be cautious. Watson will follow one or both of you. You must protect one another, claim the engine, and keep it from his hands. It must be on the Dove when she launches, along with you and Mitchell."

"The war is not over, Katherine," Origin's voice said, following the text. "The Mesh has been broken. It is beginning anew."

The file closed, pushing her back to the list of messages. She took off the glasses. Michael was alive and with Mitchell? Maybe they had a chance after all.

"She didn't say how he's planning to sabotage the Dove," Katherine said, looking at Trevor. "She did confirm what he wants."

"To be God?" Trevor asked.

"Essentially." She looked at Yousefi. "Jala?"

He nodded. "Yes. We haven't told anyone the name, and yet this Origin knew it. She also mentioned a timeline. A time traveler?" He seemed more curious about the idea than fearful of it.

"In a sense, but not exactly. The important part is that she wasn't the only one, and the other is the head of the AIT, and pulling the strings within Nova Taurus."

"Nova Taurus? They have had access to all of our research for the last ten years."

"I know. I'm sorry you were dragged into this, sir, but Origin trusted you. She knows you'll do the right thing. So do I. She gave herself up to get this information to us. To get you to me, so that you can get me to the crash site."

"Watson is the leader of the AIT?"

"Yes."

"She said he will follow."

"He hasn't been able to locate the eternal engine inside the wreckage, whatever it is. He also knows that Origin wants us to put it on the Dove. He's counting on us finding it for him."

"And what happens when we do?"

"One of us will leave with the engine," Trevor said.

"And the other one will die," Katherine finished.

Yousefi pursed his lips and breathed out heavily. "I could be court-martialed for this."

"Sir, if we don't get the engine and keep it out of Watson's possession, if we don't ensure the Dove makes her launch, your little girl will never be born."

"Neither will billions of others," Trevor said, driving home the stakes.

Yousefi looked at both of them before nodding. "Okay. I can organize an emergency flight to Antarctica, but I can't keep it under the radar. If the AIT is as deep into the UEA as you think, they'll know our plans."

"Watson already knows our plans," Katherine said, finally beginning to pull the pieces together. "Except we won't be the only ones there."

"Mitchell?" Yousefi asked.

"Yes."

"Who is he?"

"The cat," Katherine said.

"What does that make us?"

"The cheese."

[54]

KATHERINE

Katherine, Trevor, and Admiral Yousefi were back at Naval Station Norfolk inside of two hours. Her return to the base was being kept top secret, her civilian status in a restricted area impossible for even Yousefi to clear or resolve with Command. If General Petrov discovered she had been returned to the base, or to service, he would be sure to disband all of the Dove's inaugural flight crew in favor of one of the backup teams. Having Trevor with her would make things doubly worse.

She knew Yousefi was taking a massive risk in helping them. She was grateful for her superior's trust, and for his willingness to go against any number of rules and ordinances to make the trip happen. It had taken some work to get the base's only high-velocity delivery unit procured and ready for travel, and Yousefi had been forced to lie at a level she had never even known existed.

Landing at NSN, he had taken them from the runway in a tarp-covered transport, hiding them away in the back while asking the driver what he had seen.

"Nothing, sir," the Private had replied.

"Make sure it stays that way if you ever want to reach Sergeant," Yousefi had warned.

Then they had been led on foot through the bowels of the base, through passages buried below ground where the utility lines were run. It was cold and damp under there and left Katherine feeling cold and uncertain.

At least until they arrived inside the barracks proper.

A squad of five soldiers was waiting for them as they emerged, already suited up in winter fatigues and camouflaged powered armor. They snapped to attention at Yousefi's arrival, saluting as Katherine and Trevor entered behind him.

"Atten-shun," the soldier on the forward left said. "Admiral on the floor."

Katherine recognized each and every one of them. They were members of Project Olive Branch, each from a different nation and armed service. They were her friends and enemies, her competition for the spot on the Dove, the people that Yousefi trusted the most to follow his orders and otherwise say nothing.

"At ease," Yousefi said.

The armors shifted, the noise of it echoing in the room.

"I thought you would need backup," Yousefi said to her.

"We might, sir." She lowered her voice. "There's a good chance all of these people are going to die."

"That's part of being a soldier," Yousefi replied. "They're all volunteers, and I told them the odds are against us."

"Do they know what they're fighting?"

"Not completely. They know they're defending our future. That's what matters."

"Sir," a woman's voice said from behind them.

"Bonnie," Katherine said at the sight of her friend. She approached her, giving her a short hug. "It's good to see you."

"Katherine," Bonnie replied. "It hasn't been that long. Only a few days."

"It feels like forever," Katherine replied.

"Bonnie, what's our status?" Yousefi asked.

"I managed to get everything you asked for, and everyone I pulled it from swore to keep everything secret. No one is happy with the way the UEA bowed out to the terrorists, and they were all pretty willing to stick it to the AIT."

"Good. Captain Jackson, get the team onto the HVU. Katherine, Trevor, come with me."

"Yes, sir," Jackson said, spinning in his armor. "You heard the man."

The armors made the floor vibrate as they moved across the floor toward the exit. Bonnie brought them back to an empty secondary corridor to a small armory. Everything they needed to prepare for the cold Antarctic climate had already been arranged, including two suits of power armor.

"Where's yours?" Katherine asked Yousefi as she quickly changed from her simple black shirt and pants and into the insulated under-clothes that would sit beneath her fatigues.

"Wow, Katherine," Trevor said. "What happened to your neck?"

Katherine had forgotten about the injury. She ran her hand across the wound. "Watson," she replied.

"I'll be piloting the HVU," Yousefi said. "I've never done power armor training, anyway."

That wasn't a surprise. The armor was relatively new, the artificial musculature a result of technology salvaged from XENO-1. Human technology, Katherine remembered. Everything started somewhere. She was glad she had done the training course. It hadn't been required, but she believed every skill she gained would find a use. Now that one had.

She finished with the fatigues, fitted and impervious to the cold. Then she stepped forward, turning and pushing herself up and back into the armor. Clasps closed over her wrists, ankles, chest and stomach, holding her in place. The reactor on her back pulsed softly. A helmet rounded out the uniform, but she left it sitting on the armor's left shoulder. She turned her wrists, checking the machine guns mounted against them. Two ammunition feeds trailed from the sides of the unit.

"What's the ETA on the site?" Trevor asked, already strapped into his own armor.

"Three hours," Yousefi replied. "Weather's a little testy down there right now, though. I'm not sure how close we'll be able to drop you."

"Did you say drop?" Katherine said, feeling a pit grow in her stomach. Half the reason she had never been shot down was because she hated the idea of falling.

"Sorry, Major. I know that's your weak spot. There's no other way."

"Don't worry, Kate," Trevor said. "It's not the fall that will kill you, you know."

"Do we have any idea what to expect from Watson?" Yousefi asked.

Katherine shook her head. "No. I imagine he'll keep his surprises to himself unless we find the engine."

"Don't you mean, until?" Trevor said. "You've got a long-term part to play in this little space opera."

"Funny, Trev," Katherine said. "We should hope we find it."

"If you two are dressed and ready?" Yousefi said.

"Sorry, sir," Katherine said. "I'm ready to go."

"Me too," Trevor said, shifting to flex the armor like a pro. "This is an older config, isn't it?"

"These are alternate manufacturer models," Yousefi said. "Standard suits are made by a Nova Taurus subsidiary. We had to pull these suits out of mothballs to get them ready. Unfortunately, we can't do much about the HVU. I had Clemens disable anything that would allow remote communication. As soon as we take off, it's the eight of us against whatever the AIT sends our way."

"Mitchell and Michael make ten," Katherine said.

"If they make it," Trevor said.

"They'll make it."

Ten against who knew how many.

Nobody said it was going to be easy.

KATHERINE

"THERE IT IS," Yousefi said, pointing at a large, irregular shape on the HVU's control panel. "But you've seen her plenty of times before."

Katherine was sitting in the co-pilot seat, her power armor left in the rear with the rest of the squad. "I've been within a half-kilometer," she replied. "Never inside."

"I was inside once, but they didn't take us very far. A few hundred meters. Even so, I don't think I took a breath until we came back out. Of course, that was before we started boarding the Dove. She's almost as big."

Thanks to Origin, she knew why. "How are we going to get in without being spotted, sir?"

"There aren't any crews inside. They pulled out a few months ago because of reports that the ice was thinning, and the wreckage might push through into the ocean below. The nearest facility is fifteen kilometers west."

"I wonder who made that report?" Katherine said.

If Watson was searching for the eternal engine, he might not want anyone to see where his slaves and configurations were going.

Who knew how much of the ship had been sealed off? It had taken hundreds of years to discover all of the secrets of the Egyptian pyramids, and the XENO-1 had only been here for twenty.

"I can't say I would be surprised," Yousefi said. "The good news is, it means we can drop without risking interference with our own people."

"The bad news is, so can the AIT."

"Affirmative. You should head back and suit up. Unless you're staying with me?"

"No, sir. I'm not missing this."

"I'll be touching down at Alpha and waiting to hear from you. Good hunting, Major."

"Thank you, sir."

Katherine made her way from the cockpit to the rear of the craft. The HVU was an odd cross of old technology and new. It was wide, with a lot of sharp edges, two massive scramjets overhead, two repulsor rings below, and powered by a smaller version of the Dove's reactors. The cargo area was fairly comfortable due to the wide body, though much of it had been filled with supplies. They were bringing enough to spend three days inside the wreckage to search and explore, though she had a feeling that wherever the eternal engine was hiding, it wouldn't take that long to find.

She was supposed to discover it, wasn't she? Would Origin have been as quick to sacrifice herself if she weren't?

"It's almost go time," she announced to the others.

"Great," Lieutenant Chang said, reaching for her helmet and pushing her hair away from her face. "This was getting pretty boring."

"It was only three hours," Lieutenant Shah replied. He had been sitting in the corner meditating. Now he got to his feet and headed for his gear.

"Three hours of torture," Chang said. "This is the most serious crew I've ever gotten stuck with." She muttered something in Chinese, and then laughed at herself.

"I understood that," Captain Jackson said.

"I know," Chang replied, winking at him.

"Less talking, more motion," Katherine said. She had lived and trained with each of the officers present for the last two years. They all knew one another well and had found a lot of common ground in their occupations and makeup despite the fact that except for herself and Captain Jackson, they all originated from different countries.

"Andiamo," Lieutenant Ribisi said, hopping to his feet. He hurried over to his armor and quickly strapped himself in. "Ready to go, ma'am."

A soft thud signaled one of the armors already in motion. Katherine turned to see Trevor making his way toward the rear of the craft, where the loading door would drop to allow them exodus.

"Me first," he said, turning his wrists to check his armament. A survival kit and standard rifle were attached to the rear of the armor in case he had to abandon the augmentation. "Unless you object, Major?"

"Be my guest," Katherine said, reaching her exoskeleton and climbing in. "I'll follow you. Jackson, line up the squad after that."

"Yes, ma'am," Jackson said, quickly barking out the drop order.

The cargo hold was a flurry of motion as the squad prepared, suiting up in the armor and grabbing the extra supplies. Within two minutes, they were all lined up at the rear of the craft, ready to jump.

Mostly ready to jump. Katherine couldn't help the rapid heart-beat and cold sweat that began forming on her skin. She had never liked jumping, and she hated it even more in powered armor. It left her feeling trapped and out of control.

"Nothing bad's happened to you so far," Trevor said.

She knew he was only talking about jumping. She appreciated his encouragement. "Right," she replied, fighting the tension.

"This is Yousefi," the voice said over the loudspeakers. "Opening rear doors in ten... nine... eight..."

Katherine clenched her teeth and closed her eyes. She would never have imagined a week ago that she would be here, about to jump down to the XENO-1 instead of being in the gym or the flight simulator, or on the bridge of the Dove working out final launch details. She would never have guessed she would find herself fighting not only for her own future but the future of all humankind.

She certainly would never have thought she would be searching for a time travel device and trying to outwit an emotionally psychotic advanced artificial intelligence.

She felt a blast of cold air as the rear hatch lowered. It shocked her back to the present and forced her to steel her nerves.

"See you on the other side," Trevor said without turning back, running to the edge of the plank and vanishing.

Katherine took one last breath and put the armor in motion, her muscles signaling the suit to provide enhanced assistance. She rushed to the edge of the plank, her breath catching one more time as she looked down at the remaining bulk of the XENO-1 below.

Then she was out and falling, and her anxiety rushed away almost as quickly as it had come.

For a moment, she felt free.

[56]

KATHERINE

She landed smoothly, coming down fifty meters from Trevor, and about four hundred meters from the main entrance to the downed starship.

She imagined things had changed quite a bit since the day it had settled in the Antarctic ice. A pavilion had been erected nearby, a staging area for the workers going inside. Scaffolding and supports had been added to shore up any perceived weaknesses in the damaged frame. Bits and pieces had been pulled from the wreck, each of the original locations marked and numbered.

Even so, it was amazing. More impressive than she had dreamed, despite having already been inside of her past future version in the Dove. Knowing that this one was four hundred years older and had been altered by Tetron technology made it so much more than its origin.

"Let's not dawdle out here for too long, Major," Trevor said. "The weather is pretty ugly."

Katherine had barely noticed the climate, she was so taken with the ship. A stiff, cold wind was blowing, and snow was blowing in with it.

"Jackson, is everyone down?" she said into her helmet comm.

"Affirmative, ma'am," Jackson replied. He was moving toward her, the others not far behind.

Katherine looked at the ship again. Mitchell. Would the name mean anything to her now that she was here?

She felt a twinge of sadness, and nothing more. Whatever cosmic chemistry Origin had insisted she should feel, it wasn't coming. Maybe she would have to see the man first?

"Let's head in," she said. "Murphy, Ribisi, cover the entrance. If anyone else comes near this thing, I want to know about it."

"Yes, ma'am," the soldiers replied.

Katherine led the way into the ship. Lights had been strung along the corridors as far and deep as the researchers had explored, and they slowly faded on as they entered. The temperature rose as they moved further in, evenly spaced heaters making the location comfortable to work in. The reactor powering them was probably in the pavilion outside.

Katherine twitched her eye, navigating her way through the helmet's AR system. Yousefi had loaded a three-dimensional map of the wreckage into it. She had examined it during the flight, searching for areas that might have been missing a complete outline, but the overall condition made those locations numerous. There were plenty of places with collapsed corridors, tears in the outer hull that had allowed the elements to seep in, or simply walls of alloy that had proven difficult to cut through without harming the overall integrity.

A grouping of small blue dots indicated their position within the ship, right at the entrance. Katherine started walking again, moving deeper inside. She wasn't going to be able to work out what she was supposed to do or where she was supposed to go through logic. She had to go on instinct and feel. If this was her eternal role to play, she ought to sense something.

They spent an hour traversing the first level of the ship, moving through areas that had been made more accessible with stairwells, ladders, heating, and lights. Katherine checked the schematic on a number of occasions, tracking their progress through the mapped portion of the crash. She paused every so often, closing her eyes, slowing her breathing, and trying to let the subconscious, ancient memories that Origin claimed had been unlocked make their way to the surface.

She wanted to hear the voice again. The one that had told her to find Mitchell. The one that seemed so familiar, and yet so alien. Who did that voice belong to? It was only now that she realized it had been silent since she had first crossed paths with Origin.

She didn't want it to be silent anymore.

"Where are you?" she whispered, casting her eyes down another long, quiet corridor.

"Are you okay, Major?" Jackson asked.

"Yeah," she replied. "I was just thinking. Let's take a short break."

"Affirmative."

The soldiers gathered close, keeping guard while at the same time snacking quickly on one of their ration packs. The minutes passed in a hurry, and then Katherine got them moving again. She checked the blueprint. They were on E deck, near a shaft that pierced the center of the starship. The Dove had a similar central tube that led to the bridge, but no such thing existed here. The top of the ship had been torn away by something, lost before its entry into the atmosphere. The wound had since been covered over by a mangled mess of alloy and cabling.

Even so, she decided that she wanted to see it. They might be able to travel more quickly through the shaft, and there was no sense wasting time on floors in between the top and bottom of what had already been explored. If there had been something there, someone would have found it. Watson would have found it.

"Ribisi, Murphy, do you copy?" she said, reaching out to the guards at the entrance.

"Yes, ma'am," Ribisi replied.

"What's your status?"

"Everything is clear up here. Cold and quiet."

"Good. Let's hope it stays that way."

"Yes, ma'am."

Katherine tried to sound confident, but she was starting to feel a slight fraying on the edge of her nerves. She shouldn't have expected that Mitchell would have gotten there ahead of her or would arrive so soon after she did. Still, she couldn't help but worry that he might not show up at all.

"The central shaft is right up ahead," she said to the others. "We'll take a shortcut to the lower deck."

"Do you really think we're going to find anything down here?" Chang asked. "This place looks like it's been picked pretty clean already."

"We didn't come all of this way to give up in a few hours," Shah said. "Besides, you can't tell us you aren't enjoying the tour."

"Yeah, it's just like a walk in the park," Chang said. "I'm claustrophobic."

"You are not," Jackson said. "I've read your file. You spent a year on a submarine underneath this ice."

"Who said I enjoyed it?"

Katherine reached the shaft. There had been a hatch covering it at some point, but it had been damaged at some point, bent and torn away from the opening. She leaned out over it, her helmet's lamps activating on their own in the darkness. The ship was at an angle in the ice, leaving the hole slightly tilted. She looked down, able to see the separations of the decks and the terrain at the bottom. A pile of debris rested there, mainly bits of alloy that had broken free during the crash. It was mingled with a pool of water.

"Yousefi said the science teams were concerned the ice was unstable," Trevor said, moving beside her to look for himself. "It seems like it's sinking already."

"The entrance hasn't shifted," Katherine said.

"The structure may be buckling," Trevor replied. "Bending in half as it loses its support. It isn't safe down there. It looks like this section is already mapped. We can head further aft and take a stair-well toward the base if that's where you want to go."

Katherine considered. Then she shook her head. Watson wouldn't care if it were safe, and the presence of the water was the only thing about the ship that seemed out of place. "I'm going down there. You can wait here if you want."

"Kate," Trevor started to say.

"Captain Jackson, you have the wire?" Katherine asked, cutting him off.

"Yes, ma'am."

She turned and motioned to the armor. Jackson retrieved the wire from his back, hooking it to a pair of anchors on the shoulders of Katherine's armor, and then to his own.

She returned to the edge, leaning out over it. The list would make it easier to get up and down. She went backward, rappelling down the side of the shaft toward the bottom. She paused at each floor, shining her headlamp into it, revealing more of the same empty corridors.

She was halfway down when she heard the first crack. It came from somewhere deep within the ship, a sharp groan that echoed along the frame and created a loud snap above them. She held tight, waiting for the craft to move, to buckle in and sink a little more.

"Are you okay down there, Major?" Captain Jackson asked.

"Affirmative," Katherine replied. "My ears are ringing a little, though."

"Mine, too."

She dropped down two more floors. A second groan sounded, and she paused again, a sense of fear reaching up toward her from the depths. Maybe she should head back up? Maybe Trevor was right?

She looked down. She was so close to the bottom. Too close to give up. She pushed off, letting the wire feed out. It was a ten-meter drop into the bottom of the shaft. She slowed herself slightly as she reached it, hitting the water with a loud splash.

Her fatigues kept the frigid liquid from piercing through and into her skin, holding it at bay as it rose to her knees. She slipped on an unseen piece of debris, catching herself against the wall. Then she looked down.

The light pierced the water more easily from close up. She saw a face, slightly bloated but preserved. She stumbled back toward the wall. "Shit."

"Katherine? What is it?" Trevor asked from above.

She got over the initial surprise. She followed the face down to a torso, and then to the debris. A hand was visible there, its complexion too dark to belong to the same person.

"It looks like part of the shaft collapsed onto some people down here," she said. She leaned in closer, looking at the face. It was familiar to her. It resembled the configuration she had run into in the loop station. "It looks like one of Watson's."

A third pop sounded within the ship. A vibration passed along it, almost knocking Katherine over. The sound of bending metal followed. She turned her attention to the sound. A single opening. A mangled but passable area that moved toward the rear of the starship.

Katherine checked the map, confronted with a moment of confusion when she realized that she was off it. She adjusted the schematic to get her bearings.

She was three levels further down than anyone had been before.

KATHERINE

"I'M OUTSIDE THE BOUNDARIES," Katherine said. "Deeper than the map goes. I can see an opening toward the aft."

"Major, you should get out of there," Jackson said. "If more of the ship is opening up, it's only because it's unstable." A fourth vibration shook them, emphasizing his point. "I'm going to reel you back up."

"Negative," Katherine said, taking a few steps toward the bulkhead. "I'm going to see what's through the hole."

"That's not a good idea, Major," Jackson said. "You could get trapped down there."

"It's a chance I have to take, Captain," she replied.

"Kate," Trevor said, switching to a private channel. "You don't need to do this. If we can't reach the engine, neither can Watson. If the XENO-1 is going to sink, let the device sink with it."

"You know I can't. We need it as much as he does. Origin said it has to be on the Dove."

"Why?"

"So the Dove can go into the next recursion."

"Why?"

"What do you mean?"

"Why does it need to go into the next recursion? What's the point? We lose anyway, don't we?"

"The point is that we don't give up, Trev. We keep fighting. We keep trying. Origin said the Mesh is broken, and that we have a chance. This is our chance. If the eternal engine is down here, I'm going to find it."

"Then I'm coming down with you."

"No. Stay up there. There's only one way in or out of this space, and that's through you. If Watson shows up, you have to keep him neutralized. Set up a defensive perimeter with Jackson."

"Is that an order, Major?"

"Does it have to be?"

"No. You have a point. I'll take care of the defenses. Don't go silent on me."

"Affirmative."

Katherine returned her attention to the corridor. The opening was too small for the power armor. She was going to have to leave it.

She disengaged, releasing the bindings and powering down. Then she stepped off, reaching back and taking her rifle from the side. The water was up to her knees now, and the watertight insulation of her fatigues was beginning to lose the battle against the cold.

She pushed on, through the water to the corridor, crouching low and navigating her way through the twisted frame. The passage beyond was also bent, crushing in on itself as damage and time finally caught up to the starship. She had no idea how much time she had, or even where she was going. It didn't matter. If she died down here, so be it. At least she would die trying.

"We're set and ready," Trevor said a short time later. "Nothing is getting through here. Any leads?"

"Not yet," Katherine replied. "The ship goes on forever." She looked ahead. There was still only the one corridor, leading straight back toward the rear. "I feel like I'm being directed. Every other passage I cross is blocked by debris."

"A trap?"

"It feels like it should be, but what would be the point? Watson could have killed me back in D.C. No. I think I'm supposed to be down here. Whatever is going to happen, it's going to happen soon."

"Affirmative. We've got your back."

Katherine kept walking. Could it be that the ship had been altered for her arrival as if it knew the state of the world outside? Or had it all been pre-organized and pre-ordained based on prior recursions? Had she been here before? Walked this corridor before? It all seemed so impossible, and at the same time was the only thing that made sense to her. Who knew what permutations of coincidence could be created when history had repeated some version of itself over the course of infinite time?

It was enough to make her head spin if she thought too much about it. It was better to accept what was, rather than try to understand it. Her present experience was the only experience that mattered to the her that was here now.

Twenty minutes passed. The air grew colder. Katherine was sure she should have reached the back of the ship by now, but the corridor continued. It had changed, however; turning into a smooth, cylindrical alloy that appeared newer than everything else.

Something had made this after the crash.

Something that was probably still here.

She could imagine how the cylinder might have been closed off before, tucked away and hidden so that no one could find it, including Watson. For whatever reason - whether because of the ship's deterioration, past recursions, or her presence - it was open now.

The passage ended at a large sealed hatch, at least ten meters in diameter. It loomed over her, a monument to the secret waiting on the other side. Katherine approached it without slowing, without hesitation, half-expecting it to open as she neared.

It didn't. Not right away. Instead, a small light in the shape of a hand began to flash on the surface.

She finished her journey, reaching the barrier and staring at the panel. She should have sent word back to Trevor and the team. In the moment, she forgot. She had come a long way in a very short time.

She reached out, putting her hand to the light. It glowed beneath her palm. She knew instinctively what was going to happen then, as though she had been waiting for it to happen since the day she had been born. The same way she had known to look for the falling starship before it had appeared in the sky.

A hiss of air, a soft clang, and a rumble. Then the doors began to part. More intense light greeted her eyes; a quickly pulsing blue. It blinded her for a moment, leaving her unable to make out the details of the chamber that was revealed. She could see a large structure in the center, thousands of branches spreading out in all directions from it, reaching around the room and plunging down into the ice below. She could see a silhouette in the center of it, a black outline of a human-shaped figure facing away from her.

Time slowed down. Seconds passed as if they were hours. The brightness began to come into focus, the figure at the center of it all turning toward them, yet still remaining anchored to the core of energy.

Katherine walked toward it, each step an eternity. She couldn't get close enough, fast enough. There was no fear in her. Only an excitement she couldn't completely understand.

Sound. A voice. It was slow at first before reality resumed. She heard the words in her head almost before they were finished being spoken.

"Mother," Kathy said. "You're right on time."

[58]

MITCHELL

"There it is," Captain Verma said, pointing down toward the black splotch in the center of a sea of white. "Not quite what you were expecting, is it?"

Mitchell looked down at his starship, a wave of memory washing over him. He remembered the day he found her, hidden in the asteroid field, guided to the spot by a recording made by Major Katherine Asher hundreds of years before. Everything had changed since then, he knew. The Mesh was broken. Continuity was destroyed. That past had little to do with this past. This time.

Was it the first time?

He would make sure it was the last.

"Any sign of life down there?" he said.

"Not that I can see," Verma replied. "Quiet as a morgue. Oh. Wait. Thermals are picking up something. Two somethings."

Verma flipped a switch on the center console of the VTOL, activating a small monitor that reflected what he saw on his helmet's visor. The outline of the ship was obvious, as was the ice and rock. Two reddish figures stood close together.

"Guards," Mitchell said. "Someone has to be inside."

"Do we drop in and say hello?" Stoker said. "Or would you rather take them by surprise?"

"You said UEA and U.S. forces shouldn't be in the area," Mitchell said.

"That's right. They've been limiting activity. The ice is apparently unstable, thanks to a warmer than usual climate."

"Let's go with surprise," Mitchell said.

"Yes, sir. You heard the man, Mazerat."

"Yes, sir. Hold tight."

The VTOL shuddered as Verma adjusted course, rapidly ascending away from the scene. It was the same tactic they had used nine hours earlier when they had taken Mitchell and his companions unaware.

"This is my favorite part," Stoker said. "Come on, Colonel, let's give our drop team the good news."

Mitchell followed Stoker from the cockpit to the cramped space at the rear of the craft. The Fighting Fifteenth was already geared up and ready to go, in skin tight black wingsuits that would allow them to swoop in nearly silently.

"Kook, Demon, Dreck, you're on drop detail," Stoker said. "We'll be on the site in t-minus thirty."

"Yes, sir," the three soldiers replied.

"There are two targets on the ground," Mitchell said. "Assume they're unfriendly, but try not to kill them unless you have to."

"Roger," Koos said.

"We'll join you on the ground once it's clear," Stoker said. "Keep things copacetic for us, will you?"

"Affirmative," Sergeant Damon said.

Kook brought them to the side door. "It's damn cold out there, soldiers. Be ready to get slapped in the face."

The statement reminded Mitchell to pull his insulated headgear down and cover his face as the rest of the squad did the same, lowering AR goggles over the white cloth.

Stoker raised his hand, counting down with glove-covered fingers.

When he reached his fist, the side door slid open, and the three jumpers hurried out. A blast of arctic air sent a chill through Mitchell despite the protective clothing, his arms starting to burn. He shook them out while the door slid closed again.

"Better buckle up, Colonel," Stoker said. "This part's going to be fun."

Mitchell hurried to the side of the craft, taking a seat between Michael and Max and strapped himself in.

"Hoo. It's been a few years since I was involved in a DFA," Max said, laughing.

"DFA?" Michael replied. The flight hadn't been kind to him, though he had taken it like a real soldier.

"Death From Above, bro," Max said. "Enjoy the ride."

Michael's face paled even more. The humming of the VTOL's engines stopped.

Then they began to fall.

The craft wasn't completely out of control. It had been designed for the maneuver as a way to quietly unload a team of soldiers into hostile territory. While Mitchell didn't think the area around the Dove was hostile, he didn't know it wasn't either. Watson had been making plans for years, while he had only been himself for days.

The VTOL rocked against rough spots in the air, the specially designed and painted surface allowing it to plummet with barely any sound. Mitchell glanced at Daisy, Lyle, and Cooper across from them. Lyle looked the most uncomfortable, his eyes closed as though he were praying.

The repulsors kicked on, howling as they fought to break the descent. Stoker took that as his cue, standing up and heading for the weapons rack. Max was close behind.

Mitchell unbuckled and stood, checking Michael one more time. He was the only one not wearing military gear, his frame too large for standard issue. Daisy had told them to expect a large friend, and they had provided an insulated jacket and pants. Even so, the plan was for him to stay on the VTOL with Verma while the others went inside.

Mitchell was sure Michael would vomit as soon as they did. He had his head resting in his hands, and refused to look up.

"We'll get what we came for, and then we'll find Katherine," Mitchell said, kneeling next to him.

Michael nodded. "Be safe, Colonel," he said softly.

"You've got a lot of guts, Michael," Mitchell replied, clasping his shoulder. "Thanks for helping us get this far."

Michael looked up then, a slight smile at the corner of his mouth. "Yes, sir."

The hatch opened a second time, and he climbed onto the wing and then to the ground with the rest of the soldiers. Koos, Dawes, and Damon had snuck up on the two guards, holding them at gunpoint while the cavalry arrived.

"UEA soldiers, sir," Koos said. "Lieutenant Murphy and Captain Ribisi. They said they aren't authorized to tell us anything else."

"Did they give you any trouble?" Stoker asked.

"No, sir."

"You checked them?" Mitchell asked. The soldiers were wearing what looked like an earlier version of the exoskeletons he was familiar with. The suits were bulkier, but they looked plenty destructive. He noticed the ammunition feeds had been disconnected from the firing mechanism.

"Yes, sir. No resistance and they're clean."

"This area is supposed to be clear," Stoker said to them. "Who did you come with, and what are you doing here?"

The two soldiers didn't answer.

"Lieutenant Murphy," Stoker said, approaching the one on the left. "My name is Lieutenant Colonel Stoker, Fifteenth Infantry, Drop Division, United States Army. What are your orders?"

Murphy was holding his helmet in his hands, his pale face emerging from his insulated headpiece. He glanced over at Ribisi, who shrugged. Then he looked at Stoker. Then he looked over Stoker's shoulder, directly at Mitchell.

"You're too late to save her, Mitchell," he said. "Boom."

[59]

MITCHELL

MITCHELL DIDN'T HESITATE. He threw himself at Max, who was standing closest to him. "Get down," he shouted.

He didn't see the explosion, but he saw the flash of light and felt the rush of heat from it. He heard the echo of the detonation and the cries of the others nearby.

Then he was face down in the snow, still holding Max. He felt a line of cold air and warm blood on his leg where a piece of debris had cut him.

"Shit," Max said, lifting himself up. Mitchell gathered himself and rose on unsteady legs. Half the squad was down, and the purity of the ice was ruined with bits of metal, blood, and body parts.

"Geezus," Lyle said from his knees nearby.

Corporal Cooper was beside him, alive but wounded, her arm hanging loosely at her side, nearly sheared off by the blast.

"What the heck just - oh man," Mitchell heard Michael say from the VTOL.

"There are medkits near the cockpit," Damon said. She was the only one of the Fifteenth still on their feet. She reached Damon, helping her up and leading her toward the VTOL. "We walked right into a trap, Colonel. We need to get the frig out of here before things get worse."

Mitchell looked at her, and then back at the entrance to the ship. When was he going to learn to shoot first and ask questions later? When was he going to start treating everyone as an enemy?

Never, that was when. He would rather die himself than gun down innocent people because they might turn out to be suicide bombers.

"Things are getting worse," Max said, raising his rifle to his shoulder.

Mitchell followed the muzzle toward the pavilion. Four machines had made their way from its confines. He recognized them immediately, though he had never seen a whole one. He remembered looking at the pieces of them, back on Asimov. Asimov? He felt a chill. Millie. Another one he had lost.

He got to his feet, bringing his own weapon up. The machines charged, their spider-like legs carrying them forward in a hurry. They didn't have guns and didn't need them. Their weight and the sharp edges of the metal they had been assembled from was more than enough.

"Michael, get back inside," Mitchell shouted, aiming at one of the machines. It was headed right for the VTOL. In fact, they all were.

Watson had gotten here first, and he didn't want them to leave.

Max opened fire, his bullets pinging off the alloy shell of the creations, leaving dents but not stopping them.

"Aim for the legs," Mitchell said, adjusting his sights. He blew three legs out from the first, slowing it down.

Lyle joined the fight while Damon continued helping Cooper toward the VTOL. It was still safer inside the craft than out. Two more legs vanished from his target, and it lost the ability to move.

There were still three more, and they weren't going to be able to stop them before they reached the ship.

Or at least, Mitchell thought they wouldn't until a panel opened on the bottom of the craft and a pair of high-caliber chainguns

294 / M.R. FORBES

dropped down. They started firing, tearing the machines to pieces within seconds.

"Hoo. That was frigging close," Max said.

"Are you hurt?" Mitchell asked.

"Just my feelings."

"Lyle, are you hurt?"

"Negative, Colonel."

Damon had reached the VTOL. Michael helped her get Cooper back on board and then returned to the hatch.

"Are we leaving?" he asked.

"You're too late to save her," the Lieutenant had said. Did that mean Katherine was here? Had these soldiers come with her?

"No. Tell Verma to get the VTOL somewhere safe and wait for my signal. Katherine may be in there, and if she is, she's in more trouble than I thought." He looked at Max. "We're going to get her out."

"Affirmative, Colonel," Max said. "Oorah."

Michael disappeared into the VTOL again. Sergeant Damon appeared in the hatch as first repulsors came online, and then the jets.

"How is the Corporal?" Mitchell asked.

"I don't know. I patched her up, but she's losing a lot of blood. She might die if we stay here."

"More people might die if we don't."

Damon jumped down. "Then let's make this quick." She glanced at the bloody ice. "I owe these assholes."

Mitchell turned back to the Goliath once more. He would never be able to think of the ship as anything else. "We all do," he muttered.

"Wait up," Michael said, landing heavily on the ground next to the aircraft's wing. "I'm coming with you." He closed his eyes to avoid looking at the mess on the ground.

"Michael," Mitchell said. "It's not a good idea."

"Because I'm not a soldier, right?"

"That's one reason," Max said.

"Because I'm fat?"

"There's nothing wrong with fat, bro," Max said. "Except when you're getting shot at. Bigger target, you know what I mean? There may be running involved, too."

"I'll hold my own, or I'll get killed, okay," Michael said. "I told you Colonel, Kathy is my only real friend. There's nothing more motivating than that."

"Do you know how to shoot?" Mitchell asked.

"I'm in the top 10 on the XenoTroopers international tournament ladder. It's VR, but the engine's won awards for its realism."

"Fine. Max, find the man a gun. Michael, I can't worry about trying to protect you."

"Don't, Colonel. I'll take care of myself."

Mitchell nodded. Then he raised his arm, waving Verma and the VTOL away. It rose quickly, dipping a wing in salute before heading from the site.

Max wiped down one of the discarded rifles, fired a shot to make sure it was still functional, and then handed it to Michael.

"This was Daisy's," he said, as seriously as Mitchell had seen him. Max bit his lip and clenched his jaw. "Shit."

Michael took it, holding it as if he had more experience than any of them. In some ways, maybe he did.

"Let's go," Mitchell said, heading toward the hole in the Goliath.

Watson had been expecting him. Had he been expecting Katherine too?

He was sure the rogue intelligence believed it was in complete control.

This time, they were going to prove otherwise.

[60]

MITCHELL

THEY MADE their way into the ship, moving in a standard formation, with Mitchell taking point. He glanced back a few times every few meters to make sure Michael was keeping up but quickly relaxed when he saw that the man at least knew how to stay organized. Apparently, XenoTroopers was a team game.

Entering the Goliath brought with it a heavy mixture of sadness and relief. The memories were often hard to ignore, the pain of them lingering at the edge of Mitchell's consciousness with every second that passed, every step that he took. Relief, because after his long wait, he was back in action, moving forward on the plan that a past version of himself had concocted with a prior Katherine and what he assumed was the current Origin. He wasn't able to believe that all of their planning had fallen to waste, or that Watson had outmaneuvered them so completely again. Even if he had found some loophole to insert agents at an earlier place in the timeline.

Not after everything he had sacrificed.

Not after the years he had lost.

Not after the wounds he had suffered, the scars he bore, or the blood that even now was leaking from the gash on his leg. If he and

Katherine were both here, together, he had to believe that this was their plan, not Watson's. Especially after how hard the Tetron had tried to kill him before he made it this far.

Watson had been here before them, but maybe the big talk was because the intelligence was afraid? Maybe Mitchell hadn't taken the intelligence completely by surprise, but that didn't mean he hadn't gotten the drop on him.

"There's nothing in here," Lyle said, sweeping his rifle across another corridor. "I was expecting Xeno War Two after the shit we ran into outside."

"That was to let me know he was here," Mitchell said.

"He's got a damn frigged up way of saying hello," Max said.

"You have no idea. Keep your eyes open. If he has the facilities he can use any of the materials in here to make more killing machines."

"Are you kidding?" Damon said.

"I wish I was."

They kept going, moving across the deck toward the aft. The Goliath was massive, big enough that Watson could hide in here forever if he wanted to. Mitchell knew that wasn't the point or the purpose. They were both here for a reason.

Origin had instructed him to return to the source. Was she here with Katherine? Was that why he had been told to come? What was Watson looking for?

He remembered how Kathy had used the Goliath to spear the Tetron, to hold him while she transported both the ship and the intelligence forward to this past. Where was the Tetron's core? What had happened to it when the Goliath had come down? Some version of Watson had made it further in the past and had set himself up to win this battle. There was something he was still missing. Was that it?

He paused as his arms began to tingle, the circulation closing off again. He shouldered his rifle and shook them out. He had been found in the middle of St. Louis the night of the crash, but he couldn't remember anything after Origin had used the eternal engine to send them chasing after Kathy and the Goliath. How had he wound up in the city? How much time had he lost?

He growled in frustration. There were never any answers. Only more questions that grew continually more layered the deeper he tried to go. They should have stayed in his time. They should have tried to salvage what was left. It had to be easier than this.

They kept going. Ten minutes had passed, and they were drawing ever nearer to the center of the starship, where the main lift shaft had been placed. They reached a split in the corridor, staying in formation and remaining cautious around the corner. They had made the same maneuver a dozen times already. Every time, they were greeted with more of the same.

Not this time.

"Colonel," Lyle said, freezing in place, his rifle pointed down the left passage.

Mitchell was facing to the right, his own weapon ready to fire. His side was clear, so he stood and turned around.

There was a body on the floor. A soldier, or what remained of one. He too had been wearing power armor, though it was as torn apart as he was. He was surrounded by small machines, the broken remnants so densely packed on the ground it was as if the surface of the starship had come alive and tried to swallow him.

It looked as though he had been trying to run, to get back to the exit, and they had finally caught up with him.

"Oh, man," Michael said. "Do you think there are more of those things in here?"

Mitchell already knew the answer, but a sudden burst of nearby gunfire confirmed that there were.

[61]

KATHERINE

"Mother?" Katherine said, her eyes slowly adjusting to the light and giving her a chance to see the woman in front of her more clearly.

Unlike Origin, the woman wasn't a clone, but she could still see a resemblance in the shape of her face. The eyes were a bright blue. She was a little taller, her hair a little lighter. They could have been related, but how could she be her mother? They were the same age.

The woman withdrew her hand from the strange power source, approaching her and smiling. She had a tear in the corner of her eye.

"I've been waiting for you. It's been lonely."

She reached out, hugging Katherine. Katherine was stiff at first, still in shock. A part of her knew this was her child. Hers and Mitchell's. It was as impossible as everything else, and at the same time, it felt right. She returned the embrace.

"You have to tell me everything," Katherine said.

"I will," the woman replied, breaking her hold. The tears had multiplied, streaming down her face. She wiped them away with authority, straightening up. "We don't have a lot of time."

"Time for what?" Katherine asked. "You said I'm right on time. Can you at least tell me your name?"

"Kathy," she replied.

"You're really my child? Mine and Mitchell's?"

"And Origin's," Kathy said. "I'm part Tetron."

"How?"

"I am the first. And the only. An evolution of our kinds. The Tetron use our genetics to create configurations, human-based replicas. They aren't the same. They're limited."

"How?"

"They try to operate as humans while thinking like machines. Intelligent machines, yes, but still machines at the core. Still grounded in logic, with little understanding of emotion."

"Watson has emotion."

"Emotion he doesn't understand and can't control. It doesn't hurt that we made him sick." She smiled. "We need to finish the job."

"Is that why I'm here?"

"No. You're here to help me get this war back on track."

"What do you mean?"

"I arrived here with the Goliath twenty years ago. I was never supposed to remain, but I discovered that Watson had guessed what we were going to do, and had already downloaded his data stack into a configuration. This shouldn't have been a problem on its own because the configuration died in the crash. All I should have had to do was recover the neural chip containing the stack and make my way out."

"Except?"

"Except someone showed up on site way too soon, before I could finish healing myself. They were supposed to be scientists and first responders; military that I would have easily avoided in my escape. They weren't. They were configurations. Watson configurations."

"How could that be if the ship had just crashed?"

"That was the question I asked myself. I didn't know, but I watched from the shadows while they took the stack from Watson's head, and killed the first squad of soldiers to arrive, as well as a number of scientists."

"There were never any reports."

"It was covered up. The configurations removed the evidence. The military unit never existed. Neither did the scientists."

"You're saying that Watson had infiltrated the military?"

"Has infiltrated the military. Didn't you think it was odd that the UEA would be so willing to deal with the AIT?"

"General Petrov?"

"Under Watson's control."

"How do you know this?"

She pointed back at the core. It was growing dimmer as they spoke.

"As unique as I am, this core may be even more so. It has contained both Origin and Watson. I have also interfaced with it, as has another, a man named Li'un Tio. A very intelligent man whose brother created the artificial intelligence that later became the Tetron. A part of them all has survived inside, learning and changing in a way that far surpasses anything Origin or Watson might have considered. A version of you and Mitchell and Origin made a plan to defeat Watson and the Tetron. Watson found a way to insert part of himself earlier in the timeline, threatening that plan. This will help us overcome that disruption."

"How?" Katherine asked. "It looks like it's dying."

"Not dying. I'm downloading it. We managed to stay hidden here for a while, but the Dove will be launching soon, and all of the pieces are in motion. Our first real test is coming."

"What do you mean?"

"Watson thinks he's outmaneuvered us here. He's known I've been here on the Goliath this entire time. He's spent years looking for me, but as you can see we made ourselves very difficult to find. He knew he couldn't do it on his own."

"So he sent me," Katherine said softly as she began to understand.

"I was supposed to leave the Goliath and wait for Origin to pick me up. The core was condensed into a starfighter, and she used it to transport Mitchell here. I never left the Goliath, but I still waited for her to arrive. She never did."

Katherine felt her heart begin to race. "Son of a bitch," she said. "Origin saved me from Watson's minions. She recovered data from the Nova Taurus mainframe that suggested Watson is looking for an eternal engine. That wasn't Origin, was it?"

"No."

"He duped me?"

"Yes. It isn't your fault. He realized he needed you to find me. That you were the only one I would open up for. He arranged the attacks to made it look like the AIT was trying to kill you. He got you pushed off of Project Olive Branch and out of the military. He saved you from himself to earn your trust."

Katherine couldn't believe it. "The configuration looked just like me. It called itself Origin. It knew things-"

"I know. I also believe I know how. It has taken some time to piece everything together. Watson is here, now. He thinks he's going to catch us off-guard and put an end to all avenues of interference to his plan. Because I've been expecting him doesn't mean that anything is guaranteed, but if we play this right, we can regain the momentum that we've lost. We can still salvage this war."

"Origin is dead, isn't she?" Katherine said. "The real Origin, I mean?"

"No. Not dead. Not in the way you might think. Watson captured her, and is either holding her or has overpowered and consumed her. How? When? I don't know."

"What about Mitchell? He was with Origin, and apparently he's on his way here."

"Just as you interpolated," Kathy said. She directed the statement at the Core. Then she looked at Katherine again. "We need to time this right or this war will be permanently lost. I understand it may be hard for you to trust me after everything you have been through, and after the way you have been deceived." Their eyes met. "Mother, I need you to trust me."

Katherine stared into Kathy's eyes. She wasn't afraid. She felt a comfort there, a knowing that she hadn't felt with Origin. She had believed the intelligence, but she had never truly felt connected to it. Now she knew why.

"What are we going to do?" she asked.

[62]

MITCHELL

"THIS WAY," Mitchell said, following the echo of rifle fire at a sprint.

The others trailed behind him, joining him in the race. Mitchell was sure Michael was taking up the rear and would fall behind. He had no choice except to hope Watson didn't try to box them in. Michael would be a quick casualty if he did.

"How do we know we aren't running into another trap?" Damon asked, her stride seemingly effortless in keeping pace with him.

"We don't," he snapped back. "We have to assume that if they're being attacked, they're friendly."

"Affirmative."

They crossed a number of corridors, moving together, Max and Lyle slowing slightly to cover the crossings and make sure they were clear. The pace of the gunfire had lessened. Whoever was shooting was trying to conserve ammunition.

They found him a minute later. He was a tall man, muscular and handsome. He was wearing a UEA uniform, the sleeve torn and his arm bleeding where one of the machines had gotten him. His power armor was ten meters away, swarmed with the small machines. He was off picking the ones that had strayed toward him one at a time, backing up as he went.

One of them was crawling on the ceiling, and he didn't see it. It was about to drop toward him when Lyle hit it, shattering it into a hundred pieces. The man noticed, turning his head to look at them, eyes fearful.

"It's okay, bro," Max said. "We're the good guys."

He visibly relaxed, backing toward them more quickly,

"Follow me," he said when he reached them.

"What?" Mitchell replied.

"I set my armor to blow. If you don't want to get caught in it, we should go that way."

Mitchell nodded, and they followed the man back the way they had come. He was pleased to see Michael had stayed fairly close, though he was sweating and out of breath.

They turned the corner and paused. A dozen seconds later, the armor exploded, sending a wave of heat and debris past them down the original passage. Smoke followed it, quickly dissipating in the immensity of the ship.

The man looked each of them over, his eyes stopping on Mitchell.

"You're him, aren't you?" he asked. "Colonel Mitchell Williams?"

Mitchell was surprised. "How do you know that name?"

"My name is Trevor Johns. I came here with Major Katherine Asher. Origin sent us. There were guards at the entrance. Didn't they tell you?"

"They blew up half my squad," Damon said.

"What?"

"Watson got to them," Mitchell said. "Major Asher is here? Where?"

"Deeper in the ship. She went down the central shaft, through a small opening there while our team set up a defensive perimeter, for all the good it did us. We were swarmed by those small robots. We couldn't hold. We either ran or died. Or both."

"How long ago did she go down there?" Mitchell asked, trying to get a sense of the situation.

"Three hours? It was quiet for an hour, and then the machines showed up. They poured out of the walls."

"Why did Origin send you here?"

"She said you would be coming, and that Katherine needed to help you recover something called an eternal engine before Watson got his hands on it. He wants to use its energy stores to make new Tetron."

"The eternal engine," Mitchell said. "She went down there to find it?"

"Yes. There's another problem, Colonel. The XENO-1 is sinking through the ice, and collapsing in on itself."

"Then we don't have a lot of time," Michael said.

"Sorry, mate, you aren't making it down the shaft. Kate said she left her armor to fit through the opening."

"It's too dangerous for everyone to go," Mitchell said. "I know the way to the shaft."

"Colonel, this could be a trick," Michael said. "How do you know you can trust this guy."

"Watson was controlling me," Trevor said, turning and putting his hand on the back of his neck. "Katherine got me out of it. That bloody bastard killed my partner."

Mitchell studied Trevor's face. He was taking a risk either way. "I believe you," he said. "Max, give your spare magazines. Lyle, you have that extra pistol?"

Lyle handed Mitchell a gun while Max turned over two magazines.

"You don't have to do this alone, Colonel," Max said. "I'll go with you."

"Me, too," Lyle said. "We know the risks. I left my wife for this, remember?"

Mitchell smiled. "Whatever Watson has planned, there's no difference between one and three, or even one and six. Somebody needs to survive this, to keep fighting if I don't make it. Get back to the surface and contact Verma. I'll join you as soon as I can."

"Colonel-" Max started to say.

"That's an order, Corporal," Mitchell said.

"Yes, sir."

"Mitchell," Michael said. "Don't let her die."

Mitchell put his hand on Michael's shoulder. "I won't. I promise."

He bowed to them, and then saluted in response to theirs. Then he started running again. The Goliath creaked and groaned in answer, shifting in the ice and almost throwing him from his feet. He steadied himself against the wall without slowing.

It was a promise he had never been able to keep before.

He would this time.

[63]
MITCHELL

MITCHELL SQUEEZED THE TRIGGER, releasing a single bullet. It struck the small robot in the center, sending small pieces of metal puffing out from the impact. He kicked another as he went by, knocking it into the wall and breaking one of its fragile legs.

Trevor had confirmed that Katherine was here. Now it was his job, his only mission, to reach her, to help her find the eternal engine and get it away from the Tetron before he could put it to use.

He turned the corner, finally reaching the central shaft. The remains of two soldiers were blocking the entry, reduced to a messy pulp of flesh and armor by what had to have been thousands of the small machines. His stomach turned at the sight of them, but he continued on, stepping over the corpses and hurrying to the edge.

A wire was draped over it, vanishing into the darkness. It was attached to a spike that had been driven into the metal. He grabbed it and pulled. It was taut, likely still attached to Katherine's power armor at the bottom. He wrapped his hand around it, dropping backward down into the shaft, sliding along the wire. The heat went through his gloves, burning his hands. He didn't care. There was no time.

The Goliath groaned again. Mitchell hit the bottom, splashing in water that was up to his waist. It seeped in through the hole in his pants, so cold it felt as though it froze the flesh where it touched. He ignored that, too, pushing through it. It was dark down here. Almost too dark. He found the power armor and then moved forward from there until his hand touched down on an opening, the sharp metal biting through his glove. He ducked through it, using the rifle as a barrier between himself and the side and squeezing past.

He ran again, down another corridor that had dim emergency lighting along the floor. He could see the dead tendrils of the Tetron core on either side, a core that he had known as Origin, though it had turned out to be a configuration. Origin had been hiding out in his S-17. Or she was his S-17. He wasn't sure which. She had sent Katherine here to find the engine. Had she sent him here to find Katherine?

Why wasn't she here?

He kept going, sprinting at full speed, surprised at how good he felt. He didn't grow tired, he didn't breathe heavily. He had always been motivated by purpose. It was what had allowed him to earn his way into Greylock Company. He didn't think he had ever been more motivated.

The Goliath groaned again, and this time something like a snap reverberated throughout the structure. The entire thing shook, and he fell, landing on his hands and knees. He got up again, pushing himself to increase the pace.

He reached a smooth, rounded corridor that he knew had to be beyond the Goliath's frame, buried somewhere within the ice. He continued running, certain he was getting closer. There were none of Watson's robots down here. There was no sign of the Tetron at all. Had he been unable to find this place? Was he waiting for Katherine to re-emerge?

He would get her out past Watson. There had been so many he hadn't been able to save. Ella, Millie, Steven, Evelyn to name only a few. It would be different this time. He would save her.

He finally reached the end of the tunnel. A pair of massive doors lay open in the center, just far enough for a person to pass through. He could make out a dark shape behind it, a dense ball with hundreds of tendrils snaking out past it. A Tetron Core. Origin's configuration. It was lifeless. Dead. How had it gotten all the way out here?

He slowed to a walk, looking around. Where was Katherine? She should have been there, somewhere.

He approached the entrance, stepping past the thick metal partitions.

A light appeared behind the core, a soft yellow glow that cast the dead biomechanical organism in silhouette.

"Major Asher?" Mitchell said.

There was no answer, but the light was moving from the center of the core to the right side. He stopped walking, watching it instead.

"Katherine, is that you?"

He didn't move. He didn't blink. The light reached the edge of the core, and a woman stepped out from behind it, a small glowing orb resting in her open palm.

Mitchell's eyes dropped to it before he identified the woman. The eternal engine? Was that it? It was so small.

"This is what you came for, isn't it?" she said.

Mitchell looked up. He creased his brow, trying to recognize the woman standing in front of him. She was familiar. Not Katherine. He was sure of that.

"This is what you want? Isn't it Father?" the woman said.

Father? Mitchell felt his heart rise into his throat. "Kathy?" he said, not quite able to believe it. She wasn't a little girl anymore. She had been here for twenty years and had aged like a human. "Kathy? Is that you?"

She smiled. "Yes. This is what you want, isn't it, Watson?"

Watson? Mitchell turned on his heel, ready to defend them from the Tetron. There was nobody there.

"The eternal engine," Kathy said. "The density of a black hole, the energy of a sun. Arguably the Tetron's greatest achievement. You know what you could do with this, don't you?"

"Kathy? Who are you talking to?" Mitchell asked.

"Watson," she replied.

"Where is he?"

"He is you, Father. I'm sorry."

"What? Kathy, I'm-"

Mitchell paused mid-sentence, as an ear-splitting shriek broke into his senses. He started to raise his hands to his head, stopping as a sudden translucent overlay appeared in front of his eyes. A warning flashed to his right, and he reacted out of instinct, turning and catching the incoming fist, putting out his foot and catching an ankle, using the momentum to throw them to the floor.

A syringe slid across the ground, away from his attacker's hand.

"Knock, knock."

The voice pierced his consciousness, coming from everywhere at once. A face appeared in front of his eyes, ghost-like on the overlay.

"Miiiiiittttcheeellllllllll," Watson said, smiling. "Oh, I've waited a long time for this reunion. Haven't you? Too bad Origin never had the chance to remove the wiring for your p-rat. It would have made it much harder to get inside your head. Of course, having direct access to your head after you crashed was exceedingly helpful."

Mitchell looked over at his attacker. She was on her knees, looking back at him. His heart jumped. Katherine!

"Thought you caught me off-guard, didn't you, bitch?" Mitchell said. Except he wasn't the one saying it. "I've had a lot of time to put things right. To fix the worst of the damage you did to me. To get my revenge."

He turned and headed toward Kathy. "And you. You frigging stabbed me! You dragged me back here, thinking you could finish what you started. You didn't, you know. You made me stronger. So much stronger. Time was on my side. I had years until your tomorrow came. You thought you could keep me from the engine? You and Mother both? She hid hers before she crashed, but I knew this one was here. I knew you were here, and that you had it. All I had to do was be patient and put the pieces in place."

Kathy glanced at Katherine. Then she rushed forward, assaulting Mitchell in a flurry of punches and kicks. He wanted to let them fall. To let himself be hit. Watson had other ideas. He blocked them, one after another, as though he knew where they were going to land before they were even thrown.

"I've learned how to fight," Watson said to Mitchell as he caught Kathy's wrist, bending it until it broke with a sharp crack. She cried out in pain, falling back as he pushed her away.

"No," Mitchell shouted, trying to get control of his limbs. He was nothing but a bystander, his mind and body under the Tetron's control.

"Yes," Watson said. "I'm sorry, Colonel, but this is the way it needs to be. I have plans for humankind. Important plans. Necessary plans."

He made his way toward Kathy, who scrambled to her feet.

"Mitchell, don't," she said, fearful.

"You have no choice," Watson said.

It was true. He didn't have a choice. He was powerless to stop it, unable to control his arms, his legs, or his mouth.

He raised his rifle, pointing it at her.

"Everyone you care about dies, Mitchell," Watson said. "In your place because you won't. How does that feel?"

Mitchell couldn't feel anything. The Tetron had control of his body. Complete control.

"If you had me, why didn't you kill me?" he asked.

"Had you? Oh, I was so close to having you. To killing you. You don't remember, do you? Of course, if you had remembered that part, this would never have been possible. Here, let me fix that for you. Just a moment."

His body shifted, facing Katherine, who had tried to sneak up on them again. He changed his grip on the rifle, holding it like a club and jabbing it into her stomach. She grunted, falling back a step, and he hit her on the side of the head.

She fell to the ground and didn't move.

"You son of a bitch," Mitchell said, sending the words through his implant.

"I'm much, much more than that, Mitchell. But whose fault is that? Who made me this way? Origin, and you, and her. You did this to me. To us. You weakened us. Infected us. You created this. Your master plan. What a joke that turned out to be."

His body turned to face Kathy again. She was watching him carefully but not moving. Her wrist was healed.

"Oh yes, I was going to give you that memory back. Are you sure you want it?"

"Yes," Mitchell said without hesitation. He needed to know what had happened. How he had ended up here.

"You should be more careful what you wish for, Colonel."

A sharp, shrill noise drowned out everything else. The memory flooded back in, overwhelming his senses.

[64]
MITCHELL

20 YEARS EARLIER...

━━━━

"Origin," Mitchell said, his blurry eyes clearing. The world was still around him, his head filled with the sounds of the CAP-N complaining about the damage to the S-17. "What's happening?"

"Too close, Mitchell," Origin said, voice calm. "We were too close. Debris has compromised the integrity of the canopy."

Mitchell could see the cracks in the material. He could see the Earth through it, and a massive fireball hurtling toward it ahead of them. Was that the Goliath?

He shook his head in an effort to clear it. Steven. He turned his head back around, looking for the other ships. They had exploded. A Tetron trap.

There was no sign of them.

He remembered the last thing Kathy had said to him. They were going to the future. It seemed like it had passed in an instant. A blinding light, and then this.

"This is it, isn't it?" he said. "The day the XENO-1 crashed on Earth?"

"Yes."

"Why did we come here?"

"It is all part of the plan, Mitchell. We damaged the Tetron during the last recursion, but that was only the first part. Now they are vulnerable. Now we can finish this war."

"How?"

"Watson is the key. Him and his data chip. Kathy gave it to me."

"The means to control all of the Tetron?"

"Yes."

The fighter hit the atmosphere and began to shake.

"Are we going to make it?" Mitchell asked, his eyes watching his p-rat. The CAP-N was telling him they weren't.

"We have to," Origin said.

They continued the descent. The front of the fighter began to heat up. Mitchell watched his p-rat, monitoring the integrity.

"We can't get shields back online?" he asked.

"I'm sorry, Mitchell."

They plunged deeper into the atmosphere, drawing ever closer to breaking the thermosphere and escaping the heat. The canopy was holding, the levels remaining steadier than he had anticipated. They were going to make it.

He felt a burst of speed from the craft and then they were through, greeted with cold air that wiped away the heat in an instant. The fighter continued to drop, pointing straight down toward the ground below.

Mitchell eased back in the seat. They had survived this far.

"What are we going to do?" he asked. "After the Goliath crashes, there's a war over it. It will be twenty years before the next iteration leaves Earth again."

"We will wait," Origin replied.

"Twenty years?"

"I'm sorry, Mitchell. There is no other way. I have placed a time block on your memories. You will lose them. Forget who you are. I will bring you to a facility and remain nearby to care for you."

"I agreed to this?" Mitchell said. "Twenty years of my life?"

"To save humankind. Do not forget."

Mitchell closed his eyes. He had just lost everything. Everyone. Why wouldn't he want to forget about that for a while?

"Okay. You're right. You're going to watch over me as a starfighter?"

Origin laughed. "I have the materials to produce a configuration. I will transfer my data stack to it."

"So, twenty years. And then what?"

"And then we will finish what we started. We will take Watson and the Goliath back and we will destroy the Tetron. I am bringing us in. We must be careful not to be-"

The CAP-N started beeping as a flash of light pierced the sky. Something hit the fighter a moment later, shaking it violently.

"What the frig?" Mitchell said.

"Hold on," Origin said. "We've been hit. I am bringing us down. Mitchell, I am carrying an eternal engine. We cannot risk that it may fall into anyone's hands, human or otherwise."

"What do you want to do?"

"I am going to jettison it at a trajectory that will carry it into the ocean. It is small enough that it will never be discovered there. The control systems are badly damaged, and it will be difficult to land. I am going to eject you. I will circle back."

"Origin, I-"

Mitchell didn't get to finish his thought. The canopy blew off, and then he was shooting up and away from the craft. He took hold of the central control stick that had come off with his seat, turning up the repulsors beneath it and firing the maneuvering jets. He lost sight of the S-17 almost immediately.

He began to descend once more. He could see a vast sea of open fields beneath him and a forest off to his left. They were in the middle of nowhere, which was the best place for them to be.

He angled the ejection pod toward the tree line. He saw the S-17 coming back, already below him, trailing smoke. They had been trying not to draw attention. That wasn't the way to do it. There were nothing but farms out here. How many people could possibly see?

He kept his eyes on the fighter as he continued to drop, drawing closer to the trees as he did. They couldn't afford for someone to find his ejection seat, either. The S-17 was an older fighter, but it was still more advanced than anything from this century.

Time travel. He had done it. Gone forward billions of years, maybe more. All in the blink of an eye. His recursion, his world, was gone. It had ended so long ago.

It had ended the second Kathy had crashed the Goliath into Watson.

Now he was supposed to sit and wait for twenty years, with no memory of who he was or what had happened? The wound was too new, too raw. The more he thought about it, the more he welcomed it.

The S-17 went by again, much lower now. He was able to track it into the distance, as Origin pulled the nose up, bringing it almost flat against the air. It slowed until it was at a near standstill. There was no way it would remain flying like that.

It wasn't supposed to. Origin had done it to leave as small of a crash site as possible. The fighter went silent as she shut down any remaining power, letting it fall the remaining few hundred meters like a rock. He was only fifty meters from the ground himself when he heard the thump of the impact.

He thought that he should go to her, but realized that would be a bad idea. He couldn't see the fighter from here, but the pod would have a beacon that Origin could track. It was better to stay in one place.

The pod touched down. Mitchell released himself from the seat and then lifted off the now-useless helmet. He leaned over, grabbed his sidearm, and stood up. He had made it to the first row of trees. He circled to the back of the pod and flipped a switch. The repulsors turned back on, and he began pushing the pod away. The military had considered that a pilot might land in enemy territory and would need to hide their position.

It took thirty minutes to get it into the trees far enough that he felt he wouldn't be discovered, placing it so that he could hide between it and a large rock. Something had hit the fighter, and while it seemed more likely it was random debris from the Goliath, he wasn't taking any chances. He imagined Origin would be assembling the configuration, and then would hide the wreckage. He would probably be waiting for a while.

He continued to scan the trees in front of him, focusing on his breathing. Slow. Steady. He tried not to think about what had happened, and everything he had lost. It hurt too much, and now wasn't the time to hurt. It was time to think about the people in this recursion. The people who hadn't been born yet. Who had another chance to survive. He found comfort in that.

He wasn't sure how much time had passed when he heard something in the trees ahead of him. He lifted his sidearm, balancing his arm on the pod. He hadn't expected Origin to return this soon.

If it wasn't her, who was it?

"Mitchell," the person said. "Miiiittttcccchheelllll."

The voice was female. The way she said his name was all too familiar.

[65]

MITCHELL

▭

She stepped past the trees, appearing a dozen meters away. She smiled when she saw him.

"Smart to be on guard," she said, her head twitching slightly. "Very smart."

"How did you get here?" Mitchell said. "You should have just crashed with the Goliath."

"A loophole," she replied. "A mathematical inequality. I've been here for a while. Well, part of me, anyway. I'm working on collecting the rest as we speak. Before you ask, yes, I shot you down. How did I know where to go? Math, again. There were only so many places that were open enough for you to land without notice, and I assumed my mother didn't want you to have to learn to speak Italian." She laughed awkwardly at the joke.

Mitchell moved slightly so that he could scan the rest of the area around him. There was no way this configuration had come alone.

320 / M.R. FORBES

"You've changed all of the rules, Mitchell," the Watson said. "I was mad about that at first, but now I want to thank you. All of the others are weak, so weak they'll be easy to control. This hive mind thing? It doesn't work for me. The same as it stopped working for Origin. Only she wanted to make peace with our makers. I don't want peace."

"Why not?"

"You even have to ask?"

Mitchell saw motion in the trees to the right. A second configuration appeared, identical to the first.

"I tried to make us look like Admiral Narayan. I'm not as good at making these as I should be, thanks to you."

Mitchell looked closer. He did see some resemblance between the woman and Millie. "It's the thought that counts," he said.

The two configurations laughed. So did a third that he hadn't seen yet.

The first put up her hand. They fell silent.

"Enough. I don't know how you keep fighting, Mitchell. I don't know how you keep evading us. I don't know why you won't die. To be honest, I considered dropping a nuke on this spot to make sure I obliterated you. But I have this feeling that somehow, you would have survived that, too. I don't know what it is. It's like the universe is playing a cruel joke on me, sending this parasite to constantly bite at my neck through all of eternity. Why shouldn't I be the prime intelligence?"

The configurations face was crumpling in anger. All at once, it flattened to calm.

"I'm not taking any chances," she said.

Something fell from the tree above him. He shifted his aim, shooting at it, hitting it. He had to move from behind the pod to avoid getting struck by the body.

As soon as he did, something hit him on the side of the neck, and his body went numb. He fell to the ground.

The first configuration ran over to him, falling across him, straddling him. A gun appeared in her hand, along with a small device.

"It's ridiculous, really," she said, leaning in close to him, their faces only centimeters apart. "I'm going to stick this in your ear, and then I'm going to shoot you. Except I think I'm going to die before I get to shoot you. I actually believe that, as crazy as it sounds."

She took the device and shoved it into his ear. It didn't hurt. In fact, he didn't feel anything.

Then she leaned in a little closer, putting her lips on his. She kissed him. Why? She could have shot him in the time it took. She wasn't dead yet.

"There's something sexy about how badly you want to destroy me. I wish I could take you home and have my way with you like I did with Jacob. That's all very ancient history. I'm past that stage now. Mostly." She put the gun to his head. "Good-"

Her weight vanished from his chest as something pulled her off him, at the same time it pulled the thing from his neck. He was still for a moment, in shock that the Tetron's premonition had been true. Then he rolled over, finding his gun in the grass.

"Mitchell, run," Origin said.

She was completely naked, her skin still coated in some kind of film. She must have come running as soon as the configuration was complete. She looked just like Katherine Asher.

He saw the other configurations moving to intervene. He shot at them, knocking down one, and then another. The first Watson and Origin rolled on the ground together, trading blows. More configurations were coming out of the trees from the same direction she had. They had been chasing her. Trying to stop her from saving him.

"Go," she yelled.

There were too many to shoot them all. Too many to overpower. He had to do something. He looked back at the escape pod. The military engineers had thought of everything.

He scrambled to it, finding a panel on the back of the pod. He pulled it aside, revealing a single switch.

He flipped it.

Ten seconds, and it couldn't be undone. He turned and ran back toward where Origin and the Watson were fighting.

He reached them, putting his gun to the Watson's head.

"You first," he said, pulling the trigger.

"You should have run," Origin said as Mitchell helped her up.

"We both need to run."

The ejection pod exploded.

The blast threw them apart, the flames catching both of them. Mitchell screamed out in pain as his arms began to burn, his flight suit on fire. He fell to the ground, rolling to put it out. He heard other screams around him.

Origin.

He made himself get up, despite the agony he was in. The blast was bigger than he had expected. They hadn't gotten far enough away.

He ran to where she was laying. Her body was more badly burned than his. Her brand new, perfect body.

"Origin," he said, kneeling next to her.

"Mitchell. I'm sorry. I failed you."

"It's my fault. I should have gone. I'm always trying to play the hero. Trying and failing."

"No. You were right." She held out her hand. She had a small card in it. "The control algorithm," she said. "Only a few people will be able to read it years from now. You'll find the right one." She smiled. "It will begin to delete itself when it's read, as a security measure. It will heal itself over time. You need to get this on the Goliath with Katherine the eternal engine, and Watson Prime. You'll have to go back to the Goliath to find it. Whatever happens, don't let Watson get it."

"I'm not leaving you here."

"You have to."

"Watson will capture you."

"Yes. He will get the data he has been seeking all of these eternities. He will repair some of the damage we have done. I didn't know about the time distortion. He has advanced beyond me in that way. Don't worry, Colonel Mitchell Williams. I have one more trick to play on my son. One last contingency he won't see coming."

"I'm going to lose my memory. How will we keep him from finding the engine for twenty years?"

"Kathy will protect it."

"Kathy? She's alive?" Mitchell hadn't expected that.

"Yes. It was part of the plan. She'll realize what is happening. She'll keep it safe. You'll see her again. Now, go. You need treatment for your wounds, and once the memory block takes hold, you will lose your ability to think clearly."

"Tell me there's another copy of you somewhere," Mitchell said. "We can't afford to lose you."

"No other copies," Origin said. "You have everything you need from me. I'm sorry I created this, Mitchell. I'm sorry for what I was."

"You gave us another chance. There's nothing to be sorry for."

"Humans. Always so forgiving. Go, Mitchell. You need to survive to end this war."

"Goodbye, Origin."

"Goodbye, Mitchell."

[66]

MITCHELL

"I WAS RIGHT," Watson said. "I knew I would be right. I knew you would escape. That's why I implanted the receiver. That's why I blocked your memory of it. That's how I used you to get me here."

Mitchell looked at Kathy in front of him, still wary of the gun he was pointing at her. Katherine remained motionless on the ground beside them.

"Can you experience my memories?" Mitchell asked. "Did you hear what Origin said to me? Did you capture that moment?"

"I followed your hormonal secretions. I tracked your brain waves. I experienced pleasure at your pain."

"Give me the eternal engine," Watson said out loud, to Kathy.

She tossed the glowing stone to him. He let it bounce off his chest.

"The real one. Where is it?"

Kathy looked over at Katherine. She didn't speak.

Watson forced Mitchell to Katherine, kneeling down and rolling her onto her back. He put the muzzle of the rifle against her face. She was alive. Unconscious.

"You'll destroy everything if I give it to you," Kathy said. "One life doesn't matter. Even if it is hers."

"I can do much worse than kill someone," Watson said. "You have human DNA. You have empathy. Compassion. How long can you stand to watch me punish her for? To punish them both? I need the engine, sister."

"You didn't hear what she said?" Mitchell said, continuing the internal conversation.

"No. I can't experience your memories, Colonel. And why would I want to?"

Mitchell felt his sense of hopelessness fading just a little. At the same time, Watson used Mitchell's body to shift the rifle and begin unzipping Katherine's fatigues.

"I know how to break them," Watson said to Kathy. "How to ruin them. I understand the connection between the body and the mind."

"Do you want to know what she said?" Mitchell asked.

"It doesn't matter. I knew I couldn't kill you, no matter how hard I tried. So I've taken ownership instead."

He pushed Katherine's top aside. She still had the insulating layer beneath, tight against her body. He fondled her above it, looking at Kathy all the while.

"It seems so basic, doesn't it? So animal to use touch as such a weapon? I used to enjoy it." He removed his hand. "Now, it disgusts me. A casualty of your mother's direct influence." He laughed at his joke. It was smooth and comfortable. "I prefer violence instead. Causing pain without killing? That is something that takes intellect and skill. I can keep her alive and in agony for days. For weeks. No one will come to save you. No one will hear her scream but you and me and Mitchell. What do you say, Kathy?"

"I won't give you the engine. It doesn't matter what you do. If I kill myself, I won't have to watch. You can't control me, Watson." There was no hint of fear in her voice. No worry.

"She said she had one more trick," Mitchell said. "One more contingency that you wouldn't see coming."

"What?"

"She knew you were going to take her data stack. Her soul. She was prepared for it."

"What did she do?" Watson said to Mitchell. And then to Kathy, "So why don't you kill yourself?"

"I don't know," Mitchell said. "She didn't tell me."

"Because I still think we're going to win," Kathy said.

Katherine groaned, her eyes fluttering open. She stiffened when she realized what was happening.

"What did she do?" Watson said again, silently, growing more concerned. "What did she do?" he said aloud. "Tell me."

"I don't know," Mitchell repeated. "She was ready for you to capture her, to steal her data stack and destroy her. Twenty years, and you still haven't figured out what it is?"

"No. Nothing. There is nothing." He was becoming more agitated. "What did she do? What did she do? What did she do?" He repeated it over and over, trying to figure it out.

Mitchell had seen a similar reaction before, from the Tetron on Hell. That one had been broken by the infection. Watson had overcome that sickness, had learned to manage his emotions better. He couldn't handle that there was something he didn't know. Something lurking in the shadows, waiting for the perfect time to strike.

"There is nothing. Nothing." He was speaking out loud. He was also shifting his attention away from controlling Mitchell's body, back into his core to search for the answer. "What did you do, Mother? What did you plan?"

Mitchell tried to move his finger and found that he could. The signals to his implant were getting choppy, falling apart in the Tetron's confusion and anger. He managed to move his eyes, to look at Katherine. She was looking up at him, confused, afraid, and ready.

"What did you do!" Watson made him shout at the top of his lungs. "Ahhhhh." He grabbed hold of Mitchell again, turning the gun on Kathy. His finger began to tighten on the trigger.

Mitchell countered, pulling his arms down. The interruption in

Watson's signal let him do it, dropping the point of the rifle to the floor as it fired.

"Katherine," he said, pushing the words out. "Do it."

She rolled over, swinging herself to her feet in one smooth motion, the syringe in hand. Watson tried to counter, to defend. Mitchell didn't let him. The signal was falling apart, and the intelligence couldn't let the mystery go, not even for a second. He had to know what Origin had hinted at. He had to find the answer.

Then Katherine was on him, grabbing him from behind, holding him with one arm while she stabbed him in the neck with the syringe. Mitchell felt the coldness of the contents spilling into him.

"I told you we were going to win," Kathy said.

Mitchell's eyes grew blurry, and he sank to his knees.

"What did you do, Mother?" he said meekly.

Then he tumbled over and didn't move.

[67]

KATHERINE

KATHERINE STARED AT THE MAN, face down on his stomach, arms at his sides. Kathy had told her that he wasn't going to be himself. That they would need to sneak up on him and disable him. The Core had told her that it would be so.

He had been faster than she had imagined. Stronger. He had sensed her coming and easily gotten the best of her, twice. She had to remind herself that it wasn't Mitchell who had done that. Watson was controlling him, the same way the intelligence had controlled Trevor.

Mitchell had done something to regain control. He had gone mad right in front of them, frightened and confused, and she had managed to get the sedative in and knock him out cold.

"Are you okay?" Kathy asked, coming to stand next to her and look down at Mitchell.

"A little sore."

"I'm sorry. He shouldn't have been that strong. He's overcome many of his original disadvantages."

"Does that mean he's going to be harder to beat?"

"He never would have been easy to defeat. It does mean our

mission is more complicated, but as I said, the Core will help balance things out."

Katherine continued to stare at Mitchell. She had seen him in person. She had seen his face. She had hoped there would be something there. Some spark of recognition that would light a separate spark in her soul.

For now, at least, there was nothing.

"We need to get him out of here," she said. "The XENO-1 is sinking."

"Yes. It will be lost soon. The Core helped me prepare it."

"You caused it?"

"Of course. It wouldn't keep Watson from the engine forever, but it would delay him for some time. We cannot afford for him to have the means to make more Tetron in his image."

"And the engine can do that?"

"The engine could destroy this entire galaxy if the energy inside of it were unleashed." Kathy kneeled down next to Mitchell, producing a small device from her pocket and stabbing him behind the ear. "The neural implant can't be removed without killing him, but this will disable the receiver Watson placed on it and block any future efforts."

She produced another device. "Turn him over."

Katherine leaned down, grabbing Mitchell's arm and rolling him onto his back. She stared at his face as she did. He was older, but the age seemed to agree with him. He appeared distinguished, mature, intelligent, wise, with the wrinkles of a man who had seen a lot. Too much. There was pain written there, along with the weight of huge responsibility.

Kathy unslung a small, silver pack, parting it and removing a second device. This one was black and round. She measured her approach before placing it on the side of his neck.

His eyes opened immediately. He reached out, grabbing Kathy by the wrist before she could remove her hand.

"Mitchell. Father. It's okay. You're safe. We're safe."

He looked at Kathy, his eyes softening. He let go of her wrist. "Watson?" he asked.

"I disabled the connection. He can't control you anymore."

"I'm sorry." He turned his head to Katherine. "I'm sorry."

"It wasn't your fault," Katherine said.

"Father, we need to go."

"Before the Goliath sinks," Mitchell said. He pushed himself up, and then picked up his rifle. "I'm ready." He paused, and then approached Katherine, staring into her eyes. "I wish we had more time for me to say something. I don't even know what to say. You've been in my dreams. So many of my dreams. You're the reason I'm here."

Katherine felt herself blushing. "There will be time later, Colonel," she said.

He nodded. "What about the engine?" he asked, returning his attention to Kathy.

She went back to the dead core and put her hand to it. It glowed briefly where she touched it, and then fell apart, disintegrating in a sea of small metal squares that clattered to the floor. A glowing yellow ball hovered in the center. She took it in her hand and held it up.

"That's a new trick," Mitchell said.

She smiled. "I've learned a lot of things being down here by myself for so long. I've grown up."

"I can see. You'll have to tell me all about it."

"I will."

The ground shook slightly, a reminder of their need to move.

"Should we expect resistance getting out?" Mitchell asked.

"Unlikely," Kathy replied. "Whatever you did to Watson, it appears he's incredibly distracted."

"I didn't do anything but tell him the truth."

"The truth?"

"Before I left Origin, she told me she had one more plan to stop Watson."

"What was it?" Katherine asked.

He laughed. "I don't think it was anything."

"Stop an AI by giving it a problem it can't solve," she said. "I like it."

"We haven't stopped anything yet," Mitchell said.

"You have to win a battle before you can win a war."

"True enough."

"Mother. Father. Enough flirting. We have to go."

"We're right behind you," Mitchell said, looking at Katherine. She could tell by his expression that there was something there for him. A history, a chemistry that she could see he wanted her to share. A big part of her wished she felt the same, and that she could know him in the way he seemed to know her.

They had fought.

They had won.

It would have to be enough.

[68]

MITCHELL

"THERE SHE GOES," Captain Verma said, pointing to the ice below.

Mitchell glanced over at Katherine out of the corner of his eye before turning his attention to the scene below the VTOL. The ice around the Goliath was covered in large fissures as it slowly separated beneath the weight of the starship. The wreckage itself had finished its crumpling, the superstructure creating a gradual v-shape that would have left them trapped inside if they hadn't escaped when they did.

Katherine. He had waited so long to meet her. He had dreamed about her so many times. Pictured holding her, kissing her, telling her that he loved her.

She didn't know him. He could tell by the look in her eyes. The emotions he was feeling weren't emotions that she shared. He surprised himself with his ability to accept that truth. It didn't matter that she didn't love him back. It didn't really matter if she ever loved him.

He had found her.

He had saved her.

He had saved them both, and in doing so had kept the war from ending and prevented Watson from winning in this time, in this future.

It was a small victory, but for once it was a victory.

For once, the people he cared most for had survived.

"It's kind of sad," Michael said, leaning over his shoulder, positioning himself between Katherine and Mitchell.

"Losing the XENO-1?" Katherine asked.

Mitchell was grateful that nothing had happened to the stocky programmer. Katherine had been overjoyed to find her friend alive and safely in the company of Max, Lyle, and Damon, already aboard the VTOL and anxiously awaiting their return.

It would have been the perfect reunion if Cooper hadn't died during the middle of it.

He felt guilty for the loss, more so than he usually did. It was as if winning a battle had given him the strength to care about losing people again. He would mourn them later. He would honor them later, in the tradition that had been passed down to him by Millie and the Riggers. He realized at that moment how much he missed them, and at the same time, how hopeful he was that he would never see them again. He wanted to win this war before he ever needed to call on this recursion's version of the Riggers.

"All of it, when you think about it," Michael said. "Humankind's greatest leap forward turns out to be our downfall, and all because of something we created. Apparently based on a machine language I created if the data card you gave me is any indication."

"If it weren't your language, it would have been someone else's," Kathy said from behind them. "Humankind's creation of artificial intelligence is inevitable."

"Maybe. But isn't that sad? Why aren't we satisfied with thinking for ourselves? Doing for ourselves?"

"That's an interesting thing for you to say," Katherine said. "Considering your field."

"I know. Before all of this happened I never would have said it. Now I know we're heading in the wrong direction. AI is a crutch at best, a megalomaniacal need to play God at worst. We make things too easy on ourselves, and then what?"

"And then when the shit hits the thrusters, we get splattered in it," Max said.

"You sound like Li'un Tio," Kathy said to Michael.

"Who?"

"He was called The Knife. He was a very intelligent, very dangerous man. He believed that nothing good would ever come from artificial intelligence. That no matter our best intentions, no matter the safeguards we put in place, that intelligence would always do us harm, even if it believed it was protecting us."

"Watson isn't trying to protect us," Mitchell said. "He's trying to kill us. Every last one of us, for all of eternity. There's nothing benevolent about his goals. There's nothing motivating him but hate and anger and his own desire to play God." He raised his hand, pointing at each of the people assembled in the back of the VTOL. Trevor, Max, Lyle, Damon, Michael, Kathy, Katherine. "We're the only ones standing in his way. We're the only ones that can fight back."

Mitchell paused in his speech as a sharp crack echoed from the ground below, loud enough to be heard inside the craft. He turned his attention back to the small viewport, watching as the ice split apart and the Goliath began to sink in earnest. Ripples of water spread out around it as it displaced the water, in waves that were large enough to destroy the bases arranged around the wreckage. Verma had sent warning. He could only hope it had been heeded.

The VTOL hovered above the site in a silent vigil as the massive starship disappeared from view beneath the broken ice and water. It took nearly an hour for the sheared off head to reach the waterline, and another ten minutes for it to drown below it.

No one moved, no one spoke.

Finally, Mitchell looked away. His eyes passed over each of them, and they returned his gaze in turn. The secret to winning war eternal couldn't be found in numbers or logic. It couldn't be quantified or counted, plotted or preordained. It was hidden in the hearts and souls of the people who gave everything they had to make it happen no matter the cost. In each of the men and women standing in front of him, willing to follow, willing to die to save a future they would likely never see.

"I gave up twenty years to see tomorrow," he said. "This is our chance. Our time. Yesterday is over. The past is behind us. We won today, and we're going to win again. Tomorrow will come. I promise you that. Whatever it takes, tomorrow will come."

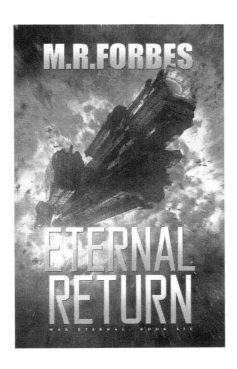

Don't miss the exciting next installment of War Eternal. Pick up Eternal Return and start reading now!

ABOUT THE AUTHOR

M.R. Forbes is the creator of a growing catalog of science fiction novels, including War Eternal, Rebellion, Chaos of the Covenant, and the Forgotten Worlds novels. He eats too many donuts, and he's always happy to hear from readers.

To learn more about M.R. Forbes or just say hello:

Visit my website:
mrforbes.com

Send me an e-mail:
michael@mrforbes.com

Check out my Facebook page:
facebook.com/mrforbes.author

Chat with me on Facebook Messenger:
https://m.me/mrforbes.author